A PERFECT LIE

LISA RENEE JONES

This book is a story of destiny, narrated by twenty-eight-year-old Hailey Anne Monroe, who is an unreliable narrator, seemingly because of blackouts. Or is she? She will lead you through her story, telling you that it's really your story as well, telling you exactly what you need to hear to believe that you are just like her. She will convince you that we are all caught in the storybook called "life," that is already written, even before we are born.

Only what if everything you think you know when the story is all but told, about yourself and her, is a perfect lie that leads to murder?

PROLOGUE

THE BEGINNING, THE MIDDLE, THE END...

They say that you are not a product of the environment that you've grown up in, that you create your own story, tell it your way. That you get to pick your own future. They lied. *If you're honest with yourself, you believed that lie, too, like I used to, because I wanted to, and even needed to believe that I had some semblance of control over my own self. The truth is that control is part of the lie. The ability to become a person of our own making is the* perfect lie. *I concede that it might appear that some people control their destiny, but I assure you, if you gave me fifteen minutes, I could pull apart that façade. We are born into a destiny that we never have the chance to escape. That's why I must tell my story. For those of you out there like me who were told that you have choices, when you never had one single choice that was your own. For those of you out there who were, who* are, *judged for decisions you've made that were directed by your destiny, not by the façade of choices. The irony of the story within this story is how one person's predisposed destiny can impact, influence, and even change the lives of those around him or her. How one destiny ties to another destiny.*

I am Hailey Anne Monroe. I'm twenty-eight years old. An artist, who found her muse on the canvas because I wasn't allowed to have friends or even keep a journal. And yes, if you haven't guessed by now, I'm that Hailey Anne Monroe, daughter to Thomas Frank Monroe, the man who was a half-percentage point from becoming President of the United States. If you were able to ask him, he'd probably tell you that I was the half point. But you can't ask him, and he can't tell you. He's dead. They're all dead and now I can speak.

PART ONE: THE BEGINNING

LISA RENEE JONES

CHAPTER ONE

HAILEY ANNE MONROE

You already know that I'm one of those perfect lies we've discussed, a façade of choices that were never my own. But that one perfect lie is too simplistic to describe who, and what, I am. I am perhaps a dozen perfect lies, the creation of at least one of those lies beginning the day I was born. That's when the clock started ticking. That's when decisions started being made for me. That's when every step that could be taken was to ensure I was "perfect." My mother, a brilliant doctor, ensured I was one hundred percent healthy, in all ways a test, pin prick, and inspection could ensure. I was, of course, vaccinated on a strict schedule, because in my household we must be so squeaky clean that we cannot possibly give anything to anyone.

Meanwhile, my father, the consummate politician, began planning my college years while my diapers were still being changed. I would be an attorney. I would go to an Ivy League college. I would be a part of the elite. Therefore, I was with tutors before I could spell. I was in dance at five years old. Of course, there was also piano, and French, Spanish, and Chinese language classes. The one joy I found was in an art class, which my mother suggested when I was twelve. It became my obsession, my one salvation, my one escape. Outside of her. She was not like my father. She was my friend, not my dictator. She was the bridge between us. The one we both adored. She listened to me. She listened to him. She tried to find compromise between us. She gave me choices, within the limits I was allowed. She tried to make me happy. She did make me as happy as anyone who was a puppet to a political machine could be, but the bigger the machine, the more developed, the harder that became. And still she fought for me.

I loved my mother with all of my heart and soul.

That's why it's hard to tell this part of my story. If there was one moment, beyond my birth, that established my destiny, and my influence on the destiny of those around me, it would be one evening during my senior year in high school, the night I killed my mother.

THE PAST—TWELVE YEARS AGO…

The steps leading to the Michaels' home seem to stretch eternally, but then so do most on this particular strip of houses in McLean, Virginia, where the rich, and sometimes famous, reside. Music radiates from the walls of the massive white mansion that is our destination, the stretch of land owned by the family wide enough that the nearest neighbor sees nothing and hears nothing. They most certainly don't know that while the Michaels are out of town, their son, Jesse, is throwing a party.

"I can't believe we're at Jesse's house," Danielle says, linking her arm through mine, something she's been doing for the past six years, since we met in private school at age eleven. Only then I was the tall one, and now I'm five-foot-four to her five-foot-eight, and that's when I'm wearing heels and she's not.

"Considering his father bloodies my father on his news program nightly, I can't either," I say. "I shouldn't be here, Danielle."

She stops walking and turns to me, her beautiful chestnut hair, which goes with her beautiful, perfect face and body, blowing right smack into my average face. She shoves said beautiful hair behind her ears, and glowers at me. "Hailey—"

"Don't start," I say, folding my arms in front of my chest, which is at least respectable, considering my dirty blonde hair and blue eyes are what I call average and others call cute. Like I'm not smart enough to know that means average. "I'm here. You already got me here."

"Jesse doesn't care about your father's run for President," she argues. "Or that his father doesn't support your father."

"Why did you just say that?" I demand.

"Say what?"

"Now you've just reminded me that I'm at the house of a man who doesn't support my father, whom I happen to love. I need to leave." I start down the stairs.

Danielle hops in front of me. "Wait. Please. I think I might be in love with Jesse. You can't just leave."

"My God, woman, you're a drama queen. You have never even kissed him. And I have to study for the SAT and so do you."

"Please. His father isn't here. His father will never know about the party or us."

"Danielle, if my father finds out—"

"He's out of town, too. How is he going to find out?"

"What about your father? He's an advisor to my father. You can't date Jesse."

She draws in a deep breath, her expression tightening before she gushes out, "*Hailey,*" making my name a plea. "I'm trying so hard to be normal. I know that you deal with things by studying. I do, but I need this. I need to feel normal."

Normal.

That word punches me with a fist of emotions I reject every time I hear it and feel them. "We will never be normal again and you know it. We weren't normal to start with. Not when—"

"After that night," she says. "We were normal enough until then. But since—after what happened, after we—"

"Stop," I hiss. "We don't talk about it. We don't talk about it *ever.*"

"Ouch," she says, grabbing my hand that is on her arm, my grip anything but gentle. "You're hurting me."

I have to count to three and force myself to breathe again before my fingers ease from her arm. "We agreed that 'the incident' was buried."

"Right," she says, and now she's hugging herself. "Because we're so good at burying things."

"We have to be," I bite out, trying to soften my tone and failing. "I *know* you know that."

She gives me several choppy nods. "Yes." Her voice is tiny. "I know." She turns pragmatic, her tone lifting. "I just need more to clutter up my mind than the SAT exam. That will come and go."

"And then there will be more work ahead."

"I need more," she insists. "I need to be normal."

"You will never—"

"I can pretend, okay? I need to *feel* normal even if I'm not. And even if you don't admit it, so do you."

My fingers curl, my nails cutting into my palms, perhaps because she's right. Some part of me cared when I put on my best black jeans and a V-neck black sweater that shows my assets. Some part of me wanted to look as good as she does in her pink lacy off-the-shoulder blouse and faded jeans. Some part of me forgot that the "normal" ship sailed for me the day I was born to a father who aspired to be President, but still, I don't disagree with her. I need to get her head on straight and maybe kissing Jesse is exactly the distraction that she needs do the trick. I link my arm with hers once more. "Let's go see Jesse."

She gives me one of her big smiles and I know that I've made the right decision, because when she's smiling like that no one sees anything but beauty which is exactly how it needs to stay. And so, I make that walk with her up those steps, climbing toward what I hope is not a bad decision, when I swore I was done with those. Nevertheless, in a matter of two minutes, we're on the giant concrete porch, a Selena Gomez song radiating from the walls and rattling my teeth.

The door flies open, and several kids I've seen around, but don't know, stagger outside while Danielle pulls me into the gaudy glamour of the Michaels' home, which is as far opposite of my conservative father as the talk show host's politics. The floors are white and gray marble. The furniture is boxy and flat, with red and orange accents, with the added flair of newly added bottles, bags, cups, and people. There are lots of people everywhere, including on top of the grand piano. It's like my high school class, inclusive of the football team and cheerleaders, has been dropped inside a bad Vegas hotel room. Or so I've heard and seen in movies. I've not actually been to Vegas; that would be far too scandalous for a future first daughter, or so says my father.

"Where now?" I ask, leaning into Danielle.

"He said the backyard," she replies, scanning. "This way!" she adds, and suddenly she's dragging me through several groups of about a half-dozen bodies.

Our destination is apparently the outdoor patio, where a fire is burning in a stone pit, and despite it being April, and in the sixties, surrounded by a cluster of ottoman-like seating and lanterns on steel poles. Plus, more people are here, and now instead of Selena Gomez rattling my teeth, it's Rihanna.

"Danielle!" The shout comes from Jesse, who is sitting in a cluster of people to our far left. Of course, Danielle starts dragging me forward again, which has me feeling like her cute dog that doesn't want to be walked. Correction: Her forgotten dog that doesn't want to be walked, considering she lets go of me and runs to Jesse, giving him a big hug. I'm left with one open seat, smack between two football players: David Nelson and Ramon Miller. Both are hot. Both have dark hair, though Ramon's is curly and excessive, and David's is buzzed, understandably since I think I heard his dad is military. Okay, I know his dad is military because I've been crushing on him since he showed up at school six months ago.

I sit awkwardly between them, and stare desperately at Danielle, who just stuck her tongue down Jesse's throat in a familiar way that says it's not the first time. *I need to leave*, I think. I'll just get up and leave, but then, what if she panics? What if she forgets that Jesse can't be in on 'the incident'? We can never tell anyone what happened. Why did I think this night was a good distraction?

"Hey there," David says, piercing me with his blue eyes.

"Hi," I say.

"You look like you want to crawl under a rock," he comments.

"Do you know where I can find one?"

He laughs. He has a good laugh. A genuine laugh and since I don't know many people who do anything genuinely, I feel that hard spot in my belly begin to soften. "I'll help you find one if you take me with you."

"You don't belong under a rock," I say.

He arches a brow. "And you do?"

"Belong," I say. "No. But happier there right now, yes."

"That hurts my feelings," he says, holding his hand to his chest as if wounded.

"Oh. No. Sorry. I just meant...I don't do parties."

"Because your dad is a politician," he assumes.

"He doesn't exactly approve of events like this."

He laughs again. "Events. Right." His hand settles on my leg and there is this funny sensation in my belly. "I'll make sure nothing goes wrong. Okay?"

"No. No, I'll make sure nothing goes wrong."

He leans in and presses his cheek to mine, his lips by my ear. "Then I'll give you extra protection." I inhale, and he pulls back, suddenly no longer touching me.

My gaze lifts and I find Danielle looking at me with a big grin on her face. David hands me a shot glass and Jesse hands Danielle one. She nods, and I don't know why, but I just do it. I down the liquid in what is my first drink ever. The next thing I know, David's tongue is down my throat and when I blink, I'm not even sitting on the back patio anymore. I'm lying on a bed and he's pulling his shirt off. And I don't know how I got here. I don't know what is happening. Panic rises with a sense of being out of control. I stand up and David reaches for me, but I shove at him.

"No!"

I dart around him and I must be drunk but I think my feet are too steady to be drunk. I run from the room and keep running down a hallway and to the stairs. I grab the railing, flashes of images in my mind. David offering me another drink. Me refusing. David kissing me and offering me yet another drink. I had refused. So why was I just on a bed and unaware of how I got there?

"Hailey!"

At the sound of David's voice, I take off down the steps, not even sure where I'm going, but I don't stop. I push through bodies and I'm on the porch in what feels like slow motion. I'm running down the stairs. I'm leaving. I have to get out of here.

I blink awake, cold, with a hard surface at my back. Gasping with the shock of disorientation, I sit up, the first orange and red of a new day in the darkness of the sky. I'm outside. I'm...I look around and realize that I'm on the bench of a picnic table. I'm in a park. I stand up and start to pace. I'm dressed in black jeans and a black sweater. The party. I went to the party. I dig my heels in. Did I get drunk? Wouldn't I feel sick? I'm not sick. I'm not unsteady. My tiny purse I carry with me often is at my hip. I unzip it and pull out my phone. Ten calls from my mother. No messages from Danielle.

"Danielle," I whisper. "Where is Danielle?"

I dial her number and she doesn't answer. I dial again. And again. I press my hand to my face and look at the time. Five in the morning. My car is at Jesse's house. I start walking, looking for a sign, anything to tell me where I'm at. Finally, I find a sign: *Rock Creek Park*. The party was in McLean. Rock Creek is back in Washington, a good forty minutes away. I lean against the sign and my mother calls again.

I answer. "Mom?"

"Thank God," she breathes out, her voice filled with both panic and anger, two things that my mother, a gentle soul, and doctor, who loves people, rarely allows to surface. "Oh, thank God. I've been so worried."

"I don't know what happened, Mom. I blacked out and I'm at a park."

"Near Rock Creek," she says. "I know. I did the 'find my phone' search but it's not exact and I was about to call the police. I just knew—" She sobs before adding, "I just knew you were dead in the woods. I was about to get help. I was about to have a search start."

"I—Mom, I—"

"Go to the main parking lot." She hangs up.

My cellphone rings with Danielle's number. "Where are you?" I demand.

"At Jesse's," she says. "Where are you? I was asleep and I thought you were in a room with David, but he was with some other girl."

"You don't know what happened to me?" I ask.

"No. Jesus. What happened?"

Headlights shine in my direction from a parking lot. "I'll call you later," I say. "I have to deal with my mother." I hang up and start running toward the lights. By the time I'm at the driver's side of my mother's Mercedes, she's there, too, out of the car and reaching for me.

"You have so much to explain," she attacks, grabbing my arms and hugging me. "I am furious with you. You scared me."

"I scared me, too," I say hugging her, starting to cry, the scent of her jasmine perfume, consuming my senses, and calming me. "I don't know what happened."

She pulls back. "Did you drink and do drugs?"

"No. I mean—one drink. I'm fine. I—"

"One drink. We both know what that means. This wasn't the first time."

"No. Mom. It was. One drink. I don't know what happened. Someone drugged me. They had to have drugged me."

Her lips purse. "Get in the car."

"Mom—"

"Get in the car."

I nod and do as I'm told. I get in the car. The minute she's in with me, I try to explain. "Mom, I—"

"Do not speak to me until I calm down." The seatbelt warning beeps.

"Mom—"

"Shut up, Hailey," she says, putting us in motion.

I suck in air at the harsh words that do not fit my mother, who is not just beautiful, but graceful in her actions and words. Perfect, actually, and everything I aspire to be. I click my belt while her warning continues to go off. She turns us onto the highway and I listen to the warning going off, trying to fill the blank space in my head with answers I can give her. But there are none and suddenly she lets out a choked sound and hits the brakes. My eyes jolt open, but everything is spinning. We're spinning. I can't see or move. "Mom!" I shout, I think. Or maybe I don't. Glass shatters. I feel it on my face, cutting me, digging into my skin.

We jolt again, no longer spinning, but the world goes black.

Time is still.

And then there are sirens and I try to catch my breath, but my chest hurts so badly. "Mom," I whisper, turning to look at her but she's not there. She's not there. Panic rises fast and hard and I unhook my belt and ball my fist at my aching chest. Forcing myself to move, I sit up to find my mother on the hood of the car, a huge chunk of steel through her body.

I scream and I can't stop screaming. I can't stop screaming.

CHAPTER TWO

I killed my mother.

I have never denied this reality, or my responsibility for her death. From the very beginning, I accepted my father's grief-fed anger that turned into his hatred. I'd been where I shouldn't have been. I'd stayed too long. I'd forced my mother to come after me. I'd destroyed my father's perfect world in the process. I understood because I'd destroyed the only perfect thing in my world.

Back then, I really did hate myself, right along with him. I really did feel that I could have made different decisions that night before my mother's death, and therefore changed the outcome of that early morning. It gutted me. It shaped my decisions going forward. It shaped my relationship with my father, which profoundly impacted my life, and his. Now, I see things differently. Now, I believe that every decision that I would have made would have ended the same: In my mother's death. It was her time to die. I was supposed to play a role in how it happened and suffer for it. My father was supposed to hate me for the rest of my life, but I couldn't accept that. I couldn't see that my mother was all we had in common, and to love. Because I wanted his love.

But back to defining my perfect lie. I never told my father I drank that night. I never told him I blacked out. Not that it mattered. It changed nothing. He still hated me. I still wanted him to love me. I melted down, and then pulled myself back together, and I did it for him. I tried to be the perfect political princess. I tried to please him. You don't

have to wait until the end of the story for the punchline to that statement. I'll tell you right now.
I failed.

THE PAST—FIVE YEARS AFTER MY MOTHER'S DEATH…

I sit in the auditorium of Georgetown University, my graduation gown hiding the conservative navy-blue dress expected of a presidential candidate's daughter, listening to our valedictorian, Rebecca Knight, ramble on about our greatness. "We are leaders," she says, when most of the time she calls herself a leader and the rest of the world idiots. "We are the future," she adds. "Those insightful enough to see each glass as half full, not half empty."

She's right on that. I've learned to see the glass as half full, not half empty, but most of the time it's still filled with blood. Under those circumstances, perhaps half empty is the better scenario. Nevertheless, or whatever the case, today my glass, is, in fact, brimming over with that blood, or perhaps the sins of my past. Otherwise, my father would be here today, but he's not. No matter how hard I tried to redeem myself with him, to recreate myself for him, I am still that girl who killed her mother. And until *he* makes me remember that girl again, I am teetering on that emotional tightrope that I've secretly walked, which is nearly too thin to walk (because a politician's daughter must always be perfect) in the years since my mother's death.

The rest of the speech is more of Rebecca's eloquently spoken fake perfection that really defines why she's headed into a career in politics. Not that my father, the master politician himself, is fake. Not that he is real either, because how would I know? He pulled favors to enroll me in this school and keep me close to him, but we share blood, too much blood, to know anything about each other beyond the past it represents.

There are more speakers and then names are called, and chaos, clapping, hugs, kisses, praise follow, all surrounding me, suffocating me. But then I am suddenly throwing my hat in the air, and it hits me that I did this. Through the tears, the pain, the loss, after falling apart and destroying my grades, I stood back up. I went to college. I fought hard. I survived, and I've secured a place here at Georgetown for law school, where political careers are groomed and bred. My father doesn't know it yet, but that's not my plan. I nailed my interview at Stanford. It's not art studies as I crave, but my father can't knock it down, and bottom line: I'm going to get out of here. I'm going to fill my glass with wine, not blood, even if I don't drink that wine. And so, I catch my hat and I shout in joy.

A few minutes later, I'm outside the building with my favorite people in the world by my side; Danielle, who is still my best friend, and Tobey, my boyfriend of a year, a regular JFK-lookalike, who thinks he knows me, but he doesn't. At least, not the real me.

The three of us stand there and play the graduation game. We laugh. We smile. We proclaim happiness when happiness is always a glass ball two seconds from shattering. "I start on your father's campaign tomorrow," Danielle says in a sing-song voice. "I'm excited. I'm going to kill it at fundraising."

Tobey sniffs and drapes his arm over my shoulder. "Of course, you will," he says. "And Hailey and I will be right here in Georgetown law school preparing to keep you out of whatever jail cell your political career tries to earn you."

There he goes embracing that political future, and the idea of me doing so as well, I think, while Danielle snarls at him. "Jail cell?" she snaps. "Why would you even say something like that?"

"Because," he replies dryly, "the rest of the world sees your pale pink dress and the pink clips in your hair and they see the sweet girl next door. The three of us know better."

It's true, of course. Danielle plays "good girl" like a perfect bad girl. A thought that takes me back to something Terrance, my father's Chief of Staff, has asked me two times in my life now: *How does the world see you, Hailey?* The first time he'd posed this question to me, my mother had been alive, and I'd said: *Smart and organized, and yet, average.* He'd replied: *Okay. Now how do you use that against them and for yourself?* The second time, I'd been in college, trying to dig myself out of a depression and poor grades. Again, he'd said: *How does the world see you, Hailey?* I'd said: *A stupid fuck-up.* His lips had curved and he'd said: *Now, how do you use that against them?* Turned out, I used it pretty darn well, but that is another memory for another time. For Danielle, I am certain her reply to the same question would be: *Beautiful, sweet, and innocent,* because she uses those things against everyone and does it well.

"Tobey!"

At the sound of Tobey's name, the three of us turn toward the voices. We find his aunt and uncle clearing the crowd, a basic middle-aged political couple dripping of money and stature. Both working in political this or that, for this or that representative. Everyone caters to politicians in this town. They arrive by our sides and hug Tobey. I'm next, of course, because I'm their nephew's girl, and Tobey's father is my father's Chief of Staff. They all think they'll get lucky in life if I, the future First Daughter, marry Tobey, and they all become some version of a royal family. They won't get that lucky and I won't make Tobey that miserable. Neither of us need fake bliss in my fake life.

At this point, the family stuff snowballs. Danielle's father, a pollster for my father, joins us, his dark hair thick, his features as chiseled and perfect as his daughter's. He's also without a wife, like Danielle is without a mother. She'd left when Danielle was a small child, and long before my freshman year in high school, when we'd met. She doesn't talk about her mother and I don't push.

Whatever the case, I set aside the baggage of the past and live in the moment. I laugh and even smile with the group, but then Terrance appears inside the huddle we've formed, a tall familiar redhead in his fifties; my father's Chief of Staff who is apparently my fake parent for the day.

Suddenly, I am still in the circle of people, but I'm standing on the outside, the absence of my mother a blade carving out my heart in what feels like slow motion. Reality chooses then to slap me a good one: *I am, as always, alone in a crowd.* Still, I manage to greet Terrance, Tobey's father, who then hugs Tobey and does a fine job of congratulating everyone. It's really all more political yip and yap, up until the moment that Terrance focuses on me alone. "Hailey, honey," he says, taking my arm and turning me away from the group, "your father—"

"Don't, please," I say, holding up a hand.

"That early debate is only a month away," he says, ignoring my objection. "And you know, there's never been one this early in the primaries."

"I know," I say, because he's clearly going to force me to have this conversation.

"And that your mother and brother—"

"Step-mother and step-brother," Tobey corrects, joining us, and sliding his arm around my shoulder again. "Susan and Bennett." He says their names with the disdain I feel.

Of course, he's protecting me, because while he knows little about the real me, he's quite aware that my father's marriage to a younger woman just a year after my mother's death is as much a sore spot as my arrogant, holier-than-thou step-brother is now and always has been.

Terrance offers Tobey a displeased look before refocusing on me. "They're a part of your father's prep team."

"Of course they are," I say dryly, and I'm well trained enough to bite back the ninety-nine nasty remarks that come to mind, but I can't seem to hold back the one hundredth. "Let's be honest here," I say. "Who better to prep my father on Russia than Bennett? He's a corporate attorney, an aspiring politician, and," I hold up a finger, "this is the big one. He's spent every family dinner for the past two years debating Russian and American ties with anyone who did or did not want to talk about it."

Terrance gives an amused smirk. "And getting most of it wrong while assuring us he's right."

I'm surprised by his comment, but it makes me laugh. I think. I at least manage some sort of choked attempt at a laugh. He smiles in reply and chucks me under the chin. "Put the shit aside. You did good, kid. And your father is proud of you. I sure am."

Emotion wells in my chest and I don't even know why. "Thanks, Terrance," I murmur softly.

He motions Tobey away, and Tobey reluctantly releases me and rejoins the huddle. Terrance steps a bit closer to me, and for my ears only says, "How does the world see you now, Hailey?"

Before I can form a reply, I'm tapped on the back. I rotate to find my father's pretty brunette assistant, Leslie, standing in front of me with flowers in her hands. "From your father," she says, handing them to me, and I swear the pink and red roses wrapped in white paper pierce me with a million thorns.

My lips thin and I look at Terrance. "Ask again," I order.

He follows my lead without hesitation. "How does the world see you, Hailey?"

"As the future first daughter," I say, because it's true. That *is* how the world sees me. The perfect girl. No one remembers the story that the flowers in my arms, delivered by my father's secretary tell me now: I'm still me.

And to my father, I'm not a daughter. I'm just a *killer*.

That's our secret that no one else knows, and one thing that we undeniably share is the hope that it stays that way.

CHAPTER THREE

A killer and the future President's daughter. There is irony there, *I think, or maybe not at all. The definition of me sounds like a joke or maybe the truth beneath it all is that I'm perfect for the world of politics. Maybe underneath my father's perfect lie I'd find that what he doesn't like about me is how much I resemble him. Whatever the case, in the month post-graduation, I began an internship in a nearby political office, while waiting earnestly for news from Stanford, which I'd soon learn was never going to come. All the while, seeing little of my father.*

The next time I would have any quality time with him, if you could call it that, was the night of the opening party debates, when he was to face ten rival candidates in challenge for the party nomination. His entire life was driven toward that night, and so was mine. The problem was that neither of us knew in what way. Neither of us knew that that night would change everything, change us, forever.

THE PAST—ONE MONTH AFTER GRADUATION, THE BIG DEBATE…

The Austin, Texas auditorium is large and cold with rows of seats facing a stage filled with ten podiums, my father set to be center stage, an indication of his top poll numbers. I'm in the front row, sitting next to my pompous, twenty-eight-year-old Ken doll of a step-brother, Bennett, who is wearing a flag-blue tie to go with his Armani suit. He's also pressing his knee to mine, in what is a seemingly crowded, unavoidable action, when we both know it's not. He's a pervert and always has been. I shift away from him, and cross my legs, resting my hand on the skirt of my also flag-blue, high-necked dress, the design nothing I'd ever choose for myself. It's from my step-mother's recently launched clothing line, and since it was delivered to my room an hour before I dressed, with a note from my father that read "for the future first daughter" and this is his night, I'm wearing it.

My phone buzzes with a text and I glance down to find a message from Danielle, who is two rows back, thanks to her seat next to her father's staff position with my father. I grimace at her text that reads: If I lick Bennett will you hate me?

I don't react. Why would I? This is nothing new. Everyone but me wants to lick the man, the press included, and Danielle has always hounded after Bennett, mostly to ignite my agitation. What she does in this case is earn me my step-mother's attention. The Audrey Hepburn-ish, sweet as sin bitch leans forward and scowls at me and my phone, which I deserve. I turn off my phone and stick it into the oddly placed pocket, in the shirt. I don't know why I'm holding the damn thing.

The moderators walk to the stage and my heart starts racing. This is huge. This is everything to my father, and everything that has shaped my life. All things aside that led us here, I am rooting for him. I inhale and force myself to calm. He's perfect for this job. He cares about this country. He's devoted his life to his service. He's intelligent and savvy in all ways, at least professionally. They announce him first, and he takes the stage and I clap fiercely. Now, I actually find myself looking at Bennett, and we both nod. No matter what our motivations, or our relationship, in this, we are together. We want the same thing. For my father to become the President of the United States.

My father appears on the stage, tall, dark and handsome, with wavy locks of dirty blond hair that look so much better on him than me. I'm average that's been polished and pressed to try to fit in, on his dollar of course, while he's exceptional in all ways. Really truly, Bennett and his playboy good looks fit my father like a glove of a son, while I am just—something else. I won't go there tonight.

He claims his podium and waves at the crowd, who gobbles him up like a fat kid does cake, me included, pride welling inside me. The other candidates follow but are dim to his greatness. Soon the show is on the road, and introductions are made, starting with my father. "I'm Thomas Frank Moore, and I want to thank the great people of America for the honor of serving this great country. And thank you to the moderators and the sponsors of this event. I have my family here tonight and I want to make them proud the way I want to make you, the American people, proud. I will serve you humbly, with grace and dignity, and protect you, and honor you."

It's a perfect opening and roars of applause follow. For the next hour and a half, I listen to my father prove why he leads this competition. Why the people trust him. Why he is the best of the candidates, both diplomatically and intellectually. We reach the closing statements and it's my father's turn. He delivers a persuasive, humble outline of his points made this night and ends with, "I will not be beat up by our adversaries, nor will this country. We will be one family, not a divided nation." When he closes, it's chaos, and we head to the stage to join him for photo ops. The minute he sees us, he grabs my step-mother and looks around, I think for me, but no. He hugs Bennett. "I couldn't have done it without you," I hear him say, and it punches me in the chest.

He's forgotten me until the photographer motions me forward, and I stand in the huddle of family, next to my father. He looks at me. "You look like your mother tonight," he says, and I see the hardening of his mouth, the condemnation in that statement that isn't a compliment, but a bitter memory.

I'm suddenly back on my tightrope and walking a thin line.

My father turns away, focused on my step-mother and a camera flashes in my eyes, reminding me that I'm on show. I can't allow the spiral of emotions inside me to reflect in the lenses of a camera with an eternal memory, much like my father's apparently. I step into the instructions I'm given by some publicity person, joining my "family" for what is an eternal photo session. When it's done, I expect dinner to follow, in some elite location where I will once again be an outsider. I dread it until the moment it really is done, and suddenly Terrance appears next to my father. I'm not really sure what happens beyond my father has to leave town. There are fake kisses on cheeks, and hugs for more cameras, and then I'm alone, that dreaded dinner no longer a threat. And I'm fucked up enough to wish it wasn't gone, when I have spent thirty minutes wishing it away.

I walk down the stairs and toward an exit. I'm led into a garage and a set of twin security guards, direct me toward a black sedan, where Tobey and Danielle are leaning against the outside. Tobey is in his perfectly tailored blue suit and Danielle is in a dress with a front zipper that is no longer to her neckline, but low to expose her breasts. Her dress is also a flag-blue to match my own, which I'm certain irritated my step-mother, making it pretty darn perfect. I stop in front of them and none of us speak. They know what happened in that auditorium. They know the outsider I am.

"Let's celebrate," Danielle says.

"Celebrate what?" I ask.

"It's over," she replies, and maybe she believes that, but the good thing about Tobey is he knows better.

His eyes meet mine, and I see understanding. He knows what I feel deep inside, with a clawing, scraping certainty: It's only just begun. I struggle with a sudden need to stop some indescribable "it" from happening. Tobey opens the back door of the car, and for reasons I can't explain, I don't want to get inside. It's illogical, irrational, even.

I get in the car.

Later, I would discover that feeling had a purpose. It was telling me not to get into the car.

CHAPTER FOUR

One drink.

For years I said that drink on the night my mother died would be my only drink for the rest of my life. I stuck to that vow through college and did so easily. No matter how illogical, and I knew it was, I'd attached drinking to death. It stayed that way all the way up until the night of my father's first debate. That's when I found out everything and absolutely nothing. Think that makes no sense whatsoever? It will, once you live the rest of that night with me...

THE PAST...

I squeeze into the back of the sedan next to the window with Tobey beside me and Danielle on the opposite side. Danielle glances at her phone and reads an address to the driver that isn't the hotel.

The car starts moving and I glance across Tobey to Danielle. "Where are we going?"

"A place where you can drown your sorrows," she says.

Tobey grimaces. "She doesn't drink. And she doesn't need to be a press magnet tonight." The driver halts us at the garage exit and Tobey leans forward and taps his shoulder. "Drop us back at the hotel." The driver nods and exits to the road. Goal achieved, Tobey eases back into his seat and flicks me a blue-eyed look. "The hotel has a bar. You can do your virgin routine there."

"She doesn't want to be a virgin for you, Tobey," Danielle snaps. "And clearly there's a reason you're going to be an attorney and I'm a fundraiser. I know what people need and want. You don't care. They have that flavored hookah vape stuff she likes at the place I'm taking her." She plants her hand on his leg, squeezes and leans forward to look at me across his lap. "You know I know you don't drink and why. You also know that I know what you need. It's the lower level in a five-star hotel, with tight security. The hookah and desserts, which means chocolate. I had to get special approval to get us in without a membership."

"What does that even mean?" Tobey demands, grabbing her hand, removing it from his leg, and turning to face me. "She knows why you don't drink? Is there more to you not drinking than dislike?"

"It's a control thing," I say, not sure if I should kick Danielle for her big mouth or kiss her for hookah and chocolate. "I can't risk being stupid drunk," I say. "You know that."

"But you can risk people thinking hookah is weed not tobacco?" he challenges. "And tobacco will kill you."

"Better me than someone else," I murmur, leaning forward to tap the driver on the shoulder. "Please continue to the bar and my apologies for our flip-flop."

"Do you know her at all, Tobey?" Danielle demands. "She uses the tobacco-free stuff. It's just like flavored herbs."

Does he even know me? No. He does not, and it seems tonight, Danielle has made it her mission to drive that point home to me and him.

Fifteen minutes later, we're at a place that is as perfect as Danielle had described. A place that combines business and pleasure, which translated to my father and his people's approval, should I have asked in advance. The door is well guarded. The music is a mix of modern and dated pop, all toned down to allow conversation. Once we're past security, we find the setup to be that of a giant aquarium with flat blue ceilings. There are stunningly wide and deep, often oddly shaped fish tanks built into concrete walls, as well as lining several walkways, that create privacy for tables.

I count three round bars at the back of the room, all side by side, with cylindrical aquariums behind the bartenders. With every table filled, we head to the crowded, far-left bar, and the three of us claim fancy high-backed stools at the counter, with me sandwiched between the two of them. I slink my tiny bag, across my chest. Tobey and Danielle order martinis, while I scout the menu.

"Coconut hookah," I say, when it's my turn, decisive as my father expects, "and the chocolate flower arrangement."

"Oh look," Danielle says, when the waiter leaves, showing me her phone with press headlines. "Frank Monroe has arrived at his hotel in Austin, Texas, with his lovely family. That's what it says. *Lovely* family. Only you're the only real family and you're not at the hotel."

And apparently my father isn't leaving town after all, I think, nor did anyone think to inform me. Tobey seems to read my reaction, lacing his fingers with mine and tugging my attention in his direction. "You okay?"

"Of course," I say, because like my father, I never give him any other answer.

"You sure? You know it's okay to not be okay?"

He's lying, and he knows it. It's not okay to not be okay. Ever. Thankfully the food and drinks arrive before I'm forced to play whatever this nonsense game is that he's playing tonight. Easily distracted, Tobey reaches for his dry martini and as an added bonus that ensures the game ends, the guy in a suit next to him speaks to him, causing Tobey to turn in his direction to reply. Good because I'm one hundred percent past an attempt at a meaningful, but meaningless, conversation with Tobey. Eager to assure it stays that way, I angle in Danielle's direction to find her holding a glass of chocolate goodness complete with marshmallows. She sips it and holds it out to me.

"You want a sip."

"No," I say. "I do not want a sip." I reach for a rose-shaped chocolate and take a bite, moaning with the glorious rich, cherry flavor inside.

Danielle finishes off her drink in a gulp and orders another, before leaning close. "Does Tobey ever make you moan like that chocolate?"

Never, I think. "Always," I say.

"Liar," she replies. "Say what we both know. You're just in a business arrangement. You look good on each other's arms to the press and the powers that be."

Terrance might see too much but Danielle sees everything. "Tobey likes it that way," I say.

"You don't."

"It doesn't matter."

She grabs a chocolate. "Because you think this arrangement pleases your father, who ignores you and fawns over his bimbo wife and Ken doll step-son." Her phone buzzes with a text message and once she reads it, her red painted lips curve. Translation, it's her man flavor of the moment, whoever that might be right now. She doesn't keep them around. I don't try to keep up unless he shows up, which is once in a few months, or a blue moon.

I grab another piece of chocolate and glance over my shoulder to find Tobey standing in a huddle of men, his jacket now removed. The tall guy across from him with thick wavy hair and a tie loosened halfway down his chest, gives me a flirty grin. He's good looking and that's why I turn away. I'm a good girl trying to forget being bad. I have Tobey. I have law school. I have a father about to be President. He hopes. I just want Tobey to be it and be done.

I inhale my coconut-flavored herbs and my dismissal of the pretty boy flirt has failed. He sits down next to me. "You're the future first daughter," he says.

"And you're an asshole."

He laughs. "You get tired of hearing that, I guess."

"Yes. I do."

"Sorry then. Let's start again." He offers me his hand. "Drew," he says.

I do the expected and shake his hand, tugging mine free when he holds it a little too long. "You did meet Tobey, right?" I ask. "My boyfriend?"

He glances over his shoulder at Tobey and back at me. "The gay one?"

I blanch. "He's *not* gay."

"He'd do me. I guarantee it."

I don't like how confident he is in this and I change the subject. "What do you do?" I ask, "and who are you really?"

"Corporate attorney." He reaches into his jacket pocket and slides me a card.

I don't pick it up. "An attorney that has time to frequent bars?"

"I've signed many a client in bars and celebrated many a win in this very bar, including today."

"What case?"

"Do you really care?"

In another life, I would. "No."

"Liar again," he says, as if he's read my hesitation. "But all that matters is that I'm here and so are you. The future—"

"Don't say it," I warn.

He laughs. It's kind of a warm, whiskey laugh. I like it. I like him, which is why I have to make him go away. "Go away," I say.

"No." He waves at the bartender. "A whiskey sour for me," he tells the guy before looking at me. "What'll you have?"

"I don't drink," I say.

He glances back at the bartender. "S'mores Martini."

"I'm not drinking that," I say when the bartender leaves.

"Let's make a bet," he says. "If I prove your man is gay, you drink it."

"He's not gay. Stop saying that."

Danielle suddenly squeezes between me and Drew, turning to Drew and saving me from his advances, but probably for greedy reasons. She likes the man, who's easy to like, outside of the insistence that Tobey is gay thing that is, and she'll like the drink I can't drink. I turn away from the two of them and grab another chocolate, this one filled with some sort of butterscotch nutty flavor that I quite like. Danielle's phone buzzes with a text message, and I don't mean to, but I catch a glimpse. It reads: Tomorrow, honey. Market Street.

I freeze with those words that feel familiar. So very familiar. There is a nagging bad feeling clawing at me, but I seem to lose the thought. I fight to get it back and then after that fight, the urge to grab the phone and read Danielle's messages. The s'mores drink Drew ordered appears in front of me, and I grab the marshmallow and take a bite, the sweet chocolate of flavored liqueur touching my tongue. I turn to find Danielle's back still firmly in place, her body turned intimately toward Drew's.

I don't think. I just take a sip of the drink and it's absolute sweet, chocolate heaven. I gulp it and order another. Tobey appears by my side, resting an elbow on the bar. "Hey, honey."

I hate when he calls me honey. My father called my mother honey. I rotate to face him. "Are you gay?"

He scowls. "Why the fuck would you ask me that?"

"Are you?"

"Do I fuck like I'm gay?"

"I don't know how someone gay fucks," I say.

His hand settles on my shoulder. "Let's get out of here and fuck. That'll end this conversation."

"No," I say, because that isn't what I want at all. "Let's talk about our arrangement."

"What arrangement?"

My new drink is set down and I grab the marshmallow, wishing we had the chemistry I had with Drew. "Taste," I order, holding it to his mouth and he studies me for several hard beats before taking a bite.

"Do you like it?" I ask, after he swallows.

"Why do I feel like that's a trick question?"

I drop the remainder of the gigantic marshmallow into my drink and sip before setting it down. "Because you're as good at the political game as me?"

His hands settle at my waist and he sets me on my feet. "There's an open table. Let's go talk."

I don't agree. I don't do anything. Not that I remember.

But I blink and I'm sitting at a table with him, and my drink has mysteriously traveled with me. "What arrangement?" he demands, leaning across the table, his eyes boring into mine, his tone snapping me right back into the here and now.

"You, and your family, want power," I say. "You see me as that power."

"I see us as a good match," he replies, smoothly, oh so smoothly, and it's not a denial. It is just what it is. The game.

"Okay," I say, reaching for my drink.

"Hailey—"

I must block out what happens next because I blink again and there is a table wrapped with people I mostly don't know around me, as if I've lost more time. Drew is directly across from me now, as Tobey was before, and I can feel his leg next to mine under the table and I seem to be allowing it. He gives me a wink and I jerk my leg and gaze away, scanning for Tobey. I find him at the far end of the table, a good six people between us. He's staring at me, anger in his eyes. Are we fighting?

Danielle claims the open seat next to me, setting a chocolate dessert between us. "I brought two forks."

I accept one of them and dig into the dessert, not because I want it but because it's here and I'm hoping food dilutes the drinks I've downed. "How much did I drink?"

"I'm not sure, but you don't seem drunk at all. You've been debating politics."

"I have?"

"Yes. And winning. Why? Do you feel drunk?"

"No. I just—I just—off. I feel off."

A guy taps her on her shoulder and she turns away from me, knocking her phone down as she does. That's when the message I'd read from earlier comes back to me. I bend down and grab her phone to read a message that says: North, South, East, West. That's what I want.

I breathe out. It's a familiar tone again. Why is it familiar? I blink and I'm no longer holding the phone but eating more dessert. I don't want the dessert. I want the phone. I want to read the messages. Adrenaline pulses through me and I stand up, looking for the bathroom sign, and finding it to the right of one of the bars. With adrenaline racing through me I head in that direction, crossing the bar, and then entering the hallway leading to the bathroom. Spying an exit sign, I charge toward it, ready to get the hell out of this prison of a bar and life, but before I can escape, a hand comes down on my arm.

Danielle whirls me around. "How about talking to me before you judge me?"

I don't know what she means, but I'm angry at her. So very angry. "I need to leave. *Honey.*" God, now I'm using my father's words. Honey. Honey. Honey.

"The real you comes out," she snaps. "Crass and bitchy."

The real me. I don't even know who that is. I turn away from her and I shove through the doorway, exiting into an alleyway...

THE PRESENT...

And that's the last thing I remembered that night, and as in the past with my first blackout, in the morning light it would prove to have deadly consequences. In the depth of my dark mind, everything I needed to know the next morning was there, and yet, I found I knew nothing at all.

The question then becomes: In ignorance is there innocence or guilt?

34

CHAPTER FIVE

The dreaded morning after is worse when you wake up with a stranger in bed with you. But what happens when the stranger is you? That would be the stranger I had to face after leaving that bar alone that night. Alone. Was I alone? That would be one of many questions that would haunt me for the months to follow...

THE PAST...

I wake up with only one immediate certainty: I don't know where I am. The next realization I have is bright light piercing my eyes. The next, a cellphone buzzing somewhere. I jolt upward and grip the blanket on top of me, scanning my surroundings and it turns out "here" is my Austin, Texas hotel room. The problem is that I don't remember how I got here. I don't remember anything. I also can't think with the sun trying to burn a hole in my corneas.

It's then that I realize that the cellphone I'd heard is buzzing again from my nightstand. I grab it and read a message from Terrance: Call me back!

I grimace and note the five missed calls, all from him, as well as about ten text messages he's sent me, all with same tone as this one: Call me. We need to talk. Now. I glance at the clock. It's seven a.m., when our plane is to leave at ten, and seven a.m. is too early to be in political puppet mode. I drop my cell on the bed, letting him believe I'm still asleep. If he and my father's posse are flying out earlier this morning, they can leave without me. I need to figure out

35

what is wrong with me before cameras are flashing in my direction simply because I'm my father's daughter.

I start to get up and purse my lips, aware that I can't actually just ignore the call, because I might not be a political puppet, but my father's running for President. That's a big deal. I dial Terrance's number and it goes to his voice mail. I leave a message, and obligation met, I toss my phone and leave it on the bed to deal with several urgent issues.

Throwing off the blanket, I walk around the bed to the window on the opposite side of the mattress, yanking shut the curtains before sinking into a soft brown high-back chair. I'm trying to remember last night, but I'm blank. Really, completely blank, but I don't feel sick. I'm not hung over. This is no different than when I woke in the park years ago. There is no excuse for what I'm experiencing which leads me to one place: I was drugged, a premise that in the years since my mother's death, I've considered as fact. I was at a party. I ended up in a bedroom, almost having sex.

But this wasn't a party. It was a bar and I was with only people I trusted.

I have a sick realization at this point. There's only three common denominators between my two blackouts: Me, alcohol, and Danielle. And on both of the nights those blackouts occurred, Danielle thought I needed to relax. Danielle, who has been known to dabble in ecstasy no matter how many times I've beat her up about it.

Adrenaline and anger rush through me, and I walk to the bed and grab my phone, dialing Danielle, who doesn't answer. I dial again. This time I receive an answer. "Officer Warner. Who am I speaking with?"

My heart sinks to my stomach, and at that moment Terrance returns my call. I panic and hang up on Officer Warner, grabbing the call from Terrance. "Why did a police officer just answer Danielle's phone?" I demand, certain we now have some sort of drug scandal that I'm going to be dragged into, and my father with me.

"Holy fuck," he growls. "Did you talk to the police?"

A PERFECT LIE

"No. I hung up, afraid we were dealing with a scandal and I didn't want to say the wrong thing."

"You called from your phone?"

"Yes. Of course. I need to call them back and now. What is going on?" My only comfort with that question is knowing that if it was too horrible, the police would have already called me back.

"Listen to me very carefully. You go to the parking garage now and don't pack your things. It will be handled. The minute you're there, waiting on me, you call me back. Do not answer your phone between now and then. Do you understand?"

"Yes, but—"

"Do you understand?"

"Yes. I'm not dressed. I—"

"Throw on sweats, and just leave. If you value your freedom, go now." He hangs up.

My freedom? I'm right. This is about drugs. I don't let myself process that fully. I look down to realize that I'm still wearing the blue dress of my step-mother's design from the debate last night. I remember the dress but not why I'm still in it. Whatever the case, I can't let the press see me in the same thing I wore last night. I run toward the closet, pull out a red dress I'd planned to wear last night, do a quick change, pull on knee high black boots, and then cover-up with a black blazer. Now dressed, I rush into the bathroom, look at the mess that I am, and quickly put on lip gloss and run a brush through my hair and not because I'm foolish and vain. Because I don't need to be fodder for the press, my messy appearance food for a headline like "Monroe's Daughter a Drug Addict." Please don't let that be the destiny already in store and I just don't know it yet.

I stop at the hotel room door and inhale when there is a knock. "Damn it," I murmur. I took too long. I'm going to have to face the police, knowing nothing.

Trapped and with a rush of adrenaline, I yank the door open to find a huge black man in a black blazer standing in front of me. "Come with me, now," he orders.

37

"And you are?" I ask, not about to be a kidnap victim, considering my father inherited money from my wealthy novelist grandfather and made a small fortune. He's rich. It's been a centerpiece his political opponents use against him.

My visitor shoves a phone at me and I accept it, sticking it to my ear. "You should already be in *the garage*," Terrance snaps. "Go now." He hangs up again.

I can almost feel the blood run from my face, and I don't reply. I shove the phone at the man. "Let's go."

He gives me a curt nod, backs up and points toward the exit door where yet another man in a suit, this one with dark hair and a scowl on his face, is waiting on us. I slide my purse onto my shoulder and hurry toward him, eagerly ducking into the stairwell. I don't want to be caught on cameras and I really don't want to talk to the police until I know what is happening. Which can't involve me, or they'd have already called me back or come after me, but my God, what is happening to Danielle? If the police have her phone, she must have been arrested.

It's right then that my phone starts to ring and I dig it from my purse to find Danielle's number on my caller ID. "Don't even think about answering that," the brute behind me warns.

Of course not. Why would I want to answer a call from what is likely the police, who I already hung up on? I stick my phone inside my purse and take a right to the next level of stairs, as I reach for my memories that I'm going to need when I finally talk to the police, which is unavoidably happening. I immediately find myself grappling with random pieces of my father's speech, which leads me to the moment he'd left me on a stage in front of a photographer, giving my step-mother's dress exposure, which was no doubt her intent. The next thing I remember is the aquarium of a bar. The last thing I remember is taking a drink of that s'mores martini. And then here, now. This hell.

I exit to the parking garage and a black sedan is idling directly in front of me. A man opens the door and motions me inside. My heart thunders in my ears with the certainty that Terrance is inside and the hell that this morning represents is about to get even more hellish. I inhale and slide into the back seat, and find that I'm, in fact, alone, aside from a driver, of course. The door shuts me inside and my cellphone rings. I pull it from my phone to find Terrance's number.

"Obviously you're not in the car," I say, as it begins to move. "I am. Now tell me what's going on."

"Listen carefully and do as I say. Call Danielle's number. The police will answer. Tell them that you're on a private plane about to taxi. Security forced you to give up your phone while you were trying to talk to him. Tell him you can call when you land. Ask him about Danielle. Be concerned."

"I am concerned," I snap. "Where is she?"

"You left her at the bar about ten. I've ensured you have witnesses."

"*Why* do I need witnesses?"

"Say nothing else," he says. "You know nothing else."

"They can check my flight details," I say.

"It'll check out," he assures me.

"*What's going on?*" I demand again.

"You know nothing else," he says. "Keep it that way until you finish that call. The driver's safe. Make the call. And remember. You're the future first daughter. Own the conversation and be worthy of your role." He hangs up.

I draw in a shaky breath, my fingers curling into my palm, and when my mind should be only on Danielle, I'm afraid for me, too. I'm selfishly afraid for me but the sooner I deal with my side of this, the sooner I can help Danielle get out of whatever trouble she is in. That's what I have to tell myself to cope with the guilt that comes at me hard and fast. I dial Danielle.

"Ms. Monroe," the same man, Officer Warner, greets me, his tone displeased.

"Hi," I say. "I'm sorry I hung up earlier, but I was in airport security and it about killed me to disconnect. This is

Hailey Anne Monroe. I'm Danielle's best friend. Where is she? Is she okay?"

"We don't know the answer to that question," he says. "We were looking for you to tell us."

"What does that mean?" I ask, confused at his tone that says "missing," not "arrested." "She was fine when I left the bar last night. Where is she now? What is happening?" I sound panicked because I feel panicked.

"You tell me," he orders, and my heart is thundering in my ears again.

"I don't know. I left her at a bar last night. A private club. I can't even remember the name. The Aquarium, I think. Damn it. We're about to lift off. We're—" I disconnect, and my gaze meets the driver's in the mirror.

"It was believable," he assures me.

"Because I am worried about Danielle," I snap, not liking this web of secrets and lies.

I dial Terrance. "Is it done?" he asks.

"Yes. It's done. Now tell me what's happening."

"Did it go well?"

"The driver says it did."

"Did it go well?"

"Yes," I bite out. "I need to know—"

"I'll explain everything on the plane. Turn your phone off. You're in the air, remember?" He disconnects, and I grimace but do as ordered.

I lean forward and speak to the driver. "What do you know?"

"Nothing," he says, and the fact that he looks like a blond, hard dictator of a soldier with sharp cheekbones, and giant hands and muscles, I'm fairly certain he'll kill for me, but he won't talk to me. This is the world I now live in and I assume with him in some version of "the know," I'll be seeing him again.

I sink back into the leather seat and try to remember anything and everything I can, but it's all about the debate. I remember the bar. I remember drinking, but very little else. It's all a fuzzy blank space, with random fluttering images finding a place into my mind's eye. Giving up, I pull out my make-up bag that includes towelettes to remove the mess on my face, before I add a fresh layer. My lips are pink and glossy. My long dirty blonde hair is now braided.

It's only a half hour later, when we reach a private airport with tight security, which I suspect is on my family's behalf. Thankfully that means no press. The brute behind the wheel parks us in a space outside the fancy globe-style building, and then calls over his shoulder. "Wait on me."

Wait for him. This is the luxury of perhaps being the future first daughter. I get to be a grown adult who is ordered around by people I don't even know and expected to just submit. The door opens, and I step outside. He motions to the door. "Who are you?" I ask.

"Your new personal bodyguard."

Great. My personal bodyguard. I'll push back on that one later. "Do you have a name, new personal bodyguard?"

"Rudolf," he says.

"Like the reindeer?"

He gives me a blank stare.

"People don't make that joke to you often, do they?"

"They used to," he replies dryly. "Then I got big."

Great. I have a bodyguard who is big with a small-man complex, named after a Christmas reindeer. There is political folly somewhere in that. I head toward the front door, and there is a whirlwind of activity that leads me straight to the rear of the building and a private jet. With Rudolf on my heels, I climb the steps and enter the plane.

Rudolf claims a seat right inside the door. I walk forward to spy Terrance sitting in a seat in the back of the plane just past a lounge area. He motions me forward and with my heart in my throat, I quickly close the space between us. He indicates the seat directly in front of him. "Buckle up. We're lifting off quickly."

I follow yet another command and do as he's ordered. I've barely secured myself when the plane starts to move, the roar of engines leaving me no room for questions. I am forced to wait until we're in the air and leveled off to speak.

Finally, I unclip my belt and lean forward. "What is happening?"

He motions to a small table in the lounge area and stands up, still holding my answers hostage. I follow him to discover we have four men who resemble Rudolf on board: big, burly, and watchful of the front of the cabin.

I slide into the U-shaped booth across from the man I consider to be my uncle, my hands in my lap under the shiny wooden surface. "Is Danielle missing?" I demand.

"Her shoe and a substantial amount of blood were found in the alleyway behind the bar you two were at."

CHAPTER SIX

Am I capable of murder?

That's inevitably the question I would ask myself over and over after that night in the bar. Right after I got over the denial that I could be a suspect in my best friend's murder. Those moments on that plane sitting with Terrance, and right after I'd found out about Danielle's bloody shoe, I wasn't over the denial. And denial is what drove every question and action I took after that point. Denial that Danielle was dead. Denial that I could really be blamed. Denial that there might be a reason.

THE PAST…

I stare at Terrance, not quite able to comprehend what he's just told me. "Danielle wasn't arrested?"

"Why would you think she was arrested?"

"I just thought—she might be in trouble."

He leans close and grabs my hand. "If you don't remember anything, why would you ask that question?"

His fingers dig into my arm and I yank against his grip, only to have him hold on tighter. "Answer," he orders.

"The police answered her phone," I snap. "My first thought wasn't that she was dead." *She can't be dead,* I think, before tugging against his grip again. "Let go of me."

Almost as if he's spitting me, he pierces me with a hard light-blue stare for several beats before he complies. "I've spent the better part of the night ensuring you do not become a suspect in her murder."

43

"Murder?!" I swallow had and try to catch my breath. "You think she was murdered?" I stand up and tower over him. "You think—"

"Sit back down and act composed, the way a—"

"Future First Daughter acts?" I challenge, pressing my hands on the table and leaning toward him. "Is she dead? Is Danielle dead?"

"Sit down," he bites out. "*Now.*"

"No, because as the future First Daughter, my best friend might be dead. And a First Daughter cares. I care."

"Sit the fuck down. *Now.*"

It's not like standing, or shaking him, which is what I want to do right now, would get me answers. I sit down. "Is she dead?"

"There is no body, but they are treating it as if it's murder. Or an abduction, but thus far there is no ransom request."

"It was supposed to be me, and I left, so they took her," I say. "That has to be it. That's why I have Rudolf."

"It's certainly a consideration," he confirms.

"Maybe they thought she was me. She had on the same color dress. Maybe when they found out it wasn't—"

"They'd still ask for money. She's close to you. She's your friend."

"Who might be dead or being raped or beaten right now, as we speak."

"Tell me what you know," he says as if I haven't spoken.

"That's just it. I don't remember. I don't know how I got back to my room. I think I was drugged. That's the truth."

"That reads like a lie meant to cover-up murder."

My reaction is instant, fierce, angry. I lean forward, and hiss a whispered, "You think I murdered Danielle?!"

"My job is not to judge you. Frankly, I don't care if you're innocent or guilty. I care about how this impacts your father becoming President, which means we're going to make this go away. Now, tell me what you will tell no one else, so I know what I'm dealing with."

"I told you. I didn't kill her."

"Actually, you didn't. You asked if I thought you did." I open my mouth to curse him before I hit him, but he holds up a hand. "Tell me what you remember."

"Nothing. I blacked out. I have vague memories after drinking a martini. The last one is leaving the bar."

"While fighting with Danielle."

"Tobey told you." Of course he told Terrance. The man is his father.

"Yes," he says. "He did, but he won't be telling the police. He doesn't want to be connected to murder either. He left with you and dropped you at the hotel early. Danielle refused to leave."

"Surely there are witnesses that will say otherwise?"

"Tobey says that's exactly what happened."

"Where is he now?"

"At the police station, answering questions and setting the groundwork for you to back him up."

"Why didn't I just stay and answer questions?"

"Tobey is not you, but he is the man who wants to be your future and in the White House. He has your back and ours."

"Why didn't I stay and answer questions?" I repeat.

"We hope that a little space and time means the mystery is solved, and you aren't in the middle of this."

"She was my best friend—*is* my best friend. I'm in this. It's going to get press."

"That I control and that means I need to know whatever it is that you aren't telling me."

"I don't remember anything after that drink, which is why I think I was drugged," I say, "and—and maybe that is proof that someone intended to abduct me." I leave out the part where I thought I was drugged by Danielle. That was wrong. It couldn't have been Danielle. "Tobey saved me," I add. "I'm sure he's told you this, too. Danielle got in the line of fire. I just need to tell the truth."

"The police don't need to hear that you were drugged. You left. Danielle stayed. And besides, Tobey says that you were perfectly fine when you left the bar and when he left you in your room. You stick to the story. You were worried about bad press and Tobey took you to your room. He said that he never even wanted to go to the bar for that very reason. Danielle convinced you to go. You left Danielle, in said bar, because it was a private club and she refused to leave. Understand?"

I stare at him two beats, but I nod. "Yes. I understand."

"Repeat it."

"I was concerned about bad press for my father and Tobey, who tried to convince me not to go out at all, was quick to escort me to my room."

"Good. We're going to repeat that story about a hundred times on this flight."

"Where is my father and what does he say about all of this?"

"Back in Washington as far from Austin, and this mess, as I could get him."

"What did he say about—it all?"

"He's worried. About you. About Danielle. About this country."

In other words, he's worried about his campaign.

"Let's review your story," Terrance says, refocusing me on his expectations, which, of course, are really my father's. "I left early. Tobey took me home. Danielle stayed at the bar." I repeat the rest of the story. I take his questions as if they are that of the police. It's a full hour later when he sends me to a seat in the back of the plane to rest.

I choose a spot away from him, alone, which is how I feel right now. I'm terrified I'm going to be accused of murder, and I hate myself for even worrying about that when Danielle could be dead. But I am, and I have questions in my mind, questions about myself, and what happened last night. About my anger with Danielle, that I somehow know exists, but I can't remember why. But I don't let myself go there. I can't go there now, because if I question myself, others might question me.

Right now, I just want to get this police interview over and I find myself thinking through the perfect story

Terrance has created. In doing so, I also find myself wondering, is a lie a lie if you don't know that it's not the truth?

LISA RENEE JONES

CHAPTER SEVEN

As I sat on that plane, the human will to survive flared inside me, and pushed aside thoughts of Danielle. I focused on what I must face in my near future: anticipating my police interview, as well as the confrontation with my father sure to await me in Washington. This lead me to something Terrance said to my father during one of the few debate preps I participated in, or rather sat in on. The dictionary defines a lie as "a false statement made with deliberate intent to deceive; an intentional untruth; a falsehood." In other words, while you do not control your destiny, you do control the lies that you tell. What I realized on that plane, is what I've known for a long time, but chosen not to see: growing up in politics teaches you that lies are avoided by the many versions of the truth. Or maybe it's my father that taught me that lesson. Which brings me to another thing Terrance said to my father during that debate night prep: own your version of the truth. Believe it. Make everyone believe it. As I moved forward from the night in that Austin, Texas bar, starting with the moment the plane touched ground in Washington, I would begin to see the lesson in those words to be profoundly necessary.

THE PAST...

It's nearly noon when the plane lands in Washington, and I meet Terrance in the center of the plane. "Are we going straight to the police department?"

49

"Rudolf will escort you to the Ritz. You'll be staying in a large suite with him."

My lips part. "You want Rudolf to stay with me?"

"I don't *want* him to. *He is.* For all we know, and as you've astutely pointed out, you might well have been the target last night. You get Rudolf until we determine if you were a target last night."

"I'm not staying with that man in a hotel room. That's not a smart decision."

"Per the Secret Service, who we consulted, it is the right decision. Rudolf will be your shadow and dealing with such things is just part of this job."

"Only this isn't a job for me," I say. "It's my life."

"It *is* your job, and like all royalty, you were born into it and you will accept the responsibility with grace and dignity. Are we clear?"

"I have never done anything but stand by my father," I reply tightly, reminded that every time this man plays nice with me, it's also his job. "Even when I melted down over my mother," I add, "aside from the teachers who saw my grades, no one knew. So don't tell me how to handle things with grace and dignity. This has been my life long before you even knew my father. Going to a hotel and hiding out makes me look guilty."

"More like it supports a real fear for your safety by your father, and as I said, it's what the Secret Service recommends." His phone buzzes in his hand and he glances at it and me. "We need to move." He hesitates and presses his hands to my arm. "This isn't about your father. I want you safe. Okay?"

What do I really say here? We both know it is, in fact, about my father. I settle on what gets me off this plane. "Yes," I say. "Okay. I'll need to pick up things at my apartment."

"We don't want to alert anyone to your arrival. Order what you need on your father's hotel account. They know to cover it and keep it nameless. Let's get moving." And that's the end of the conversation, apparently. He releases me and turns, walking away and dismissing my concerns that are still alive and well. For instance, the fact that I told the police I was headed back here. He's worried about me, my ass. This plan makes my father look like a concerned father, but how does it make me look to law enforcement? I guess that returns me to the truth that I cannot hide. There's a reason I plan to go to law school outside Washington. My life is under my father's control and he chose the Ritz for me.

Terrance exits the plane and I head down the aisle to have Rudolf step into view, waiting on me near the door. I inhale with the certainty that he's a spy for Terrance as much as he is here for my safety. I'm halfway to him when I have a flickering memory of me at the back door of the bar when Danielle grabbed my arm. I remember turning to her. I remember shouting at her, but I don't know why. The memory, what's there of it, is here and gone, and I blink to realize that I've gripped a seat and stopped walking. If Rudolf notices, his stony face gives no indication of such, and that works for me.

I charge toward him and he backs into the galley to allow me to pass. Once I exit the plane, he's on my heels, and I find Terrance climbing into the back of one of two black sedans. By the time I'm on the runway, his car pulls away and a driver opens the rear door of the second car for me. I settle inside, but after the door shuts, the man who'd held it open doesn't enter the front. Rudolf does. A man I don't know, but now have to trust with intimate pieces of my life. Until this is over, I'm being watched on a level that I want to reject, but am forced to accept. In other words, while I try to figure out my version of the truth about last night, he'll be right here supervising me.

I ride the elevator to my suite with Rudolf by my side and I don't attempt conversation with him. I just want into the room, where I can order room service, and shop for what I need to allow me to shower and re-dress. I need to be ready for whatever comes my way. We exit to my floor, and Rudolf, *my guard,* I decide to call him, since his name just makes me crazy, has my key. He pulls it from his jacket and hands it to me. "I'll need to go in first, to ensure it's clear."

"Which means anyone could grab me while I wait out here," I point out.

"The floor is secure."

"The codes on those elevators can easily be hacked."

His lips harden and his phone buzzes. He removes it from his pants, glances down at it, and then returns it to his pocket. Immediately after, he unlocks the door, and shoves it open, only to step back and motion me forward. "Ladies first," he says.

I'm no fool. I don't mistake his sudden change of tune as a win. Instead, it tells me that call he took dictated this action. Perhaps he's been told to stand down and my heart begins to race with why that might be. "Did they find Danielle? Is she okay?"

"I've not been made aware of any changes."

I narrow my eyes on him but there is nothing to read in his infuriatingly blank, hard face. Determined to find out the truth myself, and do so in the privacy of a sealed bedroom, I hurry into the suite. Once I'm past the threshold, I enter a living area done in blue and cream, stopping dead in my tracks when I realize that I'm not alone. A man in a perfectly tailored blue suit is facing the floor-to-ceiling arched window.

My father turns to face me, and as usual, his presence consumes the room. He's a powerful man. He knows it. You know it when you're with him.

In unison, we step forward, both of us stepping to the opposite sides of a square coffee table, two navy couches framing us.

"Daughter," he says, a familiar reference I know is not one of endearment but rather a reminder of family obligation.

"Father," I say, giving him the obligatory response he's looking for, and I wonder if I'm just noticing the deeper gray mixed with the blonde at his temples, or if it's newly formed, and compliments of me. I'm quite sure he'd declare the latter to be accurate.

"Terrance says that you don't remember what happened to Danielle."

"I don't," I confirm.

"You're sure?" he presses.

My defenses bristle. "You think I'm lying?"

"I need to know the facts."

"I don't *know* the facts. I know Terrance told you that I was drugged."

"You will not repeat anything about drugs beyond this moment," he snaps, his blue eyes cutting. "The last thing I need is for that to get turned into you being an addict."

"Right," I say bitterness seeping into my voice. "No worries about me or Danielle here. The only focus you have is me not making you look bad."

"You're obviously fine and there is a big picture here that involves the entire country and beyond."

"And we can't let my potentially dead best friend get in the way." I don't wait for a reply. "You do realize there is a bigger picture here, right? I might well have been drugged by someone who wanted to kidnap me"

"Which is why you're here in this room with a guard."

"And yet you don't want me to tell the police the real story?"

"What is the real story, Hailey?" he demands. "You were drugged and might have gone nuts and killed Danielle?"

"I can't believe you just said that to me," I hiss.

"This isn't about guilt," he replies. "It's about where this could go and how bad it can get no matter what your good intentions. I'm protecting you."

"You mean you."

"Both of us," he corrects. "We *cannot* risk you being turned into a fictional addict. As of right now, thanks to Terrance, this incident has been suppressed with the media. That won't last but my hope is that you get through the law enforcement interview by the time it happens."

"Or that Danielle shows up alive?" I challenge.

"Of course, that's what we all want to happen," he says, his tone agitated, "which is why law enforcement is pushing to talk to you today. They want you to help them find her."

"I can't help at all and how am I going to explain that? We just determined that I can't tell them that I was drugged."

"You say what Terrance told you to say. You didn't want to be in that bar, didn't stay, and when Danielle wouldn't leave, Tobey took you home. Don't go off that script."

"I want this over with. What time is it happening and where?"

"Here. With Bob Nickels present."

"Your attorney," I breathe out. "I need an attorney?"

"Danielle is missing," he says. "There was blood. It's standard for anyone in your high-profile position to protect themselves."

"It makes me look guilty," I say, going back to that concern.

"It makes you smart enough to know that I have political enemies that would do anything to take me down, and that means you."

"Are you suggesting someone would kill Danielle and frame me?"

"I'm telling you that when your father may soon be the most powerful man in the world, there are enemies who want blood. People can get hurt."

"She can't be dead."

"We both know that's not true," he says. "People die, often without warning." His tone is cutting, the reference obviously to my dead mother. His damning blame, a round-about explanation as to why I don't deserve sympathy or words of comfort. "Give me your phone," he adds.

My brow furrows. "What?"

"We can't risk it having anything on it that might hurt us. It'll be cleaned and returned."

"No I—"

"*Give me* your phone."

I suddenly regret not looking through it more closely before now. Why didn't I look through it for clues to last night? "I'll check it," I promise quickly, feeling stupid when I'm many things, but stupid is usually not one of them. "If there's a problem—"

"Danielle," he bites out. "I do not have time for this."

"What if the police ask for it?"

"Tell them you gave it to my security team," he says, without missing a beat. "If they want to know why, tell them you were told it was a precaution to ensure your safety. Any further details they request on the matter, should be referred to Terrance."

I purse my lips, but I unzip my purse, remove my phone but I can't let it go without confirming that there is nothing on it from Danielle that I missed earlier. I glance at my text messages, and the last thing from Danielle is the joke about doing my step-brother. "Hailey," my father snaps.

I quickly check my phone log for Danielle as well, and when there are no calls in the timeframe in question, I hand my father my phone. "What was that about?" he demands.

"I just needed to know I didn't miss a message or call from Danielle."

He arches a brow. "Did you?"

"No," I say. "There's nothing from her after the debate ended."

He doesn't comment or react. He just pockets my phone. "Get yourself cleaned up and ready for the interview. Rudolf will let you know when it's time."

Just as I thought. Rudolf will let me know.

He steps around the table and heads for the door. I stand there. I listen to his footsteps and I don't turn around. If I do, I might shout at him and I have plenty to shout. I'm angry. So very angry and not just about this. About five years of him treating me as crappy as he is today. So yes. I really want to shout at him, but I don't. I'm trained. I know that a future First Daughter does not shout or demand. That would be undignified. It would be too raw, too real, too close to my version of the truth that my father could not handle. He doesn't want to talk about our personal baggage or how that's affected me on a normal day. Today is not normal, and he doesn't care about anything but making last night go away. And that seems to mean Danielle.

CHAPTER EIGHT

How do you decide who is a best friend?

Loyalty? Trust? Love? I used to believe all of those things and more were a part of that sacred bond. I'd certainly proven myself to Danielle. I know what she did the summer we were in Europe and my silence constitutes my "best friend" status, right along with my own version of guilt. It also constitutes a secret so damning that back then, and for years after, I couldn't think about it without freaking myself out and I did think about it often. It haunted me, tormented me. Gave me nightmares. Obviously, that was before I accepted the destiny parts of our lives, that we cannot change, but eventually, the human survival instinct kicked in and I found a way to lock that memory away. It was how I stayed "best friends" with Danielle.

That is until she disappeared.

I won't say that I didn't worry about Danielle. I did but it wasn't that simple and cut and dry. There were complexities to my thoughts, layers to who and what we were together that reached beyond one night. Among them, I'd begun to obsess over the idea that she'd drugged me, the very person who'd kept a massive secret for her, at what could have been my own demise.

Spoiler alert: I would never prove that she drugged me, but from the moment I woke up in that hotel room in Austin, Texas, with her missing, on some level I declared it to be true. Therefore, every action I took, every question in my mind that would follow, would be shadowed by that certainty. What had she done to me and what had I done to her?

THE PAST...
I stand in the middle of the hotel room and listen as my father opens the door. Immediately after, he and Rudolf exchange muffled words, no doubt about my containment. Despite the fact that it's most likely the best choice before me, I resent how it was handled, as if at twenty-two years old, I'm nothing more than a dog that must be obedient or be punished. Actually, he treated our family dog when I was growing up better than he does me.

The door shuts again, and I feel Rudolf's presence. I walk to the right toward what appears to be the master suite, and I don't look back at him. I cross the living room and I'm about to escape when I hear, "Do no use the phone."

I rotate to face Rudolf. "Dial my father."

"Why would I do that?"

"He ordered me to clean up for my meeting. I have no clothes, no make-up, no products whatsoever. I'll need to have my father halt his campaign duties to make a Victoria's Secret and Nordstrom's stop for me, since I'm not allowed to use the hotel shopping service."

"We both know that you've been instructed to use the hotel shopping service."

"Was I?" I ask.

He stares at me for several hard beats and then walks to the desk on the wall right beside me, picking up the phone. In other words, I'm to make the call with him present. I could reject this idea. I could fight him, but to what end? It would get me nowhere but frustrated and exhausted when I need to get my head on straight for this meeting. I walk toward him, accept the receiver and offer him my back. Once I'm done arranging what I need, I transfer to room service, order and then hand Rudolf the menu. "You should order. You're going to need your energy to live this life with me."

He gives me a tilt of the head and accepts the phone. I head to the bedroom, and shut myself inside, aware that he'll leave the phone off the hook when he's done to prevent further usage. I'm trapped. I'm without means to communicate with the outside world and I can't even search the internet for clues as to what is happening now, or what was happening last night in Austin, as well as here.

I stare at the fancy, but generic room with its cream-colored leather headboard, and white bedding, but it's the balcony behind lace balloon drapes that draw my attention. I cross the room and open the double doors, stepping outside onto the half-moon shaped balcony, ignoring the lounge chairs and table to my right to step to the steel railing. I close my fingers around it, looking over the city. We're eleven stories up, high enough to put the swim lessons my father forced on me to use. I could easily dive to my death, a dramatic end to my life, sure to haunt my father with rumors of my guilt, and his poor parenting.

I'm not sure how long I stand there, contemplating that jump, seeing myself fly through the air, but where I land is not the ground. It's in the darkness of my mind, in the past. Suddenly I am sitting in my mother's car, reliving the moments after the crash. The moment the car jerked to a stop and I breathed out, "Mom," only to look at her and find a piece of steel inside her chest.

I sink to my knees, hard stone biting into my skin and bones, my hands on the concrete wall in front of me, and the image of my mother morphs into me in the hallway of the aquarium bar, with Danielle grabbing my arm. Anger erupts in me, but I don't know why. I want to shake her. I think I do. I know I do. Tobey is there. I think I hit him. Did I hit him? I think I—

There is a pounding sound and I gasp as I hear, "Ms. Monroe. Ms. Monroe," in a deep, urgent voice. I look over my shoulder as Rudolf charges in this direction and kneels beside me. "Are you okay?" he demands.

"Yes. I'm fine." I try to push to my feet and he helps me up, but I quickly back away, biting back a thank you that my mother would expect me to say. I cannot send a message to Rudolf that he can step into my private space. He's too sly, too sharp, and on my father's side, which is never good for me.

Instead, I snap, "Why are you in my room?"

"Why are you on the ground?"

"Bad memory," I say, recognizing his job to protect me is in play here. "Just a bad memory."

"About last night?" he asks quickly, too quickly for my comfort, which is why I snap again.

"About seeing my mother with steel in her chest," I say, admitting what I'd prefer to keep to myself, but I have no choice. I don't want him to tell someone I acted guilty of something. "Why are you in my room?" I repeat.

"I knocked and you wouldn't answer. The food is here."

My brow furrows because we just ordered.

"Forty-five minutes ago," he supplies, clearly reading my thoughts.

"They're usually slower here," I lie, the realization that I've lost time a terrifying one he doesn't need to know.

He doesn't buy my cover-up. "You lost time," he accuses.

I open my mouth to tell him I was drugged, but zip my lips on that forbidden topic. "Bad memories take up good time that should have been shared."

He studies me several beats. "A profound statement."

Profoundly brutal, I think. "Do we have a time on the interview?"

"Four o'clock. It's two now. Your clothes should be here by the time you finish eating."

"I'll come grab my tray," I say.

"I'll put in on the desk here in the room."

I nod and he disappears. I don't follow him. I turn back to the city view, picturing that dive again, and this time, it's not as palpable as it was before. I turn and lean on the railing, facing the room. The drugs in my system are clearly messing with me. I need that food to absorb them before my interview, and feeling encouraged that a meal might return my memory, I wait eagerly for Rudolf to return and depart again. It didn't work the first time this happened to me, but maybe it will this time.

The instant my door shuts with him on the outside, I hurry to the desk, sit down, and scarf down my omelet and fruit, downing two cups of coffee in the process. Once I'm done, I sit there and try to conjure memories, but there is nothing. I'm still haunted with small pieces of last night, but I can't even get back to the moments of anger I'd felt at Danielle, before Rudolf had interrupted. I can't figure out where Tobey fits and why I would hit him. Did I really hit him?

There's a knock on the door, no doubt my retail items, and I stand up, open the door, and find Rudolf holding my bags. Sixty seconds later, they're in my room, he's not, and I'm headed to the shower. Once I'm under the water, I have that same awkward sensation I'd had after my mother had died. A moment when I think how wrong it feels to be doing normal things when someone has died, or in Danielle's case, perhaps captive to some monster, who could be doing lord-knows-what to her. And yet, life goes on, even when we wish it would not.

I drown myself in hot water for an excessive amount of time, in which I remember nothing more about last night, thus forcing me to move on to a choice I've made once before in my life thanks to my Europe trip with Danielle: what to wear for a police interview. Considering my "best friend" is missing, I decide on a belted black dress, pulling my dirty blonde hair that somehow seems more dirty blonde today, back at my nape.

I've just finished readying myself, at least on the outside, for whatever comes next, when I somehow, without any obvious trigger, end up flashing through a collage of memories of my dead mother; her laughing, smiling. Yelling at me after that party, right before she died. There it is. The connection between now and then. Death. Anger. Danielle. I flatten my hands on the bathroom counter, staring at myself, preparing for what always comes right after the memory of my mother yelling at me. It's not us in the car.

It's not the impact of the crash. It's not her bloodied body. It's my father arriving at the accident site, grabbing my arms and shaking me. "You did this," he'd shouted gutturally. "She wouldn't have been here if not for you."

Emotions jab at me and I shove off the counter, walk to the bedroom, where I stop and stare at the open balcony doors. If I jumped, my father would win the sympathy vote and the presidency. He'd probably celebrate right with Mommy Dearest and her perfect son. I'd be forgotten for political gain, just as Danielle is forgotten in political crisis. Rejecting both premises, my lips purse, and I walk to the door and open it.

CHAPTER NINE

I misstated a fact in my story, which we all know is a nice way of saying that I lied to you. Maybe I'm more like my father than I like to admit. Whatever the brutal truth of that matter, here's another truth, if any human being is capable of offering such a thing: I haven't been interviewed by law enforcement two times, but rather four.

You'd assume, I'm sure, that the first time was when I was sixteen, after my mother's death, and about the crash that killed her, but it wasn't. That was law enforcement encounter number two. The first time was a year before, while on European holiday with Danielle and her father. It was then that I recounted an event that I'd witnessed, and in doing so, I told the truth and yet I told lies. That sounds like a contradiction, but it's not. Sitting across from a detective that I'd never met until that day, and would never see again, I actually believed what I told him. I, like Danielle, saw a woman take a selfie, lose her footing, and fall off a mountainside to her death.

It wasn't until later that I admitted to myself that my truth had been fiction. It wasn't until later that I admitted that I'd lied. She hadn't lost her footing at all. Nevertheless, whatever led that woman to that moment, it seemed then like a random, tragic event that shouldn't be a part of the rest of my story. Later though, much later, in fact, I'd find out that just as there is no such thing as real choices in life, nothing is ever random. But I'm getting ahead of the story. We'll come back to the woman on that mountainside.

Right now, we're focused on my third sit-down with law enforcement, which occurred the morning after

Danielle disappeared, and not long after my twenty-second birthday. What I didn't know in advance of that meeting, but you do now, is that actions had been taken before it occurred, outcomes already set in stone, and nothing that I would say, or could have said, would have changed those outcomes. In fact, I'd go so far as to say that despite it being last week, and eight years after the interview I had following Danielle's disappearance, my fourth interview with law enforcement, was the spawn of those actions and outcomes.

THE PAST—THE INTERVIEW...

My father's attorney, Bob Nickels, arrives an hour before my interview, and we gather around the massive dining room table in my suite; him across from me, with Rudolf at the end cap between us. I study Bob, and he studies a file in front of him, ignoring me, as if that file is more interesting than my words. He's mid-forties, with a GQ face and body, a Hells Angel's attitude, and in my opinion, no cares about anything but money and his own version of fame. In other words, he suits my father, and now I have to decide if he suits me.

Tired of watching him watch that file, I end the silence. "You're not a criminal attorney," I say, stating the obvious, which I doubt my father or Bob himself, gave me credit for recognizing. "Why are you the one that's here?"

"I spent two years with the DA before I decided I'd rather compromise my morals for money than a greedy DA."

"In other words," I say, "we the people should be pleased to know my father has an attorney willing to compromise his values for money?"

His lips tighten. "We the people," he bites out, "should be comforted to know the future President's daughter doesn't go to a bar and get into trouble, which," he opens a file that he doesn't look at, before adding, "I'm here to spin you as the innocent protector of your wild-child friend."

Danielle is not *my wild-child friend,* I think, but I barely manage those words without a cut of my eyes.

Rudolf laces his fingers together on the walnut finished table and looks at me. "You better lie better than that if you plan to lie your way through this interview."

"Why are *you* here?" I demand, looking from him to Bob. "Don't I have a right to client-attorney privilege?"

"He's former FBI," Bob replies. "Which makes him the perfect person to walk you through a mock interview." He holds up documents. "Danielle is working for your father. We know her party girl history, which she assured us in the interviews were long behind her. She was only hired as a favor to her father by your father, and with the understanding that if she slipped up even once, she's out."

"My father doesn't do favors he believes would jeopardize his candidacy," I retort. "In other words, he wouldn't hire her at all if he saw her as a risk."

"Your interviewer," Rudolf interjects, "will have done his homework. He'll know Danielle's history."

"There is no history," I reply irritably, "not beyond a normal college student attending frat parties and living life. And this isn't about her party history."

"Her party history doesn't fit your role in your father's life," he says. "The agent sent to interview you will look for a reason you had to kill her. Troublemaker fits."

My mind flashes back a moment in the bar when I'd read her text messages, to a swipe of unexplainable anger that I try to understand. What was in those messages?

Even while I do so, Bob eyes his Rolex that I'm sure my father paid for, about a hundred times over, and then me. "Thanks to the short notice of this incident," he says, "we have limited prep time." He flattens his hands on the table. "Let's get to work. Repeat the story your father gave you to tell."

"I didn't want to go to the bar," I say, already tired of this story. "Danielle didn't want to leave. Tobey took me back to my room. You need to know that I don't remember last night. I think I was drugged."

"Do not repeat what your father told you not to repeat."

"You're my attorney," I remind him. "And I'm stuck with Rudolf."

"You were with Tobey," Bob states. "He'll back you up. You back him up."

"What do you know that I don't know?" I ask.

"Enough to stop talking about being drugged," he snaps. "Now. Rudolf will get you ready for the actual presentation of the story we've given you to use." He motions to Rudolf. "Do it. Question her."

Rudolf complies and hits me with a question. "Why did you go to the bar last night?"

"Because my father's an asshole who ignored me after the debates," I state honestly, when honesty isn't what he's looking for, "and," I add, "I needed to let off steam."

"Holy fuck," Bob bites out. "This is not a game, little girl. Your father's running for the most powerful office in the world. Get it right and do it now. Understand?"

I purse my lips. "Yes. I understand."

"Good." He motions to Rudolf. "Begin again."

"Why did you go the bar last night?" Rudolf repeats.

This time, I offer the answer as I'm expected to offer it: politically fluffed. "Danielle coordinated a first debate celebration at a private venue that felt secure and appropriate."

"Danielle coordinated the visit to the bar?" he confirms.

"Yes," I reply, offering nothing I don't have to offer, which is also the politically fluffed version of any interview.

"Elaborate," he commands.

I arch a brow. "What do you want to know?"

His lips quirk every-so-slightly. "How did you get from the debate venue to the bar?"

"She and Tobey were waiting on me outside the debate event center," I say. "Tobey didn't want me to go to the bar because he's quite protective of my reputation. But Danielle pressed us and we caved. Or I did. Tobey only went along to look out for me."

"But you didn't leave with her?" Rudolf counters.

66

"No," I say. "Tobey's disapproval read like my father's and I just couldn't get past that. I regretted the decision to go to the bar almost immediately upon arriving. Danielle didn't want to leave when I told her I was leaving, and she chose to stay there on her own, but that wasn't unusual. Because of my father's career, I've been the one to go while she stayed during most of our college years, actually even as far back as high school."

"Like the night your mother died?"

My anger is instant, and I surge to my feet. "This is over."

"If you can't handle me," Rudolf assures me. "You can't handle this interviewer who will be looking for a reason you hate her enough to kill her."

"She wasn't even around when my mother died," I snap.

"And if she had been?" Rudolf presses. "How would things have changed?"

I wouldn't have ended up alone in a park and my mother might be alive, I think, but my self-preservation is strong enough to say, "Thank God, she wasn't," I say. "The steel went through my mother to the back seat. Danielle might have died in that crash, too."

Rudolf looks at Bob and back at me. "Good answer. Go with it."

I lean on the table and glower at him. "They won't go down this path."

"You don't know that," he states flatly. "You opened the door the minute you said high school. Don't open the door to a room you don't want them to visit."

"They wouldn't know to associate Danielle with my mother, but I know who would." I straighten and look at Bob. "My father told you to ask that question."

He doesn't even blink. His reply is instant. "Your father knew that if you could handle that, you could handle anything. He was right. You did well."

I laugh without humor. "This is priceless," I say. "My father tests me by tormenting me with my mother, knowing that I'm fearing for the safety of my best friend."

"Your father is trying to protect you," Bob states.

"My father is trying to protect himself," I counter.

"This isn't some local cop that doesn't know what he's doing," Rudolf states. "You crossed states lines and your father is a presidential candidate. This is the FBI you're dealing with, and that's another playing field."

I'm actually relieved at this new information. "The FBI has to worry about my father becoming their boss."

"Exactly," Bob states. "So if they don't like him, now's the time to use you to keep him out of the White House." There is a knock on the door and Bob grimaces. "Just like the FBI to be early. They're trying to throw you off."

"Good thing this isn't a game," I say sarcastically, referencing his prior comment before I round the table on my way to the living room.

"Come back here," Bob shouts after me, but I don't listen. Rudolf was right. If I'm going to lie, I have to lie better than I lied about Danielle's partying. Which means I can't do this their way. I have to do it my way, naturally, not scripted. Because this *is* a game and no matter how little credit my father may give me, I have practiced and perfected my responses, thanks mostly to the press always wanting more than I can give them. I *am* the future First Daughter, and that's all I've been my entire life.

I march out into the living room and straight for the door, with one thing in mind: what *I* want and should want, for that matter. Once I'm there, I open the door, and find a stocky man in a blue suit and tie on the other side, his hair speckled with gray. "Ms. Monroe," he greets, flashing me an FBI badge. "I'm Agent Clemons."

"Did you find Danielle?" I ask quickly, and I don't know where it comes from, but emotion explodes inside me, morphing into anger. "Did you?" I demand, rather than ask, this time.

"No, we have not," he replies. "But we're trying."

"Is there a ransom?"

"Not as of yet, but your father's fear that you were a target last night is valid. He was smart to get you out of there."

"Right," I say, but the very idea that my father did anything to protect me instead of himself, pisses me off.

"Can I come in?" he asks.

"If I say no?"

"I'll ask you to come with me."

"If you mean to Texas, to help find Danielle, I'm ready."

"Ms. Monroe—"

"Come in," I say, backing into the room, and leaving him there. He's a federal agent. He can get in the door without my supervision.

I also ignore Bob and Rudolf, who are now in the living room gaping at me. Bob hurries toward Agent Clemons. I cross through the living area to stand at the window. The three men exchange niceties that feel as inappropriate as my shower had felt, as living life feels when someone is dead or bleeding somewhere, who knows where. I hit my "normal" limit when the three of them gather in the living room and start in on small talk about the debate.

I whirl around to face them. "Can we talk about Danielle? *Where* is she?"

The three of them seal their lips and stare at me. Bob indicates the empty spot on the couch next to him, while Rudolf and Agent Clemons claim the ones directly across from him. I walk closer to them, into the line of the couches, but I do not sit. "I'll stand," I say, folding my arms in front of me. "What are we doing to find Danielle?"

I'm surprised when Agent Clemons stands and doesn't just face me. He closes the small space between me and him. "Talk to me," he says softly, trying to soothe the little girl who would be First Daughter into talking. "Tell me anything and everything you can remember that might help me find her."

"There's nothing to tell," I say. "I let her talk me into going to that club. Obviously, I should have tried harder to talk her out of it."

"Why didn't you want to go?"

"My father's running for President," I state. "I can't risk exposure to scandal."

"But you went anyway."

Bob steps to our sides. "Let's go sit down at the table and talk," he states firmly.

I stay focused on Agent Clemons. "The reality of being in the sights of the office of the presidency had my head spinning," I say. "I wanted to just be a little normal for a tiny window of time, but Tobey felt it as a mistake. He kept on and on, to the point that I felt like my father was in my ear. I had to leave."

"But you left Danielle," he reminds me.

"Let's go sit down," Bob insists, hardening his voice.

"She wanted to stay," I snap, ignoring Bob.

"So you cut and run on your friends easily," Agent Clemons accuses.

I laugh in disbelief. "You don't tell Danielle what to do. When she makes up her mind, you go along for the ride or get off."

"Has she ever taken you on a ride you didn't want to go on?" Agent Clemons challenges.

"Enough!" Bob snaps. "Either we sit down and formally continue, or this interview is over."

I glance at him. "I'm fine, Bob," I state. "I want to get past this and get on with what's being done to find Danielle. Don't you think we need to know what's being done to find her?"

"Of course, I do," he states, and after studying me a beat, he eyes Agent Clemons. "If this standing up and confronting her is your method of interviewing and how you plan to play this with the future First Daughter, you have five minutes and not a second more. Then you leave." He glances at his watch. "It starts now."

Agent Clemons circles back to the prior question. "Did Danielle ever push your limits in ways you didn't want to be pushed?"

"I love her free spirit," I say. "I love that she helps me see beyond the box of the presidency and so the answer is yes. She's pushed me out of my comfort zone, but I like it."

"How did she push you?" he presses.

"As recently as last year," I say. "I was afraid of rollercoasters." I leave out the part where the car crash with my mother created certain phobias, continuing on with, "Danielle made me ride one ten times until I was numb to the fear. It worked."

His lips tighten. "Being a smart-ass will get you nowhere, Ms. Monroe."

"How is sharing an endearing story of my best friend being a smart-ass, agent? Danielle is one of the only people in this world who knows me well enough to know that I need to push myself to overcome fears."

"And yet she didn't know you well enough to know that you felt you shouldn't be at that club last night?"

"She knows me well enough to know that I couldn't go to the club unless it was private and secure. That's why I caved and went with her. Because she cared enough to do that for me. It just didn't feel right when I got there. Not with Tobey yakking in my ear."

"When and where did you last see her?" he asks, changing gears.

"At the bar last night," I say, "I don't remember what time I left. It wasn't very late."

"And what did you do when you got back to your room?" he asks.

"I went to bed," I say, and I don't blink. It's the truth. I woke up in bed. Obviously at some point I went there.

"Alone?" he presses.

"That's none of your business," I snap.

"Did you go back to the bar?"

"No," I say quickly. It feels like the truth.

"Did Tobey stay with you last night?" he asks. "Can he corroborate that story?"

"I'm not telling you that," I say, unsure of what Tobey told the FBI.

"Why not?" Agent Clemons demands. "It's your alibi."

"It's also the kind of gossip that ends up all over the press," I reply.

Agent Clemons' eyes sharpen. "Are you suggesting I'll leak it?"

"Are you suggesting the FBI has never leaked information?" I challenge, reminding him of recent scandals all over the same press, I don't want to be all over.

He smirks. "Are you running for office or your father?"

"Are you Democratic or Republican?" I counter.

He scowls. "What does that have to do with this?"

"I'm trying to decide if you're trying to take down a would-be President by harassing his daughter, or are you trying to find a missing person?"

"The FBI is party-neutral," he assures me.

"I've grown up around politics," I say. "I knew by age ten that in Washington, there is no such thing as party-neutral."

His scowl deepens. "Did Tobey stay the night with you?"

"Don't protect Tobey's privacy," Bob instructs, finally getting the memo that I don't remember last night, while offering me half-placed guidance. "Answer the man's question."

"I've already said that Tobey was with me last night," I reply, still concerned about the cameras in the hotel that might call me a liar. "I told you," I add. "He's very protective."

Agent Clemons' phone buzzes and he removes it from his pocket, glances at the message, and then glances between myself and Bob. "I'm done here." He heads for the door.

I blanch. "What? No. What just happened?"

Bob's cellphone begins to buzz as well but I ignore it and him. "Agent Clemons," I bite out, in a near shout. "Stop," I order. "We are not done."

He halts and turns to face me. "I assure you, Ms. Monroe. We *are* done."

"What does that mean? Did you find her?" My heart starts to thunder in my chest. "Did you find Danielle?" I ask, more urgently.

"No," he says quickly. "We did *not*."

"Then what are you doing to find her?"

"Our jobs." He presents me with his back, opens the door, and exits the apartment.

I whirl around to find Bob grabbing his briefcase from the coffee table where it landed at some point. "Now it's time for me to do my job and talk with Agent Clemons," he says, heading for the door.

I don't try to stop him. Whatever just happened, happened, no one plans to give me details.

Rudolf crosses to the door behind Bob, and locks it, but I don't even ask him for details. He's in my father's pocket. It seems I'm the only one who's not.

CHAPTER TEN

What happened next would feel important to me at the time.

This was when I found out Danielle's fate. This was when I would fret over my choices, certain that my leaving that bar in Austin had created Danielle's destiny, but I was still confused back then. I still believed we actually have choices that change our futures. I still believed that had I stayed at that bar with Danielle, her ultimate fate would have been someone else's or even mine. I still didn't understand that destiny isn't a choice. I still didn't understand that destiny is not fickle. It's precise. It's a surgeon's blade that cuts with precision, until only those who should feel pain, feel that pain. Those who understand this feel no guilt for what cannot be changed. Those who do not, suffer.

The surgeon is immune to it all, without consequence. The surgeon is just the necessary tool.

THE PAST—THE DAY AFTER MY INTERVIEW WITH AGENT CLEMONS…

In morning light, comes breaking light.

I wake in a hotel bed alone, and jolt to a sitting position with those words in my mind. I don't know where those words came from, a quote from a book I read somewhere, I think, but it's a lie; there is no breaking light. The room dances with shadows that scream of the night hour, but a cursory glance at the bedside clock confirms the eight am hour, while the puttering on the patio door, and the rumbling of thunder in the near distance announces a storm. Fully grounded in the present now, I return to the statement "in morning light, comes breaking light" and search my mind for memories of Danielle and that night in Austin, but there is no "light" there, either. Obviously, the book I remember was a fairytale and this is not.

Glancing at the silent, but live television, a newscaster is on the screen, and the idea that the woman might be offering me updates that no one else seems willing to share, sets me into action. I hunt for the remote, looking here and there, digging around in the sheets until I finally find it under my pillow. I turn up the volume, and soon discover an oil spill to be the present highlight of the show, I channel flip, to find more of the same. Hitting the mute button, I toss the remote onto the mattress, throw aside the blankets, and sit up. I glance at the bedroom door and accept the obvious and inevitable: I'm going to have to seek out Rudolf, my guard dog, for an update.

Tossing aside the covers, I hurry to the bathroom, and five minutes later, be damned the sweats and tank, and pink fluffy slippers, I'm ready to interrogate Rudolf. I exit the bedroom to the living room and find him there, already in his basic dark suit, sitting on the couch facing me, news on the television to his right and my left.

He sets the cup in his hand on the table in front of him and stands. "Good morning, Ms. Monroe."

"Do you have any news for me?" I ask, skipping the niceties.

"No further information."

Of course not, I think. "I need a computer and a phone," I say. "At least a computer. I'm interning. I have work to do."

"Your father has taken care of your absence from work."

"I need a computer," I repeat.

"Your IP could be tracked."

"I know your company is capable of setting up a computer I can use with internet access. I understand that I can't log into my email or communicate with anyone I know."

"Which leaves room for mistakes," he replies. "That's not a risk that we're willing to take until we know the nature of the threat against you."

He's doing his job, I remind myself. He might even be saving my life. I get that, but I also know that I might well be the key to finding Danielle. "How long will we be here in the hotel?"

"Until we confirm you weren't the intended target," he states. "Or rather, until we confirm there is no danger to you."

Which would be easier if I remembered what happened last night but I'm not about to remind a man I barely know, let alone trust, about my memory loss. "Do we have intel that suggests that I'm a target?"

"Your father is a rich man who intends to run the free world. That's all the intel we need to be cautious under these circumstances."

"In other words," I say, "even if they do have intel, I'm not to be told." I don't give him time to reply. "I need to speak to my father."

"He's scheduled to contact me at noon today with updated instructions."

Set to contact *him*, not *me*.

Someone who isn't me might consider that to mean he's contacting me as well, but I am *me*, and I know my father. My new guard has also become just another new block in the wall between father and daughter. "I'll need to speak to my father when he calls," I say, offering him nothing more, most especially no fodder for the gossips, before turning and I start walking.

Once I'm inside the closet-like enclosure so many of these high-end suites call kitchens, I start a cup of coffee brewing, and press my hands on the counter. After all these years, why do I still let my father get to me? He hates me. I tell myself that I've accepted that and that it doesn't matter anymore. I mean it when I say and think it, then turn around thirty seconds later and try to please him. Danielle would call me crazy, and often did over my father, but all the while, she's working for him, and just as eager to please him.

I hope she's working for him. If she's dead—I shove off the counter before I can finish that thought and reach for my coffee, when the sound of Rudolf's footsteps have me turning to face the doorway. He appears there in the archway, obnoxiously big in a way that reminds me of the brick in that wall between me and my father that he represents. "Danielle's disappearance was leaked to the press," he announces. "We're leaving. Per your father, we're to be at his residence at ten o'clock." He glances at that expensive watch of his and then at me. "You have forty minutes to dress and look First Daughter perfect for the cameras."

In other words, my father is about to turn Danielle into a press op, and me into a press tool when I don't even remember what happened to her or me. I reject that idea. Rudolf is mistaken. I won't be in front of the cameras. My father is too smart to let that happen. Which means he knows something I don't know. I inhale a heavy breath with a realization. He knows what happened to Danielle or he at least knows something about her fate. And soon, I will too.

An hour later, passes quickly.

I'm now dressed in a black designer pantsuit, appropriate for mourning and guilt, with my hair neatly braided. It's clean but once again, it feels like the dirty blonde is extra dirty. I just feel dirty all over, for reasons that I cannot explain, but desperately need to name. I'm in the back seat of a dark sedan, with Rudolf behind the wheel. Our drive is silent. Unfortunately, so is my mind, but I push through the darkness replaying what I remember of the bar. Trying to grab new details no matter how small they may be, but I can't even name the drink I'd consumed. Each worthless, repetitive thought, drives the guilt expanding inside me. I'm guilty. I did it.

I tell myself that "it" is me leaving Danielle behind. I tell myself this ten times and still, I need to hear it eleven and twelve. Because I still feel dirty and I have a clawing sensation that I'm guilty of *more*.

CHAPTER ELEVEN

The dictionary defines the word "more" as a greater or additional amount or degree.

I know this because at one point, my father quoted that text to me, to make a point. That point being that I couldn't be "more" wrong on a topic, the details of which I don't remember or just choose not to remember. There's a lot about my father that I choose not to remember these days.

Looking back, I'm not sure why he felt the need to offer this precise definition of "more" considering his ever-liberal use of the word with phrases such as "I'm the candidate of more" and "You need to listen more and talk less," the latter of which he's used numerous times on both me and his opposing candidates. He was quite good at leveling someone into silence. Perhaps because he saw himself as king of the world. The truth is, I saw him just as favorably.

But that didn't last, not for me, at least.

Not long after that night in Austin, I began to see myself differently, and therefore, over time, I saw him more clearly. As time passed, that random quote from the dictionary stood out to me. I homed in on the way he'd defined the word "more" for me but not the word "wrong." At that point, I decided that in his eyes the definition of right vs wrong was complicated by subjectivity, and therefore indefinable, while more is simply limitless. I would later expand on that conclusion and decide that the word "wrong" wasn't a problem for him because of the nature of its subjectivity but rather its representation of morality. Something I believe he felt was better left undefined. Otherwise, he might have to look himself in the mirror and claim his sins. In case you wonder, he wasn't just the cold, hard father who believed I killed my mother. He was a man of sins that were as limitless as his greed for power.

In terms of sins, we return to where we left off, to that day the press discovered Danielle was missing. On that day, it wasn't my father's sins that were in question. It was mine...

THE PAST...

Riding in the back of that black sedan, with Rudolf silently driving me toward my father's house, I am reminded, and not for the first time today, that I am not most people. Most people obsess over normal things that fit into categories such as chocolate, wine, yoga, books, or even how many droplets of rain smashed against the windows surrounding me. I instead obsess over the idea that I might have killed my best friend, and that my father, who wants to be President, who *intends* to be President, covered it up. He would, of course. That's how much he wants to be President, and let's face it. A dead daughter represents the sympathy vote. A murderess daughter represents bad genes that she inherited from him. I'm not sure what it says about me that I know this about my father, and still crave his approval and affection. I'm not even sure what it says about me that I'm even contemplating my guilt in a calm, reserved manner. No freak-out. No tears. No shaking. I'd like to think that's because I don't really believe myself capable of such a thing. Danielle is my best friend. The two of us once vowed a blood secret and swore neither one of us would ever betray the other.

Rudolf turns us onto my father's street, and it's not long before the property is in view. It's expensive, round, contemporary, and white, in what feels like a modernized placeholder for the White House, a detail that I've never believed to be an accident. The fact that Rudolf has to avoid umbrella-toting reporters, some of which pound on our hood as we pass, to get into the gated property, must, in fact, please my father. He's the star of the hour. He's the center of attention. It doesn't matter that someone might have died to bring this particular spotlight, which is exactly why I know that press leak didn't happen until he wanted it to happen. When he discovered whatever he knows that I'm about to find out.

I note that two additional security people appear to be manning the gate, clearly a response to the potential threat Danielle's disappearance represents. In other words, my father enhanced his security in the comfort of his home, but rather than have me join him, he left me in a hotel room with Rudolf.

Rudolf is now guiding the car down the driveway, past the front lawn, where there is obviously a podium and press area setup. All of which is being pummeled with rain, a detail I'd say might save me from a public showing, but I'm back to the girl who knows her father. He'll offer some high-profile reporter a sit-down exclusive. That means the cameras, up close and personal, analyzing me for signs of being a murderous monster who killed her best friend.

We pull to the back of the house and Rudolf is clearly not a first-timer here. He hits a button and pulls us into the basement level garage, which is more like a warehouse with shiny white floors and a collection of fancy cars. Once we're sealed inside, I open my door and exit to the garage. It's then that nerves punch at my belly and weaken my knees.

I head for the door, and once inside, I walk up the winding stairs to enter the foyer, and like the rest of the house, it's all windows and high ceilings, with dangling lights and modern furniture and art, most of which was chosen by my mother. Step-mother dearest, dressed in a red dress, her blonde hair free around her shoulders, is waiting on me. "How are you, dear?" she asks, sticky sweet, her fingers laced together in front of her. Her rock of a diamond, which is bigger than my mother's was, glistens in the sheen of the chandelier of a hundred tiny lights, directly above her.

"Where is my father?" I ask, no interest in playing the fake mother-daughter routine.

Her expression tightens. "In the media room."

"Is he alone?"

"Bennett is with him."

Of course. Step-brother dearest. The son he never had. I turn away from her and she calls me back. "Hailey."

I inhale and rotate to face her. "Yes?"

"Your photo from the debate is all over the internet and you look stunning."

She means her dress is all over the internet, and since her eyes are now alight with excitement, I'm clearly not yet labeled a killer, nor is she anticipating I will be. "I wouldn't know," I say. "I've been cut off from the internet." I rotate and start walking, heading down a curved hallway that is lined by windows, before traveling down a winding stairwell that leads to a fancy den. I cross the mahogany hardwood floors, ignoring the sitting area and bar to enter another hallway, until I reach the double doors that are my destination.

I enter the home theater, with fancy red leather seats and a ceiling that is black with lights flecked like stars throughout it. The lights are on and the debate is playing on the big screen, with my father and step-brother positioned side-by-side, in the center of a row of ten seats, open seats on either side of them. Unfortunately, my step-brother is on this side of the aisle. I walk down the stairs and stand at the end cap of their row, no interest in joining Bennett, or walking across him so he can "accidentally" grab my ass. Been there, done that. Don't want the t-shirt. I have the one that says: "Monroe 2020" and that's all I can stomach.

Obviously aware that I'm present, my father hits the pause button on the remote in his hand, and Bennett stands up. He's in a suit as is my father, but then, it's a business Thursday. Why wouldn't they be? They haven't been captive in a hotel room.

84

Bennett walks toward me, and when I turn to face him, he pauses and stares down at me. "Danielle wants to *do* me?"

I am not an impulsive person, but the idea that he read my messages and then on top of that made that remark, when Danielle is in peril, is too much. I raise my hand and I fully intend to slap the living shit out of him, but he catches my wrist. "Be careful," he warns. "That temper of yours could get you into trouble." There is a flicker in his blue eyes that is one-part threat, and one-part taunt.

I'm just considering a well-placed knee when my father calls out, "Leave us, Bennett," in his most commanding tone.

Bennett's lips quirk and he releases me. "Talk to you soon, sis." He walks away and regret ticks through me. I not only lost control, I've now given Bennett the satisfaction of thinking he has that power over me, that he can push my buttons, when he does not. My father owns my anger. He gave him my phone. This idea re-ignites my anger, in a more familiar way. That low, simmering he's always a bastard to me kind of way. I step into the row of seats and sit next to my father, when I could leave a seat between us, and with good reason. He won't like it.

"Daughter," he greets.

I don't give him what he wants. I can't bring myself to even speak the word "father." "I assume that Bennett wouldn't be making suggestive remarks toward Danielle if you didn't have good news to share," I comment.

He cuts me a steely stare. "I don't know what remark you're referencing, but no. I do not have news on Danielle. The Secret Service has intervened and we're all on lockdown here, until further notice."

"They didn't approve of me in a hotel room with Rudolf and you and your family here?" I ask, flippantly, because apparently, my control hasn't returned.

"Don't start down that path again."

Again is not an appropriate choice of words, considering this is where I went when I found out he was remarrying, and just one year after my mother's death. But then, a presidential candidate needs a wife, and my mother would have been the perfect First Lady. A doctor who'd volunteered in third world countries. "What do we know about Danielle?" I ask, before this goes to a place he won't like, but I just might.

"Other than you left her in a bar alone?" he snaps, punishing me, not for my choices with Danielle, but for my choices the night my mother died.

"To protect your career," I remind him. "I left her for you."

"Is that right?"

"I've lived my life for you."

"We both know that's not true," he replies.

"Where is Danielle and why is the Secret Service involved?"

"They're involved because we have nothing but a bloody shoe right now. And since the details of such have been released to the public, the two of us will be sitting down with a reporter and pleading for help in locating her."

"How can I go on camera when I don't remember what happened?"

"Stick to the story we've established, and you'll be fine."

"Until someone you missed recognizes me and comes forward with details we aren't prepared for," I counter.

"What details, Hailey? What do you know that I don't know?"

"Nothing. That's the problem."

"It's handled."

"And if it's not?"

"Why are you so damn afraid of the unknown?"

"Why are you not?" I demand, narrowing my eyes on him.

"Because I have control that you obviously do not."

I stand up.

"Sit down," he bites out.

I inhale and force myself to obey. How can I not? I'm now a prisoner in his house, wishing I was back in the hotel.

86

I claim my seat, but do not look at him. He grabs my hand, squeezing it tightly. "Look at me."

I obey again because that is what I do. I obey my father, the future leader of the free world. "Yes, father?"

"I have this under control. Do you understand?"

"Yes," I say.

"You will do as I say. Do you understand?"

"Yes," I repeat, trained well on the script. "How is her father coping with this?"

"As expected," he says. "Not well and full of questions for you, which he'll ask when he arrives here for the press conference. Make sure you stick to the story and make him feel good about it."

His cellphone rings where it sits on the armrest between us. He picks it up. "The FBI," he says, and my fingers ball into my palms, heart racing. This is it. This is the answer I'm waiting on and I know, it's bad news. My father shows no signs of premonition or even anticipation. He simply, calmly, answers the line. "Monroe here," he confirms, before listening several beats.

"I'm about to speak to the press," he asks. "Is this public knowledge?" More silence follows and then he says, "Understood," and hangs up.

He sets the phone down and without looking at me says, "The FBI has been questioning a homeless person for the past three hours. They wanted us to know since the press knows."

I turn to him. "Did this person see something? Did this person hurt her?"

"No further details at this point, but they want us to make a plea to the public for information. We'll hold a press conference in the foyer in one hour." He stands up, the cue for me to do the same and I do. It appears that I'm going in front of the cameras whether I like it or not and my father is far too comfortable with that idea. Still, I walk with him out of the room, but my opinion of what he knows hasn't changed since I entered this house. He knows more than he's telling me.

My reunion with Danielle's father is tearful and filled with hugs. He asks me questions, but they are short and sweet, and interrupted by my father and a Secret Service agent. It's not much later that the rain pauses and allows us to gather on the front lawn. I stand at the podium with my father as he relays what the press already knows. Danielle is missing. Nothing more. Reporters fling questions at me, but my father answers for me, an indicator that he is perhaps not as comfortable with me in front of the cameras as I might have thought him to be.

We step aside, and Danielle's father takes the podium. "Please help me find my daughter. I'm headed to Austin when this is over. I will be there. If you know anything, if you are there, I can meet you. I can talk to you. I need to find my daughter. And Danielle, if you can hear this, I love you, honey. I love you so much."

I tear up. My hand balls between my breasts. I know in my heart that it covers that she isn't coming back. No sooner than I have that thought, one of the Secret Service taps my father on the shoulder. He inhales sharply, and moves forward to join Danielle's father. He whispers to him, and then grabs the microphone.

"We'll be taking a short break," he announces before turning to me and motioning me toward the house.

A bad feeling, curls in my belly and sixty seconds later, I'm standing next to Danielle's father, when my own father says, "The police have been questioning a homeless person about Danielle for the past four hours. He's confessed to Danielle's murder."

The room starts to spin, and everything seems to fade to black and then move in slow motion. Danielle's father collapses and paramedics are called. My father never speaks to me, nor does Susan or Bennett. I am pushed away from Danielle's father, but I stay close, and I watch security, and then the medical personnel work on him. He's taken to the hospital, but only as a safety precaution. Once they strap him onto a stretcher, my father finally addresses me.

"We're going back out to talk to the press." He motions to the door. "Let's go."

No "are you okay?" No "do you need anything?" Just "let's go do a job." Somehow, I slip into robot mode, and do just that. I stand on the lawn and I watch my father deliver the news to the public. I listen to him choke up. I see him grab the podium and lower his head as if he fights pain. He's full of shit. I know him. This is a show. A setup. A cover-up.

I endure what I must endure until I finally find an escape to my old bedroom, where I shut the door and sink low to the ground. Danielle is dead. It can't be and yet, I knew it would be. So did my father, I think, and before it was announced.

CHAPTER TWELVE

And so, the surgeon's blade had indeed cut with precision, though it wasn't Danielle who ultimately felt the pain but those of us left behind. Those who claimed responsibility for what we wrongly believed, could have been changed. I was one of them. I suffered. I also noticed who did not...

THE PAST...

The announcement of a confession in Danielle's murder case, is followed by chaos, questions, media, and more media. When I finally leave my father's house, it's in the back seat of that black sedan again, with Rudolf behind the wheel, and with a desperateness to reach Tobey that borders on starvation. He was there that night in Austin. He knows what I cannot remember. I need to know, too. I don't call him, though. Not with Rudolf in hearing distance. I'll be free once Rudolf drops me off at my apartment, cleared from the sights of danger. Cleared from prying eyes and ears.

Frustratingly when we arrive at my apartment, Rudolf insists on carrying my hotel purchases upstairs. I try to leave him at the door. "I've got it from here," I say.

"I'll need to check out your apartment for you," he states, towering over me and standing far too close.

"There is no threat to me. I check out my apartment every night by myself."

His hard expression doesn't change, and he doesn't move. "I'm going to need to check out your apartment," he states. "Step aside."

Unlike my normal politically-correct moments, I don't even try to hide my grimace. This feels like a power trip designed by my father, who has yet to ask me how I'm handling the potential murder of my best friend. I hand Rudolf my keys, and then "step aside" as he's ordered. He opens the door and heads inside my apartment. I lean on the wall, and wait, counting every second until I can call Tobey.

After what feels like a lifetime, Rudolf appears. I push off the wall and he announces, "All clear," before handing me a card. "Call me if you have any problems now, or ever."

I don't want to take the card, but it's expected, and the sooner I do it, the sooner he leaves. I accept it, but I don't speak. He gives me this hooded, impossible-to-read five-second stare and then turns and walks away. I enter the apartment, lock the door, and pull my phone from my purse. By the time I'm sitting on my couch, Tobey's line is ringing. He answers almost immediately.

"They freed you from captivity."

"Do you think she's really dead?" I ask, getting to the point.

"Hailey—"

"Answer," I demand.

"Yes," he says. "I think she's dead."

The certainty in his words does nothing to make me as certain. "Tell me what happened."

"You know what happened. We left. She stayed. That was a bad decision on her part."

My confession of memory loss is replaced by anger. "You're blaming her?" I demand instead. "Are you really doing that?"

"You tried to make her come home with us. She stayed."

"I'm back to, are you really blaming her for getting killed by a crazy person?"

"You want me to blame myself? I didn't even want to go to that damn bar. I told you not to go."

"And now you're going *there*? Blaming me? *Really*?"

"What do you want me to say here, Hailey?"

"I want you to tell me you remember something that helps us find her."

"You told her to leave. Hell, you fought with her over it. She lashed out at you and stayed."

I flash back to Danielle grabbing my arm in the bar and screaming at me. He's given me explanation as to why and yet it still doesn't make sense. "You and I did leave together, right?" I ask, because he's not in my flashbacks.

"Don't play that game with me," he says. "I know you remember last night. We were naked thirty-seconds after we got to your hotel room. Is that a jab? It wasn't good enough to remember. What the hell Hailey? I'm not the enemy."

"You weren't with me when I woke up," I punch back.

He laughs without humor. "You told me to leave and now you're mad that I left?"

"Nothing about this feels right," I say, remembering nothing he's saying.

"Death never feels right."

"I need to go to Austin," I say.

"Why? To stir up the press and complicate the investigation?"

"I need to know the truth, Tobey."

"The truth? What truth can you discover that the police won't?"

"Something doesn't feel right," I say.

"Leave it alone," he insists.

"I *have* to know."

"Leave *it alone*," he repeats. "I'll come over. We'll talk this through."

"No," I say quickly. "No, I don't want you to come over."

"I'm coming over."

"Don't," I say. "I won't answer the door, because frankly I can't stomach you blaming Danielle for what some monster did to her."

I hang up on him and toss my phone across the room, feeling like he's a monster and so am I.

CHAPTER THIRTEEN

I remember my mother as good and right in ways that defied her choice in my father. She was the light in the darkness of greed and power. The heart in the machine. She changed the balance of our lives. She diluted the wrong with the right. In other words, from the moment she died, I was living in my father's undiluted version of those things. His world became my only world, and as I contemplated the end of Danielle, I contemplated my role in that end. My father didn't grieve Danielle. He did, however, grieve any hit to his campaign, lashing out in response, and when I left that bar, I left to protect him or perhaps me, from that lashing. I left because I chose him—okay, myself—over her. I made him right and her wrong. It reminds me of something I once heard him say: Sometimes there is no avoiding wrong to get to the place that is right. *In other words, you can justify just about anything if you're doing it for the "right" reasons. In the days after Danielle's disappearance, I struggled with a growing sense that I'd done more wrong than right that night.*

THE PAST—SEVEN DAYS AFTER THE CONFESSION…

Still no body, I think, parking my car in the garage of the building that is my destination. It's day seven. How can there be no body? It's also day four of me being back at work, interning for the fourth time in two years for Keith Smith, a senator, who is also a brilliant Stanford graduate and attorney. The inspiration as well for my law school application, though I have yet to hear on my acceptance that I desperately crave. I need out of this town. I need away from my father. For now, though, at least work keeps my mind busy.

I exit my BMW, a gift from my father when I was accepted into Georgetown, which was all about show and the spotlight. Or perhaps it was a reward for supporting the perfect image that he requires I present as the future First Daughter. He never said he was proud of me. I start walking toward the elevators and my cellphone rings. I dig it from my purse and find Tobey's number. I decline as I have every time he's called since the night he'd blamed Danielle for her own demise. The same thing Danielle's father has done with my calls every day since as well. He hates me for leaving her in that bar. I hate me, too.

It's not long until I'm inside the tiny office where I work, and I've barely sat down at my desk when Senator Smith pauses inside my door. He's a tall man, thin, his dark hair graying at the temples. His eyes kind. "How are you?"

He's asked me this question every morning since my return to work, and he isn't doing it for formality. He cares about people and that's a trait you don't see often in politics. "Better at work where I can stay busy."

"Any word on the law school?"

"No," I say. "Nothing."

"Want me to make a call?"

"Would you?"

"Of course," he says. "I'll call today." He narrows his eyes on me. "You look thin. Go get us a bucket of those chocolate chip bagels we both love and coffee. Charge my account. When you get back, come to my office. I'll let you know about the call then." He doesn't wait for agreement. He disappears into the hallway.

I swallow hard, wondering why a man who is my mentor is more a father than my father. It cuts. It cuts deep. I grab my purse and stand up, determined to get out of this office before I do that thing my father hates and show emotion. Thankfully, my office is off the beaten path and has a direct line to the stairs, which are preferable to the elevator right now, despite a ten-floor walk in high-heeled boots.

I enter the stairwell, and my phone rings yet again. I grab it from my purse, and eye Tobey's number once more. I hit decline before shoving it into the pocket of my black dress, just one of my variations of grim and dark that I've worn these past seven or so days. Some part of me clings to the idea that Danielle will suddenly appear, and we will wear pink and red and laugh at the way some joyride spun out of control. I exit to the garage and it's not Danielle that's suddenly appeared, but Tobey. He's leaning on my car, in his expensive, politician-ready suit, arms and ankles crossed.

Clenching my teeth, I charge toward him. "Why are you here?" I demand, and he straightens to tower over me.

"We need to talk."

I realize then that I neither want to talk to him nor do I miss him or wish for a kiss or a touch that he doesn't supply. Why am I with him? We don't have chemistry, if chemistry even exists. "Actually, I need to go run an errand for my boss." I start to move away, and he grabs my arm.

"Avoiding each other looks bad to the police."

"You convinced me to leave Danielle in a bar. She died. I think it looks pretty realistic."

"Now it's my fault she died?" he demands.

"If you can blame her, I can blame you. Let go of me."

"We're a couple," he says. "I'm not letting you go."

"We're a political prop and we both know it," I say. "And funny thing about death. It makes you look at your life."

"What are you saying?" he demands.

"I'm saying we need a break."

"No."

"You can't just say no."

"I am," he says. "I'm saying no. I'll give you a few days to breathe, but Friday night, we're together. And we're working this out. We're going to have that talk you wanted to have."

"What talk?"

"The talk you wanted to have at the bar about our future that we never had thanks to Danielle." He releases me. "Go on your errand." He walks away, and I don't wait around. I hurry and get into my car, but I try to remember the "talk" I demanded and cannot. "Damn it, Danielle," I murmur, grabbing the steering wheel and lowering my head. "What did you do?"

I lift my head and stare straight ahead, picturing the moment she'd grabbed my arm, feeling the anger I'd felt when I'd turned in that hallway and faced her, one thought coming to mind: If she hadn't drugged me, maybe she wouldn't be dead.

Ten minutes later, I park and enter the bagel shop, quickly placing my order. Once I've paid, I shove my phone into the pocket of my black dress, and while the woman behind the counter speaks to me, I am in my own head. I murmur something I hope sounds polite, distracted by my internal monologue; telling myself that soon law enforcement will discover this is a big mix up, and that Danielle is alive.

With about a dozen cute wooden tables to choose from, I move toward a corner, and just as I'm about to sit down, I freeze as a headline flashes across the television screen: *The body of Danielle Parker has been located, and she has arrived in Washington.*

I can't move and yet my knees and hands are trembling, my breath lodged in my throat. She can't be dead. It's not real. This is not real. Suddenly, I flash back to Austin. I'm in the bar, charging toward an exit when Danielle catches my arm:

She whirls me around. "How about talking to me before you judge me?"

I don't know what she means, but I'm angry at her. So very angry. *"I need to leave. Honey."* God, now I'm using my father's words. Honey. Honey. Honey.

"The real you comes out," she snaps. "Crass and bitchy."
The real me.

"Hailey!" the woman behind the counter shouts with my
order, and I snap back to the present, but I can't escape
those words: *the real me*. What did that even mean?

I give myself a mental shake and rush to the counter,
opening my wallet, and setting a twenty on the counter.
"Please deliver these to Senator Smith's office." I grab a
sheet of paper and scribble down the address, but I don't
wait for agreement.

I head for the door and I am already removing my phone
from my pocket before rushing to my BMW, dialing
Danielle's father, as I do. I'm in my car by the time his voice
mail picks up. I puff out a breath and I really don't know
where to go. I need to see Danielle. That means the morgue.
I google the number and address, but I'm certain they won't
release anything over the phone.

Fifteen minutes later, I pull up to the building and park,
my fingers gripping the steering wheel, Danielle's voice is
screaming in my head: *"The real you comes out," she snaps.
"Crass and bitchy."*

Was that the last thing ever exchanged between us, or
was there more? God. I hate that damn word *more*. My gaze
lifts and lands on a man hurrying this way. Danielle's father.
I reach for the car door and exit, rushing toward him. "Is she
here?" I ask, stopping in front of him.

"Yes," he says, his voice cracking, his blues eyes swollen
and red. "She's here or her body is here. She's gone."

"You saw her?" I ask, needing real confirmation.

"Yes," he says. "I saw her, Hailey. In Austin. I was there
when they found her."

"Can I see her please?"

"She was cremated this morning."

"What? What? No. No, please tell me—"

His hands go to my shoulders, fingers digging in hard.
"You didn't want to see her like that," he bites out through
his teeth. "You didn't want to see her like that." He releases

me. "And I can't see you. You remind me—of her." He walks around me and leaves.

I remind him of her. No. He means I remind him of the friend who left her behind to die. I can't stop what comes to my mind next. I can't escape what is there, demanding it be voiced; the monster, no, *the killer* strikes again.

CHAPTER FOURTEEN

Alone.

It's a simple premise most of us make complicated. We think that if we surround ourselves with people, we can't be alone, when the reality is that we're always alone. If you look closely and objectively, it becomes clear that life is just one big revolving door of people: some who matter, some who don't. Some that matter until they don't.

Simple.

Not complicated.

The day that Danielle's body was found was a day filled with emotional blows that would eventually allow me to find that objectivity. Despite what I felt when Danielle's father blamed me for Danielle's death, time brings clarity and now, years later, I'm not sure he really did. At least not then. Then, we both wanted the same thing: Danielle to come back. Tobey and my father just wanted her to go away.

THE PAST...

I'm not sure how long I stand in front of the morgue, telling myself that Danielle isn't ashes inside. She's not inside at all. This is all one big mistake. Nothing about this feels right.

Once I'm back in my car, I force myself to call my boss. "I just heard," he says. "Are you okay?"

"I don't know how to answer that," I say, my voice barely above a whisper.

"Honestly."

"I don't even know what that means," I reply.

"Where are you?" he asks. "I'll come pick you up."

"You're a senator," I say. "You have a portion of our country to run. Why would you come here and help me?"

"You know that I'm fond of you, and not in an inappropriate way. Lord help me, like a father to a daughter, despite the fact that I don't want to be that damn old."

Like a father, I repeat in mind, that description clawing at me. Because he sees that I don't have one. "You don't have time to babysit an intern," I say. "I'm fine."

"That's a lie," he accuses.

"Well I am a politician's daughter," I say with a bitter laugh, only to realize my error. "I'm sorry. I didn't mean you."

"But you meant your father?" he queries.

"It was a bad joke at a bad time," I say, because like myself, he believes in my father and what he can do as President, but I've read between the lines; he doesn't always like him.

"Was it?" he challenges.

"Yes," I assure him. "It was."

He pauses a moment and thankfully must decide to shift directions, because his next question is, "What can I do?"

"Did you call the school?"

"Do you really want to connect this news to this day, kiddo?"

"I really want a path out of this city right now," I say, in a rare moment of daring to speak the truth. Up until now, I've told him I wanted the edge I'd gain by stepping wider with my education.

He doesn't question me, though. Not on that, at least. "You remember our agreement, correct?" he asks, instead.

"I won't tell my father you helped me."

"Then congratulations. You were accepted into Stanford."

"Thank you," I breathe out, thankful that while law school isn't my dream, I don't have to endure it while enduring this place. "Thank you so much."

"All I did was provide a reference, young lady. You did the hard work. You sure you don't need a ride?"

"Yes," I say firmly. "I'm sure."

"Then take a week off. I'll see you at the memorial service." He disconnects and leaves me with two horrible words: *the memorial service.*

There will be a memorial service.

Because Danielle is dead.

My cellphone rings again in my hand and I glance down to find Tobey's number. I answer the call. "You know," I say.

"Yes. Hailey—"

"Be careful what you say to me right now," I warn. "Because my capacity to handle more of the other night is not huge right now."

"It's not our fault," he replies, clearly not hearing me.

I hang up on him and toss the phone onto the passenger seat. It starts to ring again. I turn on the car and start driving.

Twenty minutes later, and five more calls that I ignore, I pull up to my apartment and park in the garage. Ready to be in my own space, where I can wallow in my emotions, and the tears I've somehow contained in solitude, I exit my car. I've only walked a few steps across the garage, when a black sedan pulls up in front of me and stops. Rudolf exits the driver's side, towering over the hood, and the back door pops open.

Every part of me knows who's inside the car and every part of me wants to resist getting in that car. I'm suffocating in too much of everything, and I need to breathe, but there is no escape. This isn't just my life. It's my prison and I'm a well-trained prisoner. I slide into the back seat and shut the door, confirming that I'm now alone in the vehicle with my father. "You cannot go off the deep end again," he says. "There's too much on the line."

"The deep end?" I demand, cutting him a look and well aware of what he's talking about. "Right after the crash, I faced realities that weren't easy for a young girl to face. My mother had died. My father hated me. I think I turned out pretty damn well considering all that. I have lived my life to please you. To support you."

"To support our country," he corrects. "This is bigger than both of us."

"Right," I say tightly. "Of course. Don't worry, father. I'll perform my duty and grieve in the politically correct manner." I reach for the door.

He catches my hand and I go still, as I'm sure he'd expected. How can I not? This is the first time my father has voluntarily touched me in years, outside of a formal event where it was required. "I don't hate you, Hailey," he says, his voice low, and dare I say, affected? "But I did," he adds. "I hated you for taking her from me, but that was my grief. That was my pain. That was me needing to blame someone, anyone, anything, for taking her from me. Do you understand?"

It's the closest thing to love that I've gotten from this man in what feels like a lifetime. "Yes," I whisper, fighting tears I didn't know I was still capable of shedding. "Yes, I do." And I do. I'd blamed myself. I still do. I know he does, too, and that's why I want to cry. Because I thought this would feel—different. I thought this moment would come and everything would just be—different.

"You have done what you needed to do," he says, lacing his fingers with mine. "Don't stop now. Okay?"

I can't look at him. I can't bear to see the coldness I know I will find in his ice blue eyes. Or the hardness in his perfectly chiseled face that defies any real fatherly tenderness in his touch. Not now. Not this day. So, I simply say, "Yes."

"If you feel this is going to be a blow you can't handle, you need to come stay with us."

Us.

He means him and Susan.

This isn't an invitation to go home. It's about going to his home, with her. The woman who replaced my mother. "I'm better here."

"Look at me," he orders.

I do it. I'm trained to do whatever he says. He studies me a moment and releases my hand. I'm relieved, as if captive, and freed, in some way. "I'll call you when I know the details for Danielle's service," he says. "We'll attend together."

The funeral service, I think. If you call it that when someone has been burned to ash. Maybe it's a memorial service. I just want it over with in the same breath that I don't want it to happen at all. "Do you have any idea when that will be?"

"None yet," he says, cutting his stare for several beats before looking at me again. "Is there anything about that night in Austin we need to discuss?"

Unease rolls through me. "What does that mean?"

"You heard the question. Is there anything we need to discuss?"

"I was drugged. I don't remember what happened."

"Nothing?"

"Nothing," I say, because that's what he wants to hear, perhaps a little too much but then, this is all about me not screwing up his promotion.

"And if that changes?" he challenges.

"My story doesn't change."

"Who knows you don't remember that night?"

"You. Rudolf. Your attorney."

"Tobey?" he presses.

"Not unless you told him."

"Tobey understands the value of stories that align in facts," he states. "Your memory was irrelevant when we discussed what would be spoken about that night. Keep it that way." He doesn't wait for my assumed confirmation. "Are you coming home with me or staying here?"

In other words, get out. I don't. "What happened that night? What is the 'more' in this story?"

His eyes darken and harden. "You left your best friend in a bar and a homeless man killed her. What more do you need?"

I want to hit him, but I'm the perfect future First Daughter.

I get out of the car.

CHAPTER FIFTEEN

The funny thing about suffering is that some of us do it silently and with inaction. I am not one of those people.

THE PAST—THE MEMORIAL SERVICE...

I stand in front of my closet mirror in my apartment and stare at the girl in the reflection, who I may or may not know. She—no, I—am wearing her latest version of my black uniform of grief that I've maintained for days, even when I've jogged on a treadmill four times in two days. The color of my attire is a symptom of my mood. Me trying to get out of my own head, because what's in it isn't answers, but potential alternate realities related to that night in Austin. For instance, that I, or rather the girl in the mirror, that I may not know as well as I think, killed Danielle, being the predominant fear I've battled, though I really don't know why. I wouldn't kill my best friend, but would the girl in the mirror?

I do not like this thought, and I narrow my gaze on my reflection, looking for a killer, and I haven't a clue if that is who stares back at me. All I know is that she's guilty. If not of murder, of leaving Danielle behind in that bar to die only I do not believe the story is that simple. Not the *real* story that my father, and perhaps even Tobey—who, after careful consideration, I do not believe is being honest with me about that night, knows, but I do not. I can't deal with that story until I say goodbye to Danielle. I just have to get past goodbye.

My phone buzzes and I grab it from the bathroom sink to find a text from Rudolf that reads simply: *Downstairs.*

I'd say that the short, direct message was a product of someone who didn't like me, but it's efficient, gets the point across, and does so with the same winning personality he presents in person. I grab the small black purse I have sitting on the sink and slip on the bracelet next to it that had been a gift from Danielle years ago. I stare down at it, willing it to trigger my lost memories, but it does not. I never remembered how I got to that park years ago. I don't know why I think this time will be different.

I head through my apartment and make my way to the elevator. When I exit inside the garage, a car is waiting on me. I steel myself to endure my father's "family," which I clearly am not, but when I climb inside the car, I'm alone. I glance at the back of Rudolf's head. "Where's my father?"

"There was a campaign crisis," he says, placing us in gear. "He's meeting you at the church."

My father is officially two for two.

Strike one: He didn't call me about the memorial service as promised. Step-mother dearest did, right along with an offer of a dress. "It's appropriate for the occasion," she'd said.

"The occasion?" I'd asked, in disbelief. "You mean death?"

"I didn't want to say that."

"I have a dress," I'd said and disconnected.

Strike two: He's not here in this car with me. Attend the memorial service together means we'll start and finish together, at least by normal standards for such an "occasion" as Susan had called it. Ultimately though, I decide, as I sit in that back seat alone, it's better this way. Every moment I'm with him, I'm focused on what he expects from me. I don't know if I have that capacity today. I don't even know how I will face Danielle's father today. Imagining in my head how that will play out, consumes me the rest of the drive.

Fifteen minutes later, we arrive at the church, entering what has been turned into a secure parking lot; a necessity thanks to the press's obsession with my father and murder, a biting thought that takes me back to my suspicious mind. Rudolf maneuvers us to a preferred parking area. My father does not meet us there. I know this even before I step out of the car, and Rudolf claims a spot beside me. "I'll escort you to your father."

Of course he will.

We start walking, my gut knotting with the certainty that I must face the accusation in the eyes of Danielle's father in the near future. With that in mind, too soon, we are inside the glorious spectacular church appropriate for the send-off of a girl who liked everything big and glamorous. My worry over the moment with Danielle's father quickly fades into the sorrow filled church, tissue and tears, and hordes of people around me, but the part that cuts me the deepest: neither myself nor Danielle, most importantly, knew most of them. They're here because she was my father's employee and my friend, but ironically, I'm not sure Danielle would care.

She enjoyed the crush of admiration when near my father. She never understood why I did not. She would never have understood why I'm going to school at Stanford, and I'll never have that fight with her now. A thought that twists a knife in my chest but I do not feel the urge to cry. I didn't cry at my mother's funeral, either. I think, perhaps, this bothered my father, who didn't handle that day well. I'd watched him struggle with his emotions and crumble into tears over the loss of my mother. It was, in fact, the last time I thought of him as human. I think it was also the day he ceased being human. The thing is that I didn't need to fight my emotions. I couldn't access anything real. Maybe he disliked what he perceived as me having more control than he did.

Rudolf guides me to a seat near the front of the chapel and I sit down at the end of a row, next to my father and thankfully no one else. He doesn't look at me. He doesn't touch me. He's also not touching Susan and I notice that when my step-mother touches his leg, he shoves her hand away. That's when I know that he is indeed, remembering my mother's funeral. His beloved wife's funeral and the daughter that made it possible. He loved my mother. That's why he hates me this much.

Tobey sits in front of me but I don't realize this until he stands and kneels beside me. "Can we call a truce for today?"

He extends his hand and I do not immediately reach for it or him, and with good reason. Recent days have lent to my assessment that Tobey is more with my father, than he is with me. Driving home the point that I am alone, in my grief, guilt, and in a church full of people.

"Hailey," he presses when I don't immediately respond, his tone low but fierce.

I am reaching my limit of conformity, of which I've done too much in my life, but this is not the time or place to start making changes, especially when I believe him to have information I need. I accept his hand. "Truce," I confirm.

He gives me a probing stare, his grip tightening slightly, as if he senses he's losing me, if it's not already too late. "I'll take you to get drunk on chocolate when this is over," he offers.

In this he knows me, which of course, is the point. He wants me to remember this. He wants me to know that now that Danielle is gone, the one person who knows that I don't drink, as I did in Austin, under stress, is him; I'll gain five pounds. Of which, I then run off while beating up whatever made me pig out in the first place, in my mind. I nod my agreement, simply to have an excuse to avoid my father at some point in the next few hours, not to mention my need for real answers that he might be able to give me. Tobey kisses my hand and then stands long enough to reclaim his seat.

It's not long until the service starts, and the fact that in each eulogy, it's clear that I am the only one who knew the real Danielle, which tells me that she too was alone in this world. I wonder if she has some consciousness to know this now. That I do, I decide, was her parting gift to me, when I deserve no gift at all. It's rather liberating. Why would I battle for companionship that is simply a placeholder in time? Or the love of a father that will never love me?

The ceremony continues, and I sit through it all and not once does the urge for tears find me, nor does any urge to share a look with my father, one he doesn't attempt to offer. I can't win in this, after all. I didn't cry for my mother. If I'm dry-eyed for Danielle, I remind my father of this, which he hated. If I'm teary-eyed for Danielle, I create a question of why would I cry for her and not my beloved mother.

When finally, it's time for Danielle's father to speak, he's at the podium all of sixty seconds, and his pain is radiating through me with such intensity that my stomach rolls. My fingers dig into my leg, nails biting flesh, and I can barely breathe. When he's done, the ceremony is over, and we are all invited to walk the adjoining courtyard, where random photos of Danielle will be displayed in the garden. I'm not sure how I feel about this odd format, but it doesn't matter really. It's how Danielle's father wishes to say goodbye. This type of thing is for the living, not the dead.

We all stand and my father turns to me, though he doesn't actually look at me but rather through me. He's good at this technique, really an expert, worthy of a gold medal. "I'm going to say something to her father and then depart." He doesn't offer an explanation. I don't ask for one. Why would I? He can't even say Danielle's name. Just "her."

"Rudolf can see you home," he adds.

"I'm leaving with Tobey," I announce.

He inclines his head and I turn away, stepping out of the way to allow his exit, and meeting Tobey in the aisle. I give him an "I want out of here" look, and to his credit, he understands. He nods, lacing his fingers with mine and leading me through the crowd. I think about his hand on my hand, and I wonder if people in love feel a spark when they touch. I feel nothing with Tobey, not that this is new. I've never felt anything with Tobey except comfortable, which is more than I can say I am with most people.

We're almost to the door when suddenly, Danielle's father is in front of me. "Hailey," he breathes out and before I know his intent, he pulls me close and hugs me. "She loved you so much," he whispers at my ear, all the fears I've had that he hates me seemingly nonsense. Now, my eyes prickle. He pulls back and looks at me. "Are you coming next door?"

"I can't," I breathe out, and mean it. "I just—I can't."

"I understand," he says solemnly. "But I have some of Danielle's things I want you to have. Come by the house soon."

"Okay," I whisper, but I know I won't be going to see him. Not now or ever.

He gives me a look that says he knows this, and the instant his sad eyes turn away, I hurry into the crowd and toward an escape, avoiding everyone who says my name with a wave of my hand. Once I'm at the back door exit, Tobey is there with me again, pushing it open. He motions to his black Mercedes that he's thankfully parked here, not out front. I run toward it, not dignified and politically correct at all. Tobey doesn't stop me. He unlocks the doors and in a few moments, we're sitting inside. "You sure you want to leave?" he asks.

"Completely," I reply, without hesitation, the very idea of staring at Danielle's photos, and thinking about how dead she is, pure insanity to me. "Take me home," I order.

"How about we grab one of those chocolate volcano desserts you love first?"

"Home," I say. "I need to go home." I mean those words, though the word "home" has never felt quite right on my tongue, most certainly, not now.

To his credit again, Tobey does not argue. He simply starts the car and sets us in motion. We don't speak on the ride and it's not Danielle's memorial service that's between us. It's that night. It's her death. He pulls into the parking garage and he parks, but has the sense not to reach for the door.

"Let's talk about what really happened in Austin," I say, baiting him before I turn to him.

He whirls around to face me. "You mean the part where you accused me of being gay because that asshole attorney in the bar—Drew, or whatever his name was—who wanted to get into the future First Daughter's pants, told you I'd do him?"

I don't react. I don't tell him that I don't remember a word of what he just spoke to me. "For someone we both know craves a future in the White House, you bait easily," I taunt instead, trying to pull more from him.

"Why would you bait me?" he demands.

"We all have to audition," I say, "now don't we?"

"You mean to be your husband?"

"You mean my father's son-in-law," I correct, putting into perspective what he really wants.

"I think we both know the answer to that question," I say.

"We're back to that again?" He shakes his head in disgust. "This is exactly where trouble started in Austin."

"What does that mean?" I demand, jumping on that. "What trouble?"

"What trouble? You and your accusations. I'm gay. I'm using you. I'm ten other things other than the person you've dated now for two years who gives a damn about you. All because of that asshole Drew who was—"

"*Who* is Drew?" I quickly demand, because this is twice he's mentioned him.

"That asshole attorney."

"What asshole attorney?"

"You were flirting with him in the bar," he bites out.

"That's ridiculous."

"You with him was ridiculous," he bites out.

"I wasn't with him," I insist. "You said yourself we came to my room after the bar."

"You were all in his personal space and him in yours," he corrects. "I've earned my place by your side."

"You mean by my father's side?" I snap back. "You talked to him before you talked to the police."

"The press is brutal. I protected you."

"Me? Or you? No wait. It's him. You protected him from me."

His jaw sets and there is a flicker of something in his eyes before he grabs my arm and pulls me to him. "It's done and we need to put it behind us," he says. "Do not speak of it again. Do you understand?"

I am unfazed by his temper that is not new, but rather a wicked flare, here and there, and too often, as far as I'm concerned. "What's done and behind us, Tobey?" I demand. "Should we just spell it out? What is it we want behind us?"

"What we should do is *stop* talking about *it*," he says, releasing me and facing the steering wheel. "It's over."

"Because Danielle's memorial service is finally out of the way?"

He cuts me a look. "You know that's not what I meant," he bites out.

I know nothing about this man I want to know, *nothing.* "Go home, Tobey." I grab the door. He grabs my arm.

"Don't do this," he orders.

"My best friend is dead, Tobey. I need space." He studies me several long beats, and when I think he might drag this out, his jaw sets and he releases me.

"I'll call you tomorrow," he says.

I don't reply. I get out of the car, and start walking, with those words "it's over" in my head. It's over. It's over. What is over? There is more to Austin than I'm being told, and I have to know what. By the time I exit the elevator to my floor, I'm rushing to my apartment. I hurry inside, lock up and then throw items in an overnight bag. By the time I'm done, I've made reservations, both for a flight and a hotel.

I'm going to Austin.

CHAPTER SIXTEEN

The answers are always hiding in plain sight.

That's something my father used to say. Work the equation and the numbers, he'd add, and you'll find the answer. He meant that quite literally because, you see, before my mother's death, he would help me with my homework. Back then, we weren't broken, any more than any father and daughter are broken. He mentored me on all things, especially math, because you see, while I'm skilled at math, my father was an Ivy League expert. His capacity to work out difficult equations, unbelievably genius, and he'd share that genius with me. He was even remarkably patient when he explained the equations, full of brilliant insights, to both math and life.

Applying those insights to the problem that was my memory loss, I knew that I needed to just work the equation, and my mind would reveal the truth. I just had to try to remember that night in Austin with the same fierceness that I've always tried to forget that night my mother died. The strategy seemed sound, if not for one large flaw: some doors are better left shut. Ironically though, when a door is shut, it's pure human nature to want to open it, even if we need a crowbar to make it happen.

I had my crowbar ready, despite knowing that it was better to keep the door on Austin shut. My father was the favored candidate for the presidency, after all. Dirty little secrets in his world, which meant mine too, were to be buried. The problem was that my best friend was buried as well. I knew that I couldn't bring her back but I had to know why she was gone. The real reason. I owed Danielle that much.

Later, my father would call me selfish and immature for stirring up the details of Danielle's death. He would tell me that I wasn't thinking with a head on my shoulders. The real problem, though, was that I was thinking at all, rather than blindly following his lead. And yet, he's the one who urged me to solve the problems before me. So really, truly, you could say it's his fault I went to Austin.

THE PAST—THE TRIP TO AUSTIN…

Staying in uniform, I leave my apartment in black jeans and a black long-sleeved lace top, with a scarf tied around my neck and sunglasses on my face, for no reason other than those things seem to throw off the press. Soon, I'm tucked away inside my car, driving to the airport, and within an hour, I'm at my gate, and so far, there are no press eyes on me. My wait there is short, but long enough to search attorneys in Austin with the name of "Drew." There are a number of first and last name variations of "Drew" but only one that works near the bar. My efforts to locate a photo are thwarted by lack of information, but I'm struggling right up until the moment I've boarded, and the flight attendant scolds me for using my phone.

Settling into my seat, I wait for lift off, and order a drink, not of the whiskey variety, thank you very much. Coffee. Strong. Two cups. Once we've leveled off, I down my caffeinated beverage and order another, clearing all the cobwebs from my mind possible. With a cup by my side, I open my MacBook and connect to the internet, but I still can't find any photos of Drew. I spend the remainder of the flight searching the Austin locations I know from the trip, starting at the debate site, and moving forward, while I hope for a trigger to a memory that I don't find. At some point I sleep, imagining that fight with Danielle in the bar, as I do, but still, it leads nowhere.

We're on the ground in six hours, and it's not long before I'm in the back of a cab, my preference when I don't want to talk. Uber drivers are more civilized. That means they actually look at you and notice you. *Talk* to you. The driver delivers me to the hotel where I'd stayed during the debate, where I have requested the same room. I check in and I'm at the door to the room in a flash, but then I freeze. I can't seem to lift my hands and swipe the card, as if I'm about to open the door to a bloody murder scene.

My head starts to spin and I think I might be hyperventilating. I don't hyperventilate. It's as if I'm afraid. Am I afraid? This is insanity. It's a room. Just a room. I swipe the keycard and open the godforsaken door. I enter the room and set my bag inside, my purse with it, before locking up and resting on the door. No murder scene. As I'd said in the hall, it's a room. Just a room. I stand there an exorbitant amount of time and wait for a tornado of memories that support my terror of this room, but the story is as the story was. I get nothing.

I push off the door and walk around the room, before I end up at the bed. I stare at it, remembering the moment I'd woken up disoriented. Wanting more than my mind is giving me, I walk to the bed, and lay down. That's when something Tobey said to me hits me. Something about us getting naked when we got to the room. I sit up. I wasn't naked when I woke up. I was fully dressed. He lied to me. I spring off of the bed, and rush across the room to grab my phone from my purse. Once it's in my hand and I'm about to dial Tobey, I stop myself. Why would he lie to me?

I can come up with only two answers. He knew I wouldn't remember what happened, which means he either helped drug me or knew that I was drugged. Or I got dressed again after he left and went somehow, perhaps to kill Danielle, which is illogical. They have her killer, who just happens to be a defenseless homeless person, just as Danielle was conveniently cremated, both of which read like perfect cover-ups. Of course, Danielle's father would cremate her to cover-up a crime against her. Would he? He is close to my father, and who knows what my father has on him. I don't like the places my mind is going and I want a reason to stop.

I glance at the time on my phone that reads nine p.m. and since it's a Thursday, it's the perfect time to return to the bar. Maybe there I'll find a lead on Drew. Or even better, Drew himself. I call another taxi.

Thirty minutes later I arrive at the door of the bar, which is as formal as I remember. There are well-staffed checkpoints, all men, all bulky, all formally dressed in suits and ties at the entry of the building, and then again at the elevators and even at the corner you have to turn to walk toward the club. The last bit of security between me and my destination is the man at the door. He's a tall, thirty-something guy, with sandy brown hair that I recognize from my previous visit. "You," he says, when I stop in front of him.

"Me?" I ask, my heart thundering in my chest despite what is likely a perfect innocent comment. "What does that mean?"

"You're the Monroe daughter," he replies. "And your friend—"

"Died," I say tightly. "Yes. She did."

He studies me a beat, but offers no apologies. "I can't believe you're back," he says, instead.

"Why?" I dare, both dreading and craving his answer.

"You have a history here," he says, and now it feels as if he's baiting me.

"A history with Danielle," I say. "This is the last place I was with her."

Understanding fills his eyes. "Of course," he says. "You're not on tonight's list, but—" He motions me forward. "May you find whatever peace you're looking for."

I stand my ground. "Can you ensure the press won't show up?"

"No one gets past me," he says, "And I won't call them."
If he expects that to move me along, it does not. "There
was a guy here talking to Danielle and—"

"I thought they got the killer?"

"They did," I say, sounding confident, when I am not, a
skill that is just part of being my father's daughter. "He was
talking to Danielle," I add, "and I just—I want to see him. To
hear the last words she spoke that were actually happy
words."

"Some things are better left alone," he says, as if he's
consulted with my father, and who knows? Maybe he has.

I pretend he has not. "Drew," I say, as if he hasn't
spoken. "An attorney. A regular here, I think."

"Drew Ellis," he says. "He hasn't been in since that night,
but who can blame him? The press has hounded him and
us."

"I'm sorry to hear that," I say, trying to sound sincere,
and I guess I am but not really. For all I know, any one of
these people, aided in the eventual end of Danielle or even
me being drugged. "Do you know where he lives?"

He arches a brow. "You want me to tell you where he
lives?"

In other words, he knows. "I have to leave in the
morning. I really want to see him."

"Why?"

I frown. "I just told you why."

"Right," he says dryly again. "You want to pour salt in
your wounds already festering with guilt. I have no interest
in aiding those efforts. Go inside and do that on your own."

He's a dead end, I decide then, at least for now, but he
served a purpose. I have a last name. I make a show of
frustration, and head for the door. He doesn't stop me, but
he's still here and so am I. I may not be done with him. One
way or another, I'm getting a conversation with Drew Ellis
before I leave Austin again.

I enter the bar, scanning the giant fish-filled aquariums
on the walls, and behind three bars, thirty or so people
speckled here or there in the room, memories punching at

the back of my mind. Seizing the pieces of a puzzle I don't need fitted into unknown holes, I make a beeline for the bar and stool where I'd sat that night. No one is to the left or right of me. The bartender appears in front of me. He's good looking, a tall, dark drink of delicious that I'd remember and don't. He wasn't here that night, at least, not during the part before I was drugged.

I order the same martini I'd ordered the last time I was here, with no intention of drinking it. I'm tempted to order a coconut hookah, but there is nothing in this bar that is going into my body. I'm just looking for triggers. I'm looking for my way back to Danielle, when I know I can't find that way. I shut my eyes and try to remember something, anything, I don't already have cemented in my mind, but I'm interrupted by the bartender.

"Anything else?" he asks, and I open my eyes to find my drink in front of me, with his hand planted on the bar, leaning toward me.

"Did you meet the girl who died here?" I ask, since information is the something else I want.

He doesn't blink or look away. "No. I wasn't working that night, but I know who you are. I've seen you on the internet."

"What have you heard about her death?" I ask, ignoring his comments about me.

"You had a fight with her," he says. "You two were shouting by the exit."

"And then what?"

His eyes darken. "You slapped her."

"Stories snowball here, I see," I say, dismissing the idea, when I'm panicked inside.

"So does anger when you're drinking," he comments. "Doesn't it?"

"What are you inferring?"

His lips curve. "Nothing. They got the killer. She wasn't you."

"He," I say. "You mean he wasn't me."

"He," he amends.

"What else did you hear about Danielle?"

120

"You left," he says. "She left. She died." He motions to the drink. "Anything else?"

"Do you have anything else to offer?"

His lips quirk. "Are we still talking about your friend? Or are we getting more personal now?"

I stare at him. I don't look away but there is no invitation in my eyes. "Too good for the likes of me, huh, sweetheart? I'm not royal enough for your blood. Got it." He pushes off the bar and walks away.

"I didn't slap her," I whisper to no one, since he's given me his back, but I can't know if I'm right or he's right. My gaze lowers to the drink and suddenly I realize I ordered coconut hookah and chocolates. The s'mores martini. I didn't order the drink, and my mind goes back in time. I remember Drew. He'd been talking with me. He'd ordered the drink and I'd been sandwiched between him and Danielle when her phone had buzzed with a text that I'd accidentally read: Tomorrow, honey. Market Street.

Just thinking of those words clenches my belly again and anger follows but before I can embrace the memory, another takes hold. I'm talking to Drew. "What do you do?" I ask, "and who are you really?"

"Corporate attorney," he replies, reaching into his jacket pocket to slide me a card.

I didn't pick it up. Not then, but later? I reach for my purse and start digging. In a deep scoop I pull my hand out and the card is in it. I have a work address and I even have a cellphone number. I toss money on the bar and climb off the stool, headed for the back door.

Once I'm at the exit, I pause at the door, remembering those last moments with Danielle:

Danielle whirls me around. "How about talking to me before you judge me?"

I don't know what she means but I'm angry at her. So very angry. "I need to leave. Honey." God, now I'm using my father's words. Honey. Honey. Honey.

"The real you comes out," she snaps. "Crass and bitchy."

I snap back to the present, and I shove the memory away as I had her that night, exiting to the alleyway. Once I'm there, I regret this departure route as darkness surrounds me in the narrow walkway. I reach for the door again, but it cannot be opened. I swallow hard, a chill running down my spine. This is where Danielle died. I feel it. I know it. There's a sound to my left, a cough I think, and then footsteps, but I can see no one. I dash right and start running, reaching for my phone as I do.

CHAPTER SEVENTEEN

My father once said to me that if you have an enemy, lead that enemy down a dark alleyway and make sure they can't get out. He'd been talking about his political opponents and using their own words against them in a debate. It seemed easily transferrable to life in general, though, and I remember, for the briefest of moments in that alleyway wondering if his words had been a foreshadowing of what would happen to me in the future that was that moment. I feared that someone wanted to ensure I never left that alleyway. Obviously, since I lived to tell this story, if that was their goal, they failed.

Present day, I can speculate with reasonable certainty that there was indeed more than one person who would have been relieved, if not downright celebratory, had I died that night.

THE PAST—AUSTIN PART TWO: THE BARTENDER

I clear the alleyway with my heart in my throat, but I don't stop moving. I'm on the main downtown strip, a buzzing area most nights of the week with bright lights offering safety. Still, it's not until I'm passing several busy restaurants that I breathe again. Even then, though, I turn and look behind me, feeling as if someone is there, someone is after me. Maybe it's just Danielle haunting me. It would be just like her to do such a thing and laugh as she does.

I become aware of my phone in one hand and the business card in the other. I stop walking and step to the wall, next to a sandwich shop, punching in Drew's printed cell phone number. The line is disconnected. My mind races the way my heart had in that alleyway. Why would a man who had an established career and life here disappear? It could be the press. It could be coincidence. Or it could be murder. I call a taxi again and I key in the address on the card to Drew's office, only to realize it's only a few blocks away. I glance around me, finding people walking here and there, which should feel safe. It doesn't. I wait for my taxi. It's a good decision. The car pulls up to the front door of the dark, locked high-rise, and I have no path but back to the hotel.

I enter the lobby, and I'm just passing the doorman when I hear, "Ms. Monroe."

I stop dead in my tracks, uncomfortable with the idea that the doorman knows my name, though it could simply be hotel policy to know those in expensive suites. Or perhaps my face recently slapped all across the news. Dreading what comes next for no real reason other than everywhere I step is quicksand, I turn around and face him. "Yes?"

"There was a man here looking for you. I didn't feel it was appropriate to deny or confirm your presence at the hotel."

"What man?" I ask, crossing to stand in front of him.

"He didn't leave a name."

"What did he look like?" I ask.

"Like me."

I whirl on my heel to find the bartender standing a foot away and without the bar between us, I can see that he's in black jeans, and a black T-shirt. "What are you doing here? *How* are you here?"

"I get off early on Thursdays and I took a chance that you'd stay at the same hotel the news reported you were at last time."

Early enough to follow me in that alleyway, I wonder.

"Is there a problem, Ms. Monroe?" the doorman asks.

Good question, I think, because this man is hot enough to give any woman pause, but then they say Jack the Ripper was as well. "I'll let you know," I say, walking toward my potential serial killer and stopping in front of him.

"Why are you here?"

"I wanted to buy you," he pauses for effect, "a cup of coffee. I thought we could talk."

"What do we have to talk about?"

"You seemed to want more details about Danielle's time at the bar. I thought I'd offer them."

"You said you weren't there."

"Did I?"

"Yes. You did."

"I wasn't working, but I was in the bar."

"I don't like games," I say.

"And yet you live a game of politics every single day. Coffee or no coffee?"

I don't immediately respond, and he turns to leave. "Okay, asshole," I call out. "Coffee." And because I *do* live a life of political games, playing them better than he could ever dare, I turn and start walking. I don't stop until I'm sitting at a table for two in the hotel lounge area, a cluster of empty tables around me. A wall to my right.

He, whoever he is, claims the seat across from me, an amused look on his handsome face.

"Who are you really?" I ask.

"Jake Bridges is the name," he says.

"You're not a bartender, are you?"

"Because you think I jumped behind the bar tonight just to be able to say that I made the *future First Daughter* a drink?"

A waiter chooses that moment to step to our table. "Irish coffee," I say, "but leave out the whiskey." I glance at the man. "Coffee, creamer, and whipped cream." I look at Jake and arch a brow.

"I'll take the same, with the whiskey," he says, and it's only a brief extra moment before we're alone, and he addresses me again. "You don't drink."

"I ordered a drink at the bar," I remind him.

"That you didn't touch."

"I was remembering that night," I say. "Not forgetting it."

"Most people want to forget nights like that one. Especially those in the spotlight."

I already did forget, I think, but that's not what I say. "If I forget that night, I forget the last time I saw her alive. And since she was cremated, that was the last time I saw her at all."

Our coffees are set down in front of us and this time when the waiter leaves, I get back to what's important. "Why are you here?"

"You were alone. I thought you might need company."

"I chose to be alone," I reply.

"No one chooses to be alone."

"No one who hasn't experienced what it's like to *never* be alone," I correct him, and his interest is starting to hit me all kinds of wrong. "Who are you, really?"

"I told you—"

"Who are you, really?" I press, concerned now that he works for my father.

"I don't work for your father," he says, as if reading my mind.

"That's not an answer," I reply.

"That's the one you really wanted."

"Who *are you?*" I press.

He shifts his weight and reaches into his front pocket before setting a badge on the table that reads "FBI" and now I show a reaction, sucking in air and blowing it out. "I thought an arrest was made on Danielle's murder?"

"It was, but I'm undercover in the bar investigating other activity outside of your friend's death. Which is why I was there that night."

"What else can you tell me about Danielle's last night?"

"Nothing you don't know. Well," he adds, "I might actually know a little more than you know."

"Meaning what?"

"Were you aware that after you and your boyfriend left the bar, he came back and fought with Drew Ellis in the alleyway?"

No, I think, but I stick to questions, not answers. "Was Danielle there?"

"Yes. She tried to break them up but ultimately stood back and watched."

"And?" I press.

"They threw a few punches and they must have kissed and made up, because they all went back inside and drank."

"Even Danielle?"

"Even Danielle," he confirms.

"Where were you?" I ask, deciding that's a safe question.

"Watching from the corner of the alleyway right up until they went back inside. I had another pressing issue to attend to that night. I left after that. Were they fighting over you?"

"Drew accused Tobey of being gay."

He arches a brow. "Did he?"

"Is he?" I ask.

"I wouldn't know."

But he does. I see it in his eyes. Tobey is gay and suddenly I need something real in my life, if only for now. "Let's go to my room," I say.

"You sure you want to do that?"

"Yes," I say, because another thing I learned from my father is decisiveness. Make the decision. Act on the decision. Move on. And if this man ever comes at me, he'll be the man who slept with me and has a vendetta, not the man who was investigating me.

He leans forward, seeming to read my mind. "I can fuck someone and still arrest them. You know that, right?"

"Why would you want to arrest me?"

"If I had my way, every politician that existed would be in jail. I hate them all."

"Then I think I'm in love or at least in lust."

He laughs, and it's a good laugh. A real laugh. I like real. We stand up and I don't rush as we walk across the lobby. Once we're in my room, he's quick to kiss me and push me against the wall. I don't just let him. I participate with everything I am, what no one ever sees or feels, and most certainly not Tobey. Jake feels different. He feels real. He feels like a man who wants a woman, not a politician that wants a free ride, as I now accept Tobey does.

I sink into the night, into the man, and revel in every naked moment with Jake, every kiss, and touch telling me one thing I need to hear. He's an FBI agent who wouldn't want me if he thought I was a killer.

I wake the next morning alone, and this time, I'm naked, a point that drives home the fact that I was not the morning after Danielle's death. If I'd slept with Tobey, surely I would have been. Of course, according to Jake, the FBI agent I did, in fact, sleep with, Tobey went back to the bar after we left. I wonder if he told the police that part of the story. Actually, he must have since Jake knew, or maybe he didn't. Maybe the FBI knew Tobey lied but it didn't matter since they captured the killer. Or perhaps, Tobey told them but didn't want me to know about the fight with Drew, thus he wanted me to believe he was here, and we were having sex. But why? It doesn't make sense. None of it.

I stand up and walk to the bathroom, and when I reach the sink, I find Jake's card taped to the glass, though I have no idea where he got tape. I grab it, read the FBI agent formality of his title, and then turn it over to read: *Call me if you need me.*

I frown, not sure how to take that offer. Why does he think I'll need him? Well, aside from the obvious reason, I needed him last night, and the fact that it never hurts to have a friend in the FBI. Unless of course, he's really my father's friend, and he was paid for last night. Which in premise, means he didn't care if I was a killer. He just wanted money, and to please the future President of the United States. I grimace and throw the card in the trash.

An hour later, I've gone through the motions of normalcy with the skill of someone hired to perform, or in my case, born into that responsibility. I'm dressed in jeans and a black leather waist-length jacket and boots, my hair shiny and my lips painted pink, and I stare down at the card in the trash. I snap it up, unzip my purse and stick it in my wallet. He could be useful in more ways than one. I head to the door, and thirty minutes later, I'm at Drew Ellis's office building. Fortunately, the security guard is easy to bypass, showing no signs of recognizing me, and with nothing more than a claim to an appointment with his firm, I'm offered the signature log. I sign it, using a fake name of course, and I'm on my way.

After a short elevator ride, I step into a lobby of rich hardwoods and dark brown furnishings to greet the receptionist, the kind of pretty blonde one decorates with, much like my father has my step-mother. "Hi," I say. "I'm here to see Drew Ellis."

"Drew?" Her brow furrows. "Are you sure?"

Am I sure? What kind of question is that? I think, but I go with it. "Yes. We're old friends. I wanted to surprise him."

"Oh, I'm sorry. You don't know."

"Know what?" I ask, trying not to shake the information from her.

"He took a consulting job overseas. He's in Japan now."

"Japan," I say. "I see. Is there a way to get him a message?"

"He's not working for us and he left no forwarding address."

"Is there someone here he's close to that might get him a message?"

"I really can't give out that kind of information."

"Of course not," I say. "Thank you."

I turn and head for the elevator, pausing long enough to take a photo of the list of associates on the wall.

A half-hour later, I sit down in my room and start calling them, trying to find someone, anyone that can connect me to Drew. I come up dry. Discouraged, I open my purse and dial Jake. "I wondered if you'd call," he says.

"Why did Drew Ellis leave the country?"

"I wasn't aware that he did. I told you. I wasn't on your friend's case."

"All right then. Hypothetically. Why would he leave the country?"

"Someone thought he couldn't be trusted to shut his mouth without extra incentive. In other words, he was threatened or paid off. Because some things, *Hailey*, are better left alone."

"Right," I say, and I don't ask for details. We both know he's giving me a message from my father. *Leave this alone.* I hang up.

CHAPTER EIGHTEEN

For every action, there is a reaction, my trip to Austin being no exception. I would be punished and who better to punish a daughter than her father?

THE PAST…

By six a.m., I've already boarded a Washington-bound plane. Once I settle into my seat, I breathe out relief that I have escaped any obvious notice, considering all the recent, local press. I tug away the baseball cap I've been wearing, allowing my tucked away hair to fall free, and the pressure on my head to be released.

My lucky streak ends when the flight attendant stops by my seat. "Coffee or juice?" she asks.

I look up and say, "Coffee. Three sweeteners and two creams."

The minute her eyes meet mine, hers go wide, and I see the recognition in her gaze. "Oh I—of course. Anything else?"

"No, thank you," I say, as if I don't realize that she's noticed me, the real me. "Actually," I say. "I'm going to nap. Cancel the coffee." I give her a smile and rest my head on the seat. Now there is no reason for further contact.

Once we're thirty-thousand feet above land, and I'm on my way home—if I can call anywhere home—I contemplate the sea of sharks and lies threatening my sanity, if not my safety. Tobey is somehow at the core of all of this, and I find myself questioning his character. On that note, being gay isn't a character flaw. Pretending to be straight to make it to the White House is another story. If it's true, I suppose I should be hurt, but honestly, I'm not. That in itself tells a story I've ignored. Perhaps it's the way I've insulated myself from emotions. Or maybe it's that Tobey and I just don't work. In fact, I am not even angry at Tobey, not on this. I used him as he used me. With him by my side, I pretended I wasn't alone. He was part of my insulation.

If Danielle were in my place though, she would not be as forgiving as me. She had her flaws, but we also had reasons to be loyal to one another. If she was here now and she believed Tobey had used me, she would go at him. He knows this. If Drew told me about Tobey, it's likely he also told Danielle. The question then becomes: Did that truly make Danielle Tobey's enemy? Could he kill her? *Would* he kill her? The "could" portion of this equation feels more important than the "would" at this moment as it's the prelude to anywhere else my mind might travel.

And where my mind travels is back in time, to a frat party we'd attended together in college. Tobey had always been a star frat boy for this particular organization, but that night a jock named Hensen Rogers, a new recruit who seemed to have it all—money, girls, grades, and a future in politics—decided to mock Tobey in front of an adoring crowd. Tobey had looked at Hensen with absolute murder in his eyes. Later, when Tobey didn't know I was watching, only that Hensen was not, I'd witnessed Tobey spit in Hensen's drink.

Certainly spitting in a drink does not make one a killer, but that murderous look mixed with pure hate was terrifying. I'd sensed something in Tobey that night that I never saw again, but it told a story about what was inside of him. *Oddly*, I think now just as I had back then, *Hensen had committed suicide only six months after that party.* He'd seemed an unlikely candidate for such a thing. More so now than ever. With those memories, I decide that, yes, I believe that Tobey could kill. Speculation of course, but he had a motive to shut Danielle up before she went public with his sexual orientation.

I frown. If he really is gay.

That uncertainty and the appearance of Jake and his badge tamp down my hypothesis that Tobey was the killer. Jake's involvement has my father's fingerprints all over it, but I have to ask myself why my father would protect Tobey. Perhaps to exclude his campaign from the dirtiness of murder but that doesn't feel right. Tobey isn't family, but I am, and if I did sleep with Tobey that night, at some point, I put my clothes back on. Which means at some point, I may have left the hotel room again. I may have seen Danielle again.

I exit the secure portion of the airport to find Rudolf decked out in his standard blue suit and tie, waiting on me, and why wouldn't he be? If I'm correct, he had FBI agent Jake Bridges alert him that I was in Austin, soon to be booked on a flight back to Washington. "Let me guess," I say. "My father wants to see me."

"You're very smart for someone so stupid."

"Are you sure you want to move to a new level of intimacy in our relationship?" I say. "The kind where we speak our minds? Because I have plenty I could say."

"Let the dead rest in peace," he replies dryly.

"Funny thing about resting in peace," I say. "They say the truth will set you free."

He gives me a deadpan stare, and then says, "We'll see about that." He takes my bag. "Let's go before we get attention I don't want, even if you do."

I don't argue the semantics of who wants attention and who does not. On this, I follow him to the car, thankfully without incident. Rudolf and I don't flex our new level of intimacy with conversation. We're silent, and I spend most of the half-hour drive doing word problems in my head, or rather variations of conversations I might have with my father over Austin. By the time we arrive at my father's mansion, I have about five prepared angles to every which way I think he can hit me; not literally hit me, but as his opponents know well, me included, his words pack a punch.

Rudolf parks in the driveway near the front door as if he's expecting my rapid departure, which suits me just fine. "He's in his office," Rudolf says as I reach for the door.

I don't reply. I prefer us in silence and as my mother always said, positive reinforcement feeds positive repeat results. My father, of course, never got that memo. I exit the car and walk slowly and deliberately toward the house. A brief moment later, I'm on the porch, skipping the bell. I enter the house, finding the foyer free of people, otherwise known as my fake family or my father's trophy family. I walk the same path I had before to reach the theater room, but instead of heading down the stairs, I walk up to the private loft-style room that is my father's office.

I find him sitting behind the heavy walnut of his half-moon-shaped desk, with a window directly behind him, hugged by bookshelves. He stands when I enter. "Shut the door," he orders, "and sit down."

I do it because what's a daughter supposed to do if not obey and respect her father? Once I'm settled in the seat in front of his desk, he sits down, his blue tie resting against a perfectly pressed white shirt. "You had to go to Austin, didn't you?"

"Yes, actually," I say. "I did. Because we both know a homeless man didn't kill her."

He leans forward. "The police said he did it. Her father accepts that they have the guilty party."

"If that's the case, why would you care that I went to Austin to say my goodbyes?"

"She's not in Austin, or on this planet Earth, daughter. She's dead," he says. "She's gone. Lord fucking knows I know what it's like to face that fact. I was left with you to take care of and you, Hailey, are supposed to take care of me like I take care of you." He reaches in a drawer and tosses an

8" x 11" envelope in front of me. "I tried to suppress those, but I failed."

I'm trained too well to react. I count to three and then reach for it, opening it to remove a photo of me on the street in the process of falling over, then in various awkward poses as I hit the ground. There are shots of me holding my face, my hair. There is a man whose face I can't see helping me into a car, but based on his build, he's not Tobey or Drew, well, what I remember of Drew. I'm wearing my dress from debate night, which places the time as the night of Danielle's disappearance, which must thrill step-mother dearest. The final picture is actually not a picture, but a collection of headlines:

Hailey Monroe, daughter to top presidential candidate, Thomas Frank Monroe, spent the night her best friend was murdered sloppy drunk.

Hailey Monroe, daughter to the widely believed top contender for the presidency, leaves her friend in a bar to die only hours after her father murdered his opponents in a debate.

I don't read the rest. I shove them back inside the envelope to clarify my thoughts, at least some of them. I was on the right track on the plane. My father isn't protecting Tobey. He's protecting me, or rather himself and his candidacy. "Who really killed Danielle?"

He stands up and presses his hands to the desk. "They have the man that killed her," he repeats. "What I didn't want was for them to know that you let it happen while you were on a binger."

My fingers curl on the arms of the chair. "I didn't do that," I hiss, and in that moment, I believe it. I didn't. I wouldn't.

"Didn't you?" he demands, and he doesn't give me time to reply. "The school threatened to pull your entrance into the law program," he announces.

I stand up. "I'm going to Stanford anyway."

"Stanford? You're not going to Stanford on my dime. I convinced Georgetown that you'll be entering a rehab counseling program and staying off the radar until next fall when you begin classes."

"I wasn't drunk," I bite out, anger coming at me hard and fast. "I was drugged. What part of that do you not understand?"

"Like you were drugged the night your mother died?"

"Yes," I breathe out. "Exactly."

"Do you have a drug dealer that follows you around, and then decides randomly when to ruin my life on your behalf?"

I feel those words like a slap and physically take a step back, managing to tumble back into my chair. "What do you want me to do? Give an interview? Talk to the press?"

"I want you to disappear until I nail the party nomination."

"What does that even mean?"

"Rudolf has arranged an apartment in Denver for you to stay at with plenty of money in your account, and a cover identity using your mother's maiden name. You'll leave now."

I've wanted an escape from Washington, thus why I'd chosen Stanford, but the idea that I might have lost that opportunity, along with the one here twists me in knots. "I'll go," I say, eager to get out of this room to make a phone call. I stand up and head for the door.

Just as I'm about to disappear into the hallway, he says, "Hailey."

I turn to look at him. "Yes?"

"Leave the past in the past. Move forward and do it quickly and quietly. Understand?"

No, I whisper in my mind, but I say, "Yes, father."

I exit his office with this feeling that I will never be back, which is crazy. Of course, I will, unless my "drug dealer," whoever that might be, decides I'm next to die.

I climb in the car with Rudolf behind the wheel. "I need to go by my place and pack."

"You can shop in Denver," he says, as if nothing I own is personal enough to matter.

"I'll be gone for months," I say. "That will be expensive."

He eyes me in the mirror. "Good thing your father is a rich man. We can't risk the press getting a hold of your location and following us."

I don't argue. If my father wants to pour money down the drain, so be it. If he wants me to go to Georgetown, he can forget it. I'll go to Stanford, and once I'm in Denver, I'll put in for a scholarship. I keep my mind on my plans and Stanford, because it's easier than thinking about all the other horrible things my father said to me. I'll deal with those when I'm alone, in Denver.

I sink back into the leather seat, and I don't allow myself to replay the conversation with my father. I won't let my mind go to the many places it could go if I let him take me there right now. I pull out my headset and I turn on my music, repeating the words in my head. When we finally stop, we're at a private airport. At the steps leading up to the plane Rudolf hands me an envelope. "Everything you need to know when you land is inside. The address to the apartment you'll call home. An ID with your mother's maiden name. Your cover story. A bank card with that new name on it. And a deposit of ten thousand dollars in your new bank account."

I frown. "I need a fake ID and a new bank account? Am I in witness protection or just laying low?"

"There is a reason movie stars use aliases. Once someone puts the face with a name, for instance, at the bank, the press is alerted. The idea here is to give them time to refocus on someone else."

"Can I use my phone?"

"Yes, but it would be advisable to keep your location private and communication limited. Exclude all things about Danielle which I would argue will be easier, if you give it some time. Take a step back, Hailey, and breathe. If you run into trouble, you call me immediately."

"Why not Jake?" I ask, seeking a solid link.

"I don't know Jake. I don't want you to talk to Jake. You call me. Understand?"

"I guess my father doesn't connect the dots between minions," I say. "But okay. I'll call you, not minion number two, Jake." I start to turn, and he catches my arm.

"Who the fuck is Jake?"

"Ask my father," I reply, pulling away from him and walking up the stairs.

I enter the cabin, a typical small private jet, and walk past the random seating area to sit in the back. I buckle up and I turn my music back on. I half expect Rudolf to follow me, but he doesn't appear. It's ten minutes later when we start to taxi; clearly, my father was eager to get me in the air.

Once we're there, and I'm thirty-thousand feet up for the second and last time today, I let myself have a real thought. I don't analyze the photos or why I was alone with some man I don't know. The bottom line here is that I don't have to look for answers anymore.

I'm a killer again. My father said so.

PART TWO: THE MIDDLE

CHAPTER NINETEEN

HAILEY ANNE PITT

My mother's maiden name was Pitt, which made her Caroline Beth Pitt before she married my father. On some level, even before arriving in Denver, I knew that becoming Hailey Anne Pitt would connect me to her in ways I'd long ago disconnected. Ultimately it did more than rekindle old memories. It changed me. She changed me, and ultimately—ironically, considering she was everything good and light in my life and I'd been forced to embrace everything dark and wrong—it would be my dead mother who opened my mind enough to find the truth in that sea of lies. And she who would give me what I needed to keep from being eaten alive by the sharks. That sounds profound and even touching, but don't let that fool you. It was that connection to my mother that also taught me to kill or be killed.*

THE PAST—DENVER, CO…

It's not until seven p.m., when the plane is landing, that I open the envelope Rudolf gave me on the other side of the flight. Inside I find exactly what I was promised: a new version of my driver's license with the name Hailey Pitt on it, and I don't ask how my father made that happen. This is my father. There is also a detailed outline of my cover story, which has me working for an art dealer. I ball my fingers into a fist and shove that part of the package back in the folder.

Moving on, I find a debit card with my new name and a deposit slip indicating a ten-thousand-dollar balance, along with a note:

Some things are better left alone.
—Your father

In other words, me. I'm better left alone. The wheels to the plane hit pavement and I key the apartment address into my phone and then shove all the paperwork back in the envelope. Once the doors open, I'm on my own. There is no Rudolf waiting on me, and for that, I'm happy. I'm also somewhere around sixteen or seventeen hundred miles from Washington, not by accident I'm sure, and it's unlikely I'll be recognized.

Embracing that freedom, I don't bother to cover-up, but when I reach the taxi station outside the airport, a cool breeze lifts off the Rocky Mountains. My jacket, of course, is in my suitcase back in Washington. Luckily, I snag a car quickly and dictate the address I've been given to my driver, an old man who tries to ignore me, which makes him just about perfect. It's a full forty minutes before he pulls us into what my phone GPS says is our location. He halts in front of a house that is in a nice, cozy neighborhood.

"Are you sure this is it?" I ask.

"That's the address," he assures me.

"It's supposed to be an apartment."

"It's a house," he says, as if I can't see that.

I frown. "I need to make a call," I say. "I'll pay for your time."

"You're paying," he says. "I'm staying."

I dig for Rudolf's number and then key it into my phone. "Trouble already?" he asks dryly.

"You said that my new residence was an apartment," I say, "but the taxi has taken me to a house."

"Did you try the key I gave you?"

I check the envelope for the key and find it, but that's irrelevant. "I wasn't going to stick a key into a strange house when you said apartment. You said—"

"It's a house," he repeats. "Anything else?"

My answer is simple. I hang up and the driver looks at me in the mirror. "Problem?"

"No," I say, "but can you drive me around the surrounding areas, so I can get the lay of the land?"

"If you're paying," he says again. "I'll drive where you want to go, honey."

"Thanks, *honey*," I say, because my mother would want me to check his "honey" with mine, and I am officially a Pitt right now.

He doesn't reply, but he puts us into drive. I study the view out my window and find a quaint area, with houses surrounding rows of galleries, stores, restaurants, and salons. There is a gym a short walk away, and even a mall, movie theater, library and finally, a Whole Foods. Obviously, this location was chosen to try to confine me to a small space in this country we call the good ol' USA. I could rent a car, but why? I have everything right here.

I check my watch and have the driver drop me at the mall, where I pay him to wait. I have just enough time to hit a couple key spots for a few clothing items, as well as toiletries. Next stop is a twenty-four-hour grocery store just a short drive outside of my neighborhood, then finally I'm back at my new house. I stick the key in the lock and open the door to my new life as Hailey Pitt. Just putting the name Pitt next to mine threatens a flashback that has me swallowing hard. I don't think about that night. It's too brutal. The steel. *The blood.*

Shoving aside those thoughts, I flip on the light and take in the shiny dark hardwood, a stairway in front of me with industrial-style black railings that are sleek and modern. To my left is an open concept living area with a kitchen and built-in island that is a cream-colored stone. Everything is pretty much all cream and browns, with all the normal high-end expectations that come with what I suspect is a million-dollar house. Obviously, my father wanted me a) secluded from watchful eyes an apartment ensures and b) feeling cozy enough to stay a while.

I set all my bags by the door, lock up again, and note the security system that doesn't appear to be armed. Grabbing my kitchen items, I head that direction, unpack, and take a bag of chocolate with me—otherwise known as all three meals of the day. Once I'm loaded down with my bags, I hurry upstairs and find a number of rooms, but the master is my focus. It takes me three trips, but it's not long until I'm settled into a spacious bedroom with a four-poster bed, sitting area, and of course, a giant bathroom awaits me, with a walk-in closet. I unpack, sort, and end up sitting on the edge of the claw-foot tub, just listening to the silence. The sound of being completely alone, my proof that I was always alone. It's just more obvious now.

I think that this is like Tobey potentially being gay. I should be upset, but I'm not. Accepting what was obviously always in front of me is rather liberating. The man in my life is likely gay. My best friend who likely drugged me not once, but twice, is dead. My father hates me. I could go on, but what's the point?

I grab my purse and the envelope that is on the bathroom counter, before exiting to the bedroom and settling into the cushion of a fluffy gray chair in the corner. I set my phone on the chair and open the envelope, pulling out my new driver's license that reads Hailey Pitt. The name that is really my mother's cuts through me and I try to picture her, with all her pale blonde beauty, but I cannot. I grab my wallet and stick the license inside and in doing so, thumb to a photo inside.

I drop my purse to the side of the chair and stare at the image of myself standing with my mother and her father, my grandfather Pitt. My mother was gorgeous and my grandfather, tall, lean, and brilliant, like her, or rather her like him. He was a brain surgeon renowned for his skill in the medical world, and his hatred of my father. Ironically, he died in a car accident three years before my mother. I'd wanted to be a doctor because of them, and then I didn't.

I flash back to the night my mother died, and for a moment I am in the car. It's after the impact and those moments when I first come back to reality.

My chest burns. My head spins. Every part of me aches with the impact of the car with another car. I look at my mother, steel sliced into her body, and I don't scream. It's not real. None of this is real. I need to prove it's all one big nightmare and I lean forward and press my hands to her chest, warm sticky puddles consuming my hands. I lift them and stare down at the blood on my hands, so much blood.

I snap back to the present and drop the photo, tunneling fingers through my hair and standing up. And there it is. The reason I decided I was better suited to be a cold, calculated attorney. That night was the reason. I pace for several moments, or maybe it's minutes even, I don't know, but I need to do something. I need to just do *something*. I'm coming out of my own skin. I grab the envelope I'd taken from my father's office and pull out the photo of me getting into a car with some strange man helping me. There is only one person who I can think of that I could actually ask about him with any chance of a real answer, and a limited risk of it backfiring. There is only one person who might know. One person who could shut down all my fears. I walk to the chair and grab my phone, punching the redial on Jake's number.

He answers on the first ring. "I saw you on the news."

"As did the rest of the world," I say. "Did my father pay you to sleep with me?"

"I'm an FBI agent, sweetheart," he says, his tone less than amused. "I'm not on your father's payroll."

"Yet," I say, "if he becomes President—"

"He has a long way to go to claim that title."

"Few would dare to say that."

"I'm fairly certain we passed niceties when we took our clothes off."

"Getting naked with someone means nothing," I say. "So said you in a power play before we took our clothes off."

"And the fact that it didn't scare you says something about you."

"What does it say?"

"What indeed," he replies giving me nothing.

"If you don't work for my father, why tell me that some things are better left alone?" I ask.

"Why indeed," he says this time.

He says those words as if I should know what they mean. As if we're winking over a secret he's covered up for me or because of me and I don't like it. "Who was the man who helped me get into a car when I left the bar?"

"I didn't see you get into a car," he says, "and why are you asking? You don't remember who you were with?"

"I don't remember *him*," I reply quickly.

"I guess I should be flattered you remember me," he replies dryly.

"I wasn't drinking the night I met you, nor do I drink in general."

"Right. Just *that night.*"

"I don't drink," I repeat, "and that night, I was—" I stop myself from uttering the word drugged.

"You were what?"

"I wasn't feeling well."

"Good thing we caught the killer and you made a friend at the FBI. That kind of answer would have turned you into a suspect."

"Are you a friend Jake?"

"As long as you let me be a friend, Hailey."

"All right then, *friend.* You said that if I needed help, to call you. I can't afford some sudden tabloid scandal. I need to know who that man was."

"You don't need to know. Stirring up trouble where trouble no longer exists creates a problem for those who don't like to have problems." He softens his voice, a low warning rasping in his tone. "Listen to me and walk away from this, Hailey. If you struggle to follow this simple instruction, come see me. I'll give you something else to think about that won't get you in trouble with anyone but me. Now hang up."

I hang up.

CHAPTER TWENTY

Silence is only golden to those who want to shut you up.
I was fine with the silence Jake proclaimed necessary, if not
in so many words. I just wanted to be in on the secret. No,
not just. Danielle's death was at the core of this secret and
if my gut was right, I knew I was, too. I needed answers
and if Hailey Anne Monroe couldn't hunt them down, then
Hailey Anne Pitt, would. Once she convinced the world, she
was just a girl, being just a girl.
As if I could ever be anything but my father's daughter.

THE PAST—BECOMING HAILEY ANNE PITT...

I wake my first morning in Denver with a mission:
Convincing those watching me that I've moved on from that
night in Austin; giving myself space to find answers on my
own. I decide the best way to do this is to appear busy and
working toward goals that support my father's run for
President. That means I need a job, an internship perhaps,
but how I pull that off without a real resume, I'm not sure
this idea works for me or my father. Not if I want to avoid
bad press. First things first, though, I need my life fully set
up here. I shower, throw on the sweats, a tee, and sneakers
that I bought in a rush the night before, and I head to the
mall.

I spend several hours shopping before I head home with
a MacBook and a full wardrobe, including interview attire. I
even do it all without being recognized, which is as liberating
as being alone, without surrounding myself with

149

placeholders to make me feel better about it. I'm Hailey Pitt now and as long as the world watching me believes this, I'm free, at least for a time, and far more than I would be by simply changing my law school choice from Georgetown to Stanford. This privacy is something I want to guard, to lavish inside, for me, not my father. Which is exactly why I google ways to search for recording devices, downloading several apps that declare me clear of watchful eyes. It's not full-proof, but it's better than nothing. For extra safety, I call the security company and activate the system installed in the property.

Next, I settle down with a cup of coffee I've made with the Keurig that came with the house, which has me curious about who owns the property. Living by my mother's favorite saying of "better safe than sorry," I setup my computer and then dig deeper. Two cups of coffee and a protein bar later, I can finally satisfy my curiosity. I type in the address of my rental and find it is owned by Newman Wright Investments, which leads me to nothing interesting. Apparently, they own a vast expanse of properties in the Denver metropolis, which means rental properties. And they cater to executives that travel, which explains the fully furnished property. At least one mystery is solved without incident, and I'm assured the homeowner won't be surprising me with a visit. Still, I email the leasing company's name to myself to be safe. A woman, especially one in my circumstances, should know the local people involved in her life.

Out of pure habit, I glance at my iMessage and note the blank logs. Not only did my father scrub my phone, he scrubbed my iCloud. I have no past history chats with Danielle at all. To me, that looks more suspicious than just leaving our chats. What was there that I didn't see? What did I miss the morning she died?

"Damn it," I murmur, shoving fingers through my hair.

She's dead.

She's gone.

That is not something I can change.

I reach for my purse when my phone rings, and I swear I shiver, certain that it's going to be Danielle, telling me she's still alive, and to stop freaking calling her dead. With an out-of-character shaky hand, I grab my cell and glance down to find Jake's number. I hit decline. I've said too much to him. I'm not tempting fate. I wonder if that's what Danielle did when she drugged me again, despite how horrific the first time had turned out. I wonder if I found out before she died.

"Stop!" I bite out fiercely. "Stop now."

I need out of this house. I need to do what I did to survive my mother's death: yoga. I quickly google a location nearby and find one easily. I head for the door. I'll check out the studio and find a schedule. Heck, maybe I could become an instructor. I'm certified. I taught in college as part of building a "diverse resume," as was preached by my advisors, to look good to the law school I was assumed to be entering there at Georgetown.

A plan in place, I exit the house, lock up, and only a few minutes later, I'm strolling the quaint, calm neighborhood that reminds me of an upscale beach town minus the beach. Cars pass by, but they are few and far between, while residents stroll from place to place. I use my phone's navigation and turn right down 3rd Avenue, passing one of many galleries in the area only to halt at the sight of a painting. A beautiful black stallion that is so alive, it feels as if the magnificent creature might jump from the page. It reminds me of a time when I'd painted, when the brush in my hand, and the paint on the canvas, had been an obsession I'd shared with my mother.

Until she was gone, and I couldn't pick up a brush. I couldn't, I *can't* paint ever again. *Never* again. That part of me is as dead as Danielle and my mother.

I turn away from the gallery and start walking again, faster now, with intent in my steps, old memories I've long suppressed trying to surface, while the ones I've been trying to remember, that night with Danielle, stay buried. I reach the yoga studio, and walk inside, talking to the girl behind the desk about the schedule and pricing. I inquire about a job and I'm given a card for the manager. I leave five minutes later with plans to return tomorrow. I'm going to need my yoga to survive the trigger Hailey Anne Pitt appears to be for me.

As I step onto the street, I find myself stopping to stare at the sign just across the street: *Creatively Wined and Caffeinated* with a paintbrush at the end of the scripted words. Unbidden, I'm back in time, to another coffee shop where I'd visited with my mother on a girls' night out, an image of the two of us sitting at canvases, painting and drinking hot cocoa has me telling myself to turn away. I'm done painting. Never again will I hold a brush in my hand.

Even so, I find myself crossing the street toward the shop. I don't stop until I'm opening the door and entering, to find myself standing on a landing, a stairway leading downstairs where the wooden bar is surrounded by bookshelves and cute wooden tables. There are paintbrushes, as well as mini coffee cups and wine bottles dangling from the ceiling. It's adorable. There are two open arches, one labeled "Art" and one labeled "Books." There are people milling around here and there, and I imagine on the weekend it must be quite packed. I inhale with the realization that it's not so unlike the very first place my mother took me to paint. She would love this place, which is exactly why any other day, I'd leave but I'm Hailey Pitt right now and the Pitt part of me is the part that represents all that has been good in my life.

I head down the stairs and walk toward the bar, where I climb on a stool and eye a menu with wine and booze presented as options, that I mentally decline. A pretty woman with pale blue eyes and a mess of light brown hair piled on top of her head stops in front of me. "What can I get ya?"

"Skinny white mocha," I say, the skinny request giving me room for my added request of, "Lots of whipped cream."

"Is there any other way to drink it?" she asks, giving me a friendly, genuine smile, not the fake, plastic, obligation smile I'm accustomed to receiving and delivering. "I'm

Michelle," she adds, "the owner here, and if you need anything else, let me know, but for now, a white mocha, whipped to perfection, coming right up."

"You're the owner?" I query. "You look very young to be the owner," I add, guessing her to be in her late twenties.

"Thirty-six is not all that young," she says, wiping her hands on a towel. "But that compliment earns you extra extra whipped cream on your next coffee."

She's charming and I find myself liking her, when I like so few.

She departs, leaving me in the unfamiliar state of alone, and I have this sudden wish for my computer, for something to do that is not just sitting here. I glance toward the room labeled "Art" and find myself curiously craving a peek inside, but no. No. I'm not doing that. It's just then that a man sits down several seats away from me, setting off alarms with his choice of a seat near me rather than further down, at any of the many other open stools. I glance his way, sizing him up as tall, dark and good-looking in an expensive suit, with a briefcase he sets on the bar. He's also wearing a Harvard class ring, which I know because I'm one of those rich, privileged people I hate, even when I, like my father, declare that to be untrue. Michelle waves at him and his, "Hey, Michelle," says this isn't his first visit, as does Michelle's comfort in turning from him and returning her attention to the espresso machine. She has no choice. She's alone and I wonder where the rest of her staff is at present.

The good news in Harvard being a repeat customer is that this indicates his visit is not about me, at least not solely for me, but that doesn't mean he has not been recruited to watch me. With that sour idea, I scoot off the barstool, and walk toward the bookstore, but somehow, I end up under the archway leading to the art room. Painting stations with easels line a walkway on each side, and I'm framed by walls decorated in murals of Italy and Paris but it's the wall of rolling hills directly in front of me that has my attention. Specifically, a whiteboard positioned in the center of a grass-green hill that lists out "Paint and Wine" hours. My lashes lower and for just a moment, I'm back at that first paint night with my mother, her soft laughter playing in my head. The next moment, she's screaming at me right before she died.

My eyes pop open, acid burning my throat, and without another look around, I step back into the coffee shop, and make my way to the bookstore, the cute, airport-style bookstore setup, an easy distraction from the past. That is until I home in on a center display of hot new releases that features a much-anticipated book about my father: *The Unauthorized Biography of Thomas Frank Monroe.* Because why wouldn't his book be here? He's everywhere and the only good thing about that book is how much he doesn't want it to exist.

Which is exactly why I have to fight the urge to pick it up and devour the contents, but I don't need the attention purchasing it might deliver. Besides, what's the book going to tell me that I don't know? He's a power-hungry monster who will spin that as being a fighter who won't take no for an answer when it comes to this country and its needs.

"White mocha!" is shouted out and I leave the book behind, hurrying toward the bar where I claim my seat in front of a giant whipped cream concoction that looks like heaven. I can also feel Harvard staring at me. I ignore him. I'm good at that. You learn the skill of being obliviously aware when you're in a life like mine. I grab a slice of chocolate from its spot inside my whipped cream and take a bite.

Harvard moves to the seat next to me, a wave of musky woodsy cologne, teasing my nostrils. "That looks like dessert," he comments.

I now have a mouth full, and a good-looking man with an agenda next to me. An agenda and attention I can't afford to entertain. "I like dessert more than I like most people," I say, once I manage to swallow, "which likely includes you."

He laughs, low and full. "Is that right?"

"Yes," I say. "It is."

At that moment Michelle sets a cup of very plain coffee in front of him and glances at me. "How's the white mocha?" she asks.

I laugh and lift a spoon, scooping up whipped cream. "I haven't found my way to it yet, but I love the path I have to travel."

"You're my soul sister," she says, giving me a wink. "But you know who to bitch at if you don't end up liking it." She glances at Harvard. "I already know what you like."

She disappears, and Harvard returns his attention to me. "Still like that cup of whipped cream more than me?"

"I didn't actually say that I liked it more than you," I reply, glancing his direction. "Just that I most likely would."

"And you base this assumption on what?" His cell phone rings and he grimaces, reaching for it. "Hold that insult for just a minute." He glances at the number. "I'll be right back," he says, as if he expects that I'll be here when he returns, which proves exactly why I already don't like him. He expects. Just like every other man in my life.

He pushes off his seat and walks away, I eye the stack of papers on the bar a few seats down and the legal pad with scribbled notes with further disdain. He's an attorney, like so many of the men in my life. Scanning the end of the bar, I find a stack of cups, quickly grabbing one, filling it with my drink, and topping it off with a lid.

It's at that moment that a woman steps to the bar with an armful of books, including the one about my father, because apparently the register behind the bar, is *the* register and of course, she wants a book about *him?* "I'll be right there," Michelle calls out, sounding frazzled as additional customers enter through the front door. I decide to help her. I lift the wooden arm to the bar, and step behind it, grabbing a scanner. I ring up the order, take the credit card, bag the books and ask, "Anything else?"

"What are you doing?" Michelle demands, appearing beside me, her voice more frazzled than ever now.

"Helping," I say, turning to face her, my hands on my hips. "If you need more help, I'm new to the neighborhood.

I'll be back tomorrow." I don't wait for a reply. I lift the arm to the bar again, round the end cap, grab my coffee, and head for the exit. Just as I reach the top of the steps and would push open the door, Harvard claims the space just in front of me. Taller and broader than I'd realized until this moment, his penetrating blue eyes meet mine. "You leaving?" he asks.

"Yes," I say. "I am."

"I can't let you go until I convince you to like me."

"Are you an attorney?"

He narrows his gaze, surprise in his stare, a hint of what I'll call a "mid-thirties" line feathering by his eyes. "Yes. Why? And how did you know that?"

"How did I know? The Harvard ring. The notepad. The suit. The attitude. And why do I ask? Because I don't like attorneys. *Ever.*" I step around him and I leave.

I've made it a few steps down the sidewalk and he's by my side. "Why do you hate attorneys?"

"They're arrogant assholes who only want to win."

"I could argue that with the goal of winning, but somehow I don't think that helps my case. How long have you hated attorneys?"

I flick him a glance. "It's a recent decision."

"I see."

"I doubt that very much," I say.

"Brought on by a particular asshole, I assume?"

"A cluster of particular assholes," I amend.

"I see," he says again. "And what do you do?"

I stop and look at him, "I start at Stanford law school in a few months."

He laughs. "Are you serious?"

"Yes. I am."

"But you hate attorneys," he confirms.

"Yes. I do."

He gives me a deadpan stare. "You're staying in the area?"

"Yes."

"Going back to the coffee shop?"

"Yes."

He arches a brow. "When?"

"Tomorrow."

"Time?" he presses.

"Whenever I decide to go."

He laughs. "All right then. Maybe I'll see you there."

He starts walking the other direction, a snake charmer like my father, who would make just about any woman want to see him tomorrow, *except me*. I turn sharply away from him and start walking, and I'm back in time. I'm sixteen, standing outside my father's home office as he speaks to Frank Genks, his attorney who is much like Harvard—good-looking, charming, and smart—and I'd had a crush on him.

"End him," I overhear my father order Genks, and with a peak around the corner, I see my father standing behind his heavy oak desk. "End Desmond Johnson and do it now."

End him, I repeat in my mind, Genks forgotten, the words, the command, radiating through me. What does that even mean?

Suddenly, my mother grabs my hand, whirls me around and presses a silencing finger to her lips. I nod and she leads me down the stairs, toward the lower level of the house. Once we're in the foyer, she ignores what just happened. She deflects, "I thought you were at Danielle's tonight?"

"She blew me off for a date," I say.

"Well good. You can be my date then. Grab your purse. It's time we had a mother-daughter day."

"Where are we going?"

"A field trip," she smiles, but it's a brittle, strained smile. I don't question her. Not yet. Not when I'm smart enough to know that her silencing finger and her unease come together with uncomfortable clarity. She wants me, or maybe us, out of here. I hurry to the kitchen where I've left my things and then return to the foyer, and it's not long before we're inside the shadowy darkness of my mother's Audi. "What did that mean, mother? End him?"

She stares forward for several beats and then glances over at me. "Political and legal wars come with strong language, that amounts to nothing more than winning." She starts the car and turns on the radio, effectively telling me to let it go.

I blink back to the present that has little to do with attorneys, Harvard included, but rather my mother. It's not even about my father. It's about my mother and I let myself ask the question I've never let myself ask before now: If my mother, who was brilliant and obviously far from naive, was as pure and good as she seemed, why would she choose my father? She heard the same conversation I did. She saw the things that I saw and things beyond that, that I did not. She was my father's confidante. Why would she allow him to "end" someone, and still wear his ring?

Was my father her snake charmer, or was there more to the story? To her story?

CHAPTER TWENTY-ONE

When you paint, really paint, and allow everything that you are to be poured onto the canvas, the result is captivating. This is a lesson I learned from Neal Baker, a famous artist my mother introduced me to as a way to nurture what became my teenage obsession with art. More an obsession with expression through art. From the moment I picked up a brush, it was the one place I could tell a real story. The one safe place that I could tell the truth, admit fear, anger, confusion. I could see me on the canvas, and as long as I could see me, then the story of Hailey Anne Monroe, the future First Daughter, the one the world was told, because it suited my world, didn't have to be real. Painting was my separation from that person, my sanity in the insanity.

Until the crash.

After that day, I didn't want to see the real me and neither did my father. He just wanted me to be the future First Daughter and after my initial meltdown, being that person was how I survived. That person wasn't my creation, and that was a good thing. I wanted to live anywhere but inside the nightmare that I'd created in the real me. I think as you read along it's pretty clear, that at some point, I'd suppressed anything but my father's creation to the point that I knew no one else.

Until that trip to Denver, when I picked up another paintbrush, and expression rather than suppression, lead me to—well, me. I found me again, the real me.

Ultimately, sending me to Denver was a mistake, at least for my father.

THE PAST—DAY TWO IN DENVER…

I wake early despite binge watching two seasons of Dexter, who turns out to be an oddly likable serial killer that I understand and accept simply because he reminds me of my father. Not literally, of course. I don't know if my father "ends" people by way of murder, though it's doubtful. Body counts would be trouble for him, which is why I'm in Denver, not Washington right now. I have a body count.

I brush my teeth, throw on clothes, and head to yoga class, which is exactly what I need. It calms the storm inside me, one that is secretly always just beneath the surface. That calm is the good, while the bad is me walking out of that session with the confirmation that I won't be getting a job at the studio, or likely any studio nearby. Those jobs are filled with rich, stay-at-home housewives who, like me, just want to fill a void. I doubt their void is one of blood and death, but I get it. They need stuff to do and I'm left with a mission to find a purpose. I suspect the First Daughter persona is still ruling my roost, because the things that come to mind are things that will not please Stanford when they discover my drugged up "drunk" photos in the press.

For the briefest of a moment, I consider calling Senator Smith, but what can I really say to the man? He will have seen the photos. He put his name on the line for me. There will be no return to his offices and no entrance to Stanford. I should feel disappointed, but the truth is, I'm not disappointed over Stanford. It's not like I want to go to law school, and that was my dream school. I'm simply disappointed that I'll be stuck in Washington.

An hour later, I've showered and dressed in blue jeans and a long-sleeved black T-shirt, which I pull off and replace with an emerald green shirt. I can't do funeral wear. It's not that season anymore, not if I'm going to find a way to get beyond this. Not if I want to keep my hard-earned, well-crafted armor fully in place. I grab my newly purchased Burberry briefcase, shove my MacBook inside, and decide that I'll head to a healthy spot I saw down the road for lunch, then to the coffee shop, and not because of Harvard. I really need to define the new me with habits, and I like that coffee shop and Michelle.

Heading out, it's not long before I've lunched on fake spaghetti—otherwise known as spaghetti squash—and I start walking toward the coffee shop again. Only a block away, I detour to a gift shop, buy a card with flowers on the front, because flowers say "I'm sorry" better than most things I know. Which, I think, stopping at a counter to grab a pen, in hindsight must be why my mother was always getting flowers from my father.

Shoving that pretty thought about my parents aside, I instead ponder the one that I'm about to ink to Senator Smith. Settling on short and sweet, if an apology can ever be sweet, I neatly print:

I won't explain myself. I will only thank you for everything, and one day, if the opportunity presents itself, I will pay you back, with a favor.

Your friend,
Hailey

I stare at the word "friend" and decide I'm comfortable with that reference. If Danielle and I were "best friends," certainly I was at least a "friend" to the senator. Which simply means different levels of placeholders. It's a cynical thought, but then, I am my father's daughter far more than I am my mother's daughter. It's true. I don't like it, but that is just a fact. I seal the envelope, write the address on the outside, buy a stamp, and stick it inside the mail slot. Now, when I do see Senator Smith again, and of course, I will if my father wins the party election, it will be just a little more palpable.

Make friends, not enemies my mother always said. In truth, the senator was helping me work against my father's wishes. He could have turned my father into an enemy, and considering how powerful my father is, that is a rather curious choice on his behalf. It's really not, actually, I decide. The senator had an agenda I simply do not know. Everyone in my world has an agenda, and I am but a mere token, being played in games I too often, unwittingly enter.

Setting aside this factual, but unpleasant thought, I exit the gift shop and walk to the coffee shop, entering the cozy little spot, to discover that mid-day on a Saturday is busy. I hurry down the steps and since the bar is packed, I settle at a table, and by the time I have my MacBook open, someone sets a white mocha in front of me.

I look up to find a blonde with a pixie cut and pink-ish lipstick standing in front of me. "On the house," she says. "No idea why." She smacks her gum and walks away without asking if I want anything else, but not before I noted her badge that reads: Ashley.

I glance toward the bar to see Michelle wave at me. I smile and wave back. I like her again. Adding the "again" to that sentence is big for me. By meeting number two, people usually prove they know my father and want to get to him through me. Of course, I've barely spoken to Michelle, but she's different from the people I know in D.C., and by different, I mean genuine, like her smile. It's refreshing. Pure. I wonder if that's a quality that can be contagious the way corruption can be. If it is, am I so corrupted that I corrupt her, or is she so pure that she purifies me?

Contemplating those questions, I reach for the spoon on my saucer and scoop the whipped cream that my spaghetti squash and morning yoga earned me. I then bite the chocolate piece included, and the idea of corruption delivers my new purpose, at least for this day: I need to know what's in that book about my father, because like it or not, I'll be drilled about the bad parts, and not by him. By the press.

I can't exactly buy the book here today, any more than yesterday. Not without practically screaming "I'm his daughter" to everyone in the place who might have seen me in the news, and just hasn't placed me. Instead, I purchase the e-book online. Once it's downloaded, I resist the urge to skip to the bad parts. That's not how you make, or defend, a prosecuting case, which is what the press and the opponents to my father will be trying to do. I need, and want, to know the entire picture, and how it comes together.

I start to read, and I'm not sure how long the first half of my father's family history takes to get through, but considering it's also my family history, I devour every pebble. At some point, I order a second coffee and one of the best brownies of my life, but even that doesn't distract me from the book. For the most part, it talks about my father's financial empire, foreign links to banks, property, and a history of those connections that link back to his father, my grandfather that I never knew. He died the year before I was born, while my father's mother died in childbirth. According to the writer, my grandfather was nothing shy of the devil himself. Of course, the book is written by an enemy of my father, so the accusation of both his and his father's foreign interests over America are painted one-sided. Are they true? Even if it was, my father isn't foolish enough to make it traceable.

The chapter that has me sitting up a little straighter is called "The Women," and I struggle to even read on to the next page. I don't want to know what I'm about to learn and yet, my questions about my mother force me to go on. I'm on what the writer calls "Affair Number Three" when I down my coffee to keep from throwing my cup. My reaction is based on the familiar name. I set the cup down and my fingers curl into my palms. My gaze rockets to the art room with the realization that a stranger's words have now spoken one of the truths that I have refused to paint, but was before me all along.

CHAPTER TWENTY-TWO

There's a long list of Presidents and their infidelities, but I'll spare you the names to avoid any implication that I have a party preference. I don't. I hate politicians. All of them. My father included. I'm that equal opportunistic in my hate. Back then I believed that infidelity and lies were just different variations of the same word, therefore worthy of equal opportunity hate as well. That changed when I realized that there is no justification for infidelity, but some lies are necessary. I guess that means I don't hate lies as much as I do infidelity. Sometimes lies are about survival and even saving someone who might otherwise be destroyed. Infidelity is always about hurting someone.

That doesn't mean lies are without consequence. In fact, these revelations about my father, had me asking, what's the price for a lie? If you tell just one, do you get a pass? What about two lies? Or three? When do you stop getting passes and does size matter? What if it's just one lie, but it's as big as the one I told the police with Danielle in Europe? That question opened up the floodgate of possibilities and the door to more questions. For instance, is one kind of lie, better than another? One punishable, when the other is not? And who should deliver the punishment? That's an interesting question that I've since answered, but we'll save that for the end of this story.

For now, I'll stay focused on the question that would burn a hole in my mind over my father's infidelity. If a lie is a perfect lie, the kind that is undetectable to the human eyes, does it even count? Perhaps not unless you make a mistake and it's exposed, as is my father and his lie. As I'd sat at that table in Denver, staring at the pages of the book before me, one thing became clear: My father, who had always been a perfect man to me and so many, was no longer perfect to me at all. The book is filled with dirty secrets, really my father's dirty secrets. Does that mean they're mine as well?

Maybe.

THE PAST...

I'm still staring at the name of my father's "third" mistress, when I hear, "Do you want another coffee?"

That question brings me back to the coffee shop, my gaze lifting to find a new waitress standing in front of me, her brown hair cut in a bob. "Black, please," I say, the taste for sweetness I normally favor replaced by the bitterness on my father's infidelity. "Just black."

"Sounds horrible," she says dryly. "But you're the customer." She glances down at the mug. "You can keep that mug you're clutching like you want to throw it. I'll bring you another. Then you'll have two weapons."

I eye the mug now too, finding my fingers clutching it. I give a practiced bark of laughter. "I'm reading a horror novel on my MacBook. A gift from my father that apparently has me a bit on edge."

"I love horror novels. What's it called?"

I shut my computer. "Over," I say. "Not even my father can make me enjoy this one."

She arches a brow. "Sounds like your father is out of touch."

"Is yours in touch?" I ask, instinctively moving away from the subject of my father that was better left unspoken, not to mention, I get my dose of "normal" through other people.

"Mines dead," she says flatly and then gets back to her job. "You sure you don't want another white mocha, right?"

In other words, she'll make small talk, but she doesn't like to get personal. She's wounded, damaged in some way, and while I do not wish these wounds upon her, it makes her safe. She won't ask more question because she doesn't want to be asked any herself. "Actually," I say, getting to the simple matter at hand and it's so very nice to have a simple matter at hand, "I'll take the black coffee I ordered but with creamer and another brownie. Maybe if I add a little chocolate to the mix of sugar I'll drown out the bitter horror story."

She gives me a strange look I deserve with that stupid comment, then nods and turns away. I like that she gave me the look I deserve. No one treats me like I'm just another human being. I could really like it here. I watch her walk away—the briskness of her walk, the curl of her fingers into her hand, which has me looking at my hands where I'm still gripping the mug. My lips thin and I force myself to release my hold on the ceramic, flattening my hands on the table. I have a momentary flashback of my mother picking me up from junior high that has me sinking back in time. *The two of us settle into the car, but my mom doesn't turn on the engine. She stares forward, before saying. "We do not act out," she says, before looking at me. "Do you understand me? I can't believe you said that to her. Where is your restraint?"*

"I used restraint," I say. "I sat there the entire time she read that ridiculous essay criticizing my father's senatorial politics, quite patiently and politely. When the teacher asked for comments, I simply stood up and offered mine by stating the obvious. She's a puppet to her parent's opinions, who would never amount to anything. Simple. Obvious. Correct."

"As I said, where was your restraint?"

"You're suggesting we don't defend our own?" I demand.

"Of course, we defend our own," she says. "But we choose not only our battles, but how we fight them."

"I chose this battle."

"And made yourself look like an arrogant bully. That's not who I want my daughter to be. And how do you think getting suspended looks to medical schools?"

"Yes, but—"

"No but about this," she says. "Your father and I will discuss this with you at home."

I momentarily return to the present, staring at the wood of the table, but I can't pull myself fully out of the past. That discussion my mother wanted to happen, didn't happen, at least, not as my mother had planned. She was called to the hospital, leaving my father in charge of my punishment. My father called me into the living room and we'd sat on the couch, in front of the fireplace, hot cocoa in my cup and something stronger in his. I shut my eyes, and I can almost feel the heat of the fire.

"Your mother is angry with you," my father states staring into the fireplace, before glancing over at me. "I should be as well."

"But you're not?

"Of course, I am. Your temper gets the best of you and that has to stop."

I don't agree, but as he's taught me in the past, I remember that "my words are weapons to be used against me," thus I make my words few, and listen to those spoken by others, in this case, him.

"If you are attacked," he says, "or fight back after being attacked, and end up bloodied, you lose the battle. You lost today." He downs his drink, sitting the empty cup on the table, and lowers his voice, as if he fears my mother will walk in any moment, and he doesn't want to risk her hearing. "I don't want a daughter who loses."

I don't flinch. I agree with him. I don't want to be the daughter that loses. "Clearly you and mom are on different pages."

"We're on the exact same page," he assures me. "You were expelled, the other girl was not. She won. She goaded you. She pushed you over the edge. You gave her that control. That's your mother's point."

I lower my head, feeling those words like a punch. He's right. Despite Kathy's tears, she outsmarted me.

"Approach your enemies the way you would a math equation," my father continues.

My chin snaps up. "There isn't always time," I argue.

"Take the time," he bites out, his tone hard. "Everything doesn't have to be now. Take the time and use it to think about your next move, and act precisely, not rashly. Sometimes you don't act at all but if you do, you know from our efforts with equations that sometimes you have to simplify. Make it as painless for yourself as possible."

"I don't understand."

"Sometimes you need to come at a problem from the side, not the front. And we've talked about this over and over. Just because you don't get credit for your work, doesn't mean you don't do the work."

I snap back to the present, a splinter sliding into one of my fingers, where I have been rubbing the table, but I don't yank my finger back, or inspect the injury. I'm not angry and out of control as my mother believed me to be that day. I'm angry and *in* control. I'd understood what my father was saying to me and I've wisely put that advice to use. He wasn't telling me to let go of an attack. He was telling me to administer those attacks more covertly. I remember telling Danielle about his advice and she'd summed it up quite eloquently: *"In other words, he just told you to cut her, make her bleed, and ensure it looks like someone else is holding the knife."*

Danielle's way of looking at things had always shaded toward the dark side. From my perspective, the lesson wasn't dark, but rather crystal clear, and all about self-preservation; above all else, look out for number one, yourself, a skill my father excels at better than most. What he doesn't realize is just how good at doing just that I've become, as well, but he's doesn't need to know. *I know.*

I open my computer again and stare at the name of mistress number three: *Susan Patterson*, now known as Susan Monroe, step-mother dearest. Confirmation in my mind, of what my mother really meant to my father; she was the perfect First Lady in his eyes, while his mistress was always his backup plan. In other words, his anger at me since her death isn't about me stripping the woman he loves from him. It's about me cracking the picture-perfect glass he'd wanted the world to see, that was never perfect at all.

I consider a call to my father, but as he taught me, I analyze it first, imagining how it will go:

"Daughter," he'll answer, as if that is an endearment, not an insult.

"I read the book," I'll reply.

"Don't believe everything you read."

"Did mom know about your affairs?"

"Holy hell, daughter. I never cheated on your mother."

"What do you want me to say when the press corners me?"

"The truth," will be his reply because that's one of his campaign policies. If it can't be proven, and it's hurtful: deny, deny, deny.

"Why didn't you warn me?" would be my reply, since we both know the truth is dirty and ugly, just like the lies he's just told me.

"Why?" He'll demand. "It's all lies and surely you know this. She was the love of my life."

The call would end abruptly with some muttered excuse. And there it is.

The call I don't need to have. I just completed it in my head. A conversation with my father that isn't the answer I'm looking for right now, anyway. It doesn't tell me how I defend my mother, who can no longer defend herself, and it seems, didn't, or couldn't, when she was alive either. I want to know which. I must know more, because as my father said himself: We defend our own. And now, the one person in my life I've ever felt like was mine, is not someone I knew, therefore was she mine at all?

Harvard suddenly appears at my table, and today he's traded in his suit, for a black, long-sleeved shirt, and black jeans, his dark hair thick and tousled in that way that says wind or woman. Well for some, wind or man, as is the accusation about Tobey, which is neither here nor there for me, unless said man is in my bed.

"Can I join you?" he asks, motioning to the table.

There's interest in his eyes, the kind a man has for a woman, but who knows, maybe it's real or maybe it's not real. Maybe he knows who I am and sees a path to power and fame. The way Tobey wanted me for money and power, right up until the moment I'd called his number aka his agenda; thus, he has not called me since I left. Maybe Harvard will lie even better than Tobey did. Maybe Harvard will at least kiss better than he did, and the lies would taste like temptation rather than convenience. At least then, if I'm used, I'll enjoy being used.

Whatever the case, it's clear I might actually be angry with Tobey and that aside, the interest that Harvard has shown in me, must be controlled before my Denver sanctuary is destroyed. "You can join me," I say, "but only because I'm trying to save the rest of the place from the attorney in the house."

I am pleased when Harvard laughs, where Tobey would have scowled, proving that Harvard has a sense of humor, which is rare for those in my life. I've barely completed this thought when he moves forward and claims the seat next to me, not across from me, settling his briefcase on that chair instead. In the process, his leg brushes my leg and for the briefest of moments, I'm transported back to the place that I'm now trying to forget: to Austin, to Drew's leg next to mine, his wink, and I do now what I did then. I jerk back. If Harvard notices he doesn't react. "Since we haven't been formally introduced," he says, resting his naked hands on the table. "I'm Logan. Logan Casey."

"Logan Casey," I repeat trying to ground myself in the present, at least for now, but some part of me is still swimming in that memory, which naturally has me wondering if this man is a shark in the water around me. "Two first names," I add. "Sounds like your parents fought over who got to pick your first name. Did they draw straws for which choice became your middle name?"

"You're actually right on target," he says, laughing again, and it's a nice, masculine laugh, and oddly this thought feels familiar while Logan does not. "No one has ever guessed that," he adds. "My mother won the name war. The women always win. Speaking of names. Do you have one?"

"Hailey Anne Pitt," I say, "and in my house, my father won the name war." Because in my father's world, I add silently, the women don't win the wars. At least, not that he knows, not in an obvious way. I've learned this well.

"Well then, Hailey Anne Pitt," he says, "what's a Stanford girl like you, doing in a place like this? You're a long way from school."

I'm smacked in the face with a lesson I've long ago learned and forgotten with this man; strangers do not always remain strangers and all offhanded remarks can come back to haunt you. "That was a joke," I say, shutting the door connected to my real life, and a path that leads to my father. "I hate attorneys remember?"

He narrows his eyes on me, and for no reason other than instinct, I believe he's looking for a lie that he won't find. I'm simply too well-taught from birth, too skilled at being more than one person to allow such a detection. Well that, and the fact that I really *do* hate attorneys, which is why I'll be a good one.

"That was a joke?" he confirms.

"Yes," I say. "Are you amused?"

"Yes, actually. I am. What does a lawyer-hating smart ass like yourself do for a living?"

"When not busy taunting those who went to law school," I say. "I'm an aspiring artist." Both honest answers, if you put a "was" in front of the "aspiring artist" which I'd thought that I'd come to terms with, but the knot in my stomach says I have not.

Logan motions toward the art room. "Your career explains why you ended up here."

"I guess it does," I say, as this place serves me well to reconnecting to the Pitt part of my life, which is a place I really need to be right now, for all kinds of reasons.

"Are you good?" Logan asks, as if he's read my mind.

My father's words answer him in my head. *Art is useless unless you're famous*, he used to say often, because of course, it was inconceivable that I might be good enough to be famous. "Art is like movies and food," I say, shoving aside that bad memory. "Good is subjective." I don't give him time to reply. I ping the conversation back toward him. "What kind of law do you practice?"

"Corporate," he says, and this time he pings back to me. "Do you live in the neighborhood?"

"Yes," I say simply. "Do you?"

"I bought a building a few years ago where I live and work which means this is my home turf, and why I know you're new here."

"I am," I say and since he's clearly going to ask for details, I quickly preempt with an on-the-fly story. Actually, it's the suggested story, Rudolf included in my file. "I came here for a job, and my new boss owns a house he's rented to me for dirt cheap."

"And what does an artist do but create art for a living?"

"I'm working for a private art acquisitions firm. I now hunt for treasures for a living." This lie is actually my dream job that I've never been allowed to entertain.

The horror flick loving waitress delivers my coffee and brownie. "Thank you," I say, because every politician's daughter has manners beaten into her.

"No problem," she says, "but if you come to your senses and want a better version of that coffee, just shout." She eyes Logan. "I already know you want a crappy tasting coffee, on endless pour and a chocolate chip cookie. Coming right up."

"Thanks, Megan," he says, giving her a wink that I don't classify as flirtatious, just friendly, and Megan is gone.

"Obviously you're a regular," I comment, "and they even like you."

"And they like me," he confirms, "despite knowing I'm an attorney.

"Because you're good looking and use it to your advantage."

He arches a brow. "You think I'm good looking, do you?"

"Oh, come on," I say, crinkling my nose. "Everyone thinks you're good looking. I'm simply stating a fact. We use what we have and those of us that are smart, know what we have." I move on from what is really quite inconsequential. "Why work here, not at home, or in the office?"

"I find I get a lot of work done with a cookie, coffee, and no access to streaming television," he explains.

No one in my D.C. crowd would make an admission of being human and distractible. Some people in my situation might take comfort in that fact, but I don't. Logan's an attorney, and my gut, which I'll confirm with research, says he's a powerful one, the kind that radiates toward my father. Maybe that's a coincidence and maybe it's not. Maybe he's testing how well I execute my cover story. The possibilities are many. Though in all fairness to Logan, perhaps I'd lean toward his innocence, if not for the laundry list of recent events such as Tobey being gay and the FBI agent, who is likely working for my father, that I slept with to prove I was a) still desirable and b) not a killer.

I decide right then that my father's saying of "shut your mouth" applies to me with Logan as easily as his other favorite saying of, "keep your friends close and your enemies closer."

"Can I leave my computer with you?" I ask, establishing that friendship.

"Of course," Logan agrees graciously, warmly, and I find myself hoping that warmth is real, as real is something missing in my life.

I stand up, intending to walk to the ladies' room but I find myself walking toward the room labeled "Art," and even when I tell myself to turn away, I do not. There is a flutter in my chest that tells a story; one of heartache, loss, and even love lost in all kinds of ways. My art. My mother. My life. I pause in the archway, willing myself to turn away, only to find Michelle placing a sign on the front easel that sits center stage that reads: *Classes cancelled until further notice.*

Frowning, I walk down the aisle framed in the center of the room, a few random people sit with coffee and paintbrushes to join Michelle at the front of the room. "Why are classes cancelled?" I ask.

She puffs out a breath, her light brown hair fluttering over her brow. "Our instructor quit without notice." She throws up her hands, seeming to need an outlet I've become. "I don't know why I opened a place that revolves around creating art. I mean, yes. I love art but as far as creation, I can't even get stick figures right. It's very upsetting. It's a part of what we are here. And yes, I know. It was stupid to open a place with a premise that I can't fulfill."

Seeing her fret, makes me fret when I don't fret. The next thing I know, I'm spurting out, "I can do it," in a rare moment of spontaneity. "I'm qualified."

"Really?" she asks, her tone one part hopeful, one part skeptical.

"Really," I assure her, the idea of doing this expanding my chest with the first real excitement I've felt in a very long time.

"Show me," she says, pointing to a blank easel.

This will be the first time I've touched an easel since my mother's death, but I don't hesitate. This is my craft. This is what I love and it's like riding a bike. Certain skills never go away and I'm at home with a brush, or any artistic tool, in my hand. I sit down, grab a thick art pencil and in a quick few minutes, I've sketched her. "*Wow*," she murmurs. "You're good."

I stand and face her. "Thank you. Do I get the job?"

"It doesn't pay much," she warns.

"Keep the money," I say, remembering my father talking about the poor return on a coffee shop investment some years ago. "I have income. I need a hobby. I'm free for a few months. Use the extra cash to grow your business."

She blinks. "What? No. I have to pay you."

I wave that off. She's giving me a gift. I'll give her one back. "You don't have to pay me. Coffee and art make me a happy girl." *Happy.* I used the word happy. "I need the class schedule," I say, excitement welling inside me.

"A hobby is something you do and forget," she says. "I need someone who can be here and be reliable."

"A hobby is something you love and don't get paid for performing," I say. "I'm reliable but get a replacement if you must. I'm here until you do."

She hesitates. "You're sure?"

"Completely."

"Okay then. We can set it up to meet your schedule, but Wine and Painting on Saturday nights is big."

"It's Saturday now."

"Exactly. Tonight's our big night."

"I'll start tonight."

"Really?"

I laugh. "*Really.*"

We chat a few minutes, and she promises me unlimited free white mochas, which based on my consumption capabilities could get expensive for her. She brings me an application, which I fill out with my new identity, and a fake Denver phone number, deciding I need a temporary phone. When finally the formality is done, Michelle departs and I'm left standing in the middle of the art room, *my* room now. A place where art will be my world again. A place where I must face all the broken pieces of myself, but I know now that I have no choice. I cannot discover what I do not know or understand about my mother and her motivations without discovering what I don't want to see or know about me, the real me. What if she wasn't as pure and good as I think she was? What does that make me? *Who* does that make me? I *need* to know.

I sit back down on a stool, staring at the paper covered canvas with Michelle's image, without seeing her. I just see the darkness of my mind, where there should be light. I need that light, I need the answers it will deliver. I tear away the page with Michelle's image and with a new plain white sheet exposed, I pick up a pencil, and this time, I intend to do what I've always done in the past; let the instrument in my hand answer to the questions weighing on my mind. Let my craft become a tool that reaches inside me, and touches all those dark places in my mind that I never allow myself to touch. It's what my mother wanted, for me to confine all of my uncontrollable impulses on the canvas, not in the world.

I intend to draw my mother, hoping that in my creation I'll find the answers to the questions I have about her life, and therefore the questions I have about mine. From the first stroke of my pencil on the canvas, I am lost in my work, in *creating* for the first time in so very long that I lose time. Footsteps sound, jolting me to the present and suddenly Logan steps behind me to study my work, and so, I study my work. It's then that I discover my brush has a mind of its own. My mother is not on the canvas. Instead, it's Danielle.

CHAPTER TWENTY-THREE

A secret; defined by the dictionary as something that is kept or meant to be kept unknown or unseen by others. *We all have at least one secret, if not more, most likely. Stating the obvious here, but a secret is yours to keep and yours to share until you actually share it. Owning a secret wholly to yourself though, is lonely. It can make you alone in the middle of a room. Alone in the middle of the world. Looking back, alone is what started wearing me down. I, of course, knew that once my mother died, I was alone in the plastic world of Washington, but once I was in Denver, once I was so easily displaced, by all those who knew me, I started to realize how empty that really feels. How empty I was. I began to see that no one truly missed me. I began to not just see the token I was to them all, but feel it. That's how cold and guarded I'd become before Denver. I didn't know how cold I'd become. I didn't know what I was becoming. I realized then too, that if I was being watched by my father, it wasn't out of concern. It was out of his need to control me and protect himself.*

Knowing this had long clawed holes in me, that sealed and reopened on a quite regular basis, but once out of his direct spotlight, I was so hungry, so very hungry, for someone who saw me and not my father, that my guard began to lower. That's dangerous when you have a secret shared with someone who is missing. Someone in the back of your mind, you fear you somehow made disappear. I didn't protect her. I didn't save her. I hurt her. I had no idea at that point what happened. I had no idea if someone else knew what I should know.

And yet, as I stood in that art room with Logan staring at my work, at Danielle instead of slamming shut a door on him, I felt as if a tiny piece of my armor began to peel away, like I shoved it open just a tiny bit. I gave him room to open it. I, Hailey Anne Monroe, the political warrior, started to become Hailey Anne Pitt, the woman and artist. The problem though was that both people were me, and I still had a secret or perhaps, more than one secret.

Which brings me back to Logan, staring over my shoulder, at Danielle, the root of all of my secrets, at least back then...

THE PAST...

"You're talented," Logan says from behind me, close enough that his energy crackles along my shoulder blades. Close enough that he can trace every line of Danielle's face with his intelligent eyes. "Downright gifted," he adds.

It's something my mother would say to me and I swallow the tightness in my chest, angry with myself for just standing there, when there is so much on the line. When Danielle, who has been on the news, and by my side often, is on my canvas. Angry with myself for feeling the compliment like a balm to my hungry soul; a soul that wants to live with a paintbrush in my hand.

Jolting myself into action, I murmur, "Thank you," tearing away the disposable paper off the easel and folding it in half, not about to leave it behind, "but," I add, turning to face him, "right now it's not brilliant to me. I don't like anyone to see my work until it's done."

"Just like I don't like to read my closings to anyone until they're being delivered."

I seize this as an opportunity to turn the conversation to him. "You don't practice your closing?"

"You ask that likes it's unheard of, and like you know from experience."

"I didn't decide I disliked attorneys by watching them on TV," I say, quick with my rebuttal.

"Who was he?"

Who was he? I laugh bitterly, because somehow this man has hit yet another nerve. "Who wasn't he?" I ask, only now admitting to myself that Tobey's betrayal, his silence now after this betrayal tells a painful story of who and what we were together, that I denied until I couldn't any longer; we were as fake as a billboard sunrise in a Hollywood parking lot.

"You come from a family of attorneys," he assumes. "And therefore, you've dated attorneys."

"Smart observation counselor," I say. "Closing statements—"

"Have to be magical to win, which is why I need to choose mine with you cautiously. Come have that coffee with me so I can assess you and decide what my next move should be. Tell me more about your work, as I'm certain now that the last thing we should talk about is mine."

I stare into this man's once penetrating, now warm, blue gaze, and I feel that spark of attraction to him I've denied by brushing him off until this moment. I do not want to connect with anyone right now. I can't be cut again and aligning myself with someone who could be with my father, or become a token that my father later uses against me, is as good as handing that person a knife, when I'm already bleeding. "I'm the new instructor here now," I say. "I really want to paint, and get ready for class."

"New instructor," he repeats. "What happened to the new buyer's position?"

"This is more of a side gig," I say. "I think they need me here."

"Well judging from the work you did, I do as well. Paint. I'll be here when you're done but I want to see your next masterpiece." He pauses. "When you think it's ready, of course."

When I'm ready. When has anyone in my life ever cared if I was ready for anything? If he's with my father, he is his best pick, his best actor.

Logan turns and walks away. I watch him, something bothering me that won't materialize fully in my mind, something obvious but out of reach. Wait. *Wait*. It is obvious. He didn't ask who I'd painted which means he either already knew—or—or maybe he didn't care, because he was too interested in me, but I dismiss that fantastical idea. I hate that I've allowed myself to have that thought. I hate how much I crave being just a woman with just a man attracted to her.

I turn away from the door and face the blank page I've left myself. Staring at it, I pick up a pencil, and start sketching. This time, it's Logan I draw, Logan who has me looking for his perfect lies but when I'm done, when he's on the paper, the way he is in my mind, I don't find them. I'm not sure what I see but it is not what I expect. I'm not clear at all on this man but then, I considered myself a master at reading agendas, but missed Tobey's true alignment with my father. It hurts. I didn't love Tobey though, I remind myself. I didn't. I knew. He was just my comfort zone. The one person, outside of Danielle, that was there for me after my mother died. Now Danielle is dead, and Tobey is gone.

I tear the page with Logan's image on it off the easel as well, and fold it, sliding it over the top of the page that holds Danielle's image. I need to keep sketching, but not here. Not around other people. I need to be alone, to find me again and maybe with me, I'll find Danielle again. Maybe I'll even find a way back to the mother that I thought I knew, but now—I just don't know anymore. I need art supplies. I need time alone. I walk back toward the coffee area and exit the art room to find Logan sitting at the table we'd shared together this morning, his hair rumpled, his attention on his computer. In that moment, I dare to appreciate the fact that there is a quality about him I find appealing, some something that I cannot name, but it sets him apart from the normal stuffed suits I frequently encounter.

I cross to join him, claiming my seat in front of my computer that still rests on the table under his protection, while stuffing the folded pages in my hand under my purse on the chair next to me. He grimaces at whatever he's working at and tosses down the pen in his hand. "How's sketching?"

"Apparently better than being an attorney. Something wrong?"

"Nothing that won't bore you out of your mind or piss you off since you hate attorneys."

"Try me," I say. "You might be surprised."

"I'm preparing a filing and I don't feel like it's strong enough to make my case."

"Why?"

"It lacks facts."

"I'm good with facts," I say, seeing an opportunity to get to know this man in his world, not mine, and size up his true motives. "I'm free. I can help you research."

Surprise flickers in his eyes, followed by warmth. I've pleased him, and for this moment, it feels real. I try to think back to meeting Tobey, to any moment like this that felt real, but if it exists, it was long ago forgotten. "Keep me company," he says. "That will motivate me."

In other words, he's a smart man who doesn't want me in his business, and that sets off alarms. He wants me close, but not too close, and I decide that I've imagined that moment of genuine warmth in him as a person when it was about reeling me in; keeping me close.

"I'm antsy for something to do," I say. "I'm going to head out and let you work."

"Stay," he encourages, his hands sliding over mine, the touch rocketing up my arm and stealing my breath.

I'm disarmed and after my newfound conclusion about his motives, and those of everyone around me, I do not like being disarmed. Not one bit. "No," I say, jerking my hand back. "I really need to rest up before the class tonight."

"What time is class? Maybe I'll be your student."

I laugh. "I'm doubtful that you're a good student."

"Every good attorney is a good student. It's part of winning."

And winning is all that matters. Oh, how I understand that attitude. It's exhausting. It's what I want to escape. I stand up, pack up my bag, and settle it on my shoulder. "Good luck finding your facts." I walk away and consider that maybe, just maybe, I'll walk away from more than one attorney. I'll walk away from them all. I'll decide the possibility of a presidency doesn't get to rule my life. I'll do what my mother never did. Of course, that fact of her life is no secret. We all know she stayed.

Right up until the moment she died.

I step onto the street and start walking toward the Bed and Babbles down the road after a quick google search produces a result in Cherry Creek. Apparently, it operates like the area's everything store and I'm hoping to find art supplies. Turns out, they really do have a bit of everything and while the supplies are not perfect choices, they'll get me by until I can have the proper choices delivered.

An hour later, I walk into my rental, setup a little studio in a garden room off the kitchen. I'm glad I walked away from Logan today. Alone is what I do best. Alone is safe. Maybe one day it won't be, but right now, there are too many unknowns and too many of the wrong certainties, like my father's candidacy.

I pull out my paintbrush and as much as I want to stay in this new reality, I have another reality that is icy and cold, settling in every warm spot my new teaching job has created. I know why I drew Danielle and not my mother. She was erratic, unpredictable and yet the one person I shared a dangerous secret with, but I knew her, we were bonded. I could control her, or so I thought. I'm the one who ended up drugged, not once, but twice and yet, our secret died not with me but with her. This idea slides into my mind as if it was my decision, and I quickly shove it aside. No. That is *not*

184

what happened, but something did and someone knows what that something is, and that's dangerous. I have to remember that night.

I start to paint. First producing what seems like a simple memory; the drink that was not so simple at all. The drink that was drugged, by Danielle. I shut my eyes, searching the black hole that is my mind:

The s'mores drink Drew ordered appears in front of me, and I grab the marshmallow and take a bite, the sweet chocolate of flavored liqueur touching my tongue. I turn to find Danielle's back still firmly in place, her body turned intimately toward Drew's.

My eyes snap open. Her back was turned. My brow furrows. When did she drug me? Did the bartender drug me for her? I stand up and start to pace. I want to go back to Austin, to find him, to confront him, but I know that would bring attention to myself that I can't afford. I inhale and force myself to reach into the deep, dark depths of that black hole again. I'd gulped the sweet chocolate drink and I go back to that moment.

Tobey appears by my side, resting an elbow on the bar. "Hey, honey."

I hate when he calls me honey. My father called my mother honey. I rotate to face him. "Are you gay?"

I think back to that question I'd intentionally thrown at him with such accusation and I know why. He'd not only called me honey right after I'd seen that text message— maybe I even thought he'd sent the message back then—but Drew had also hit a nerve, something I'd sensed with Tobey. Something between Tobey and I that just didn't feel real. Passion that was never quite ripe. The idea of him faking desire for me had cut deeply.

Tobey had scowled and snapped back at me, *"Why the fuck would you ask me that?"*

"Are you?"

"Do I fuck like I'm gay?"

"I don't know how someone gay fucks," I say.

His hand had settled on my shoulder and I remember wanting to feel something, wanting a spark that didn't exist to exist, "Let's get out of here and fuck," he'd said. "That'll end this conversation."

And so I'd woken up in a hotel room, where he claims we did just that—fuck—and yet I had my dress on. Not that taking off your dress is a requirement to fuck, but one would think that if Tobey was trying to prove he was into me, he'd want me naked. One would think I'd remember such a display of manliness, but then, sex with Tobey was never overly memorable.

I tear away the page that displays the drink and stare at a blank page, furious with myself for what I don't know. I grab a pencil this time and I start creating again, letting my mind lead me. I draw myself and Danielle on a mountaintop with a woman between us right before she fell to her death. I don't like it. I don't like it at all. Why is this what is on the page? *Why* am I going there?

I flashback to that shove before the fall. I bury my face in my hands. I believed what I told the police. I really did, but my silence turned it into a lie, a damning, poisonous lie. It became my unwanted secret that I don't get to own alone, a constant hammer hanging above me, ready to fall. I know why I drew this now. I know the warning my mind is giving me. Remember *or else*. Remember *now*.

Standing up, I tear away the drawing and carry it to the kitchen where I turn on the stove top and set the edge on fire. I then stick it in the sink and let it burn until the fire alarm goes off, and then I wash it down the drain. I leave the alarm on for a full minute, the screeching sound a warning that echoes the one in my mind: Someone has a secret about that night and I need to be very, very concerned that it's someone other than me and about me.

Of course, my father would bury that secret to protect himself, to protect the presidency but this is no comfort. My father would bury Danielle, or maybe even me, to protect that future. Is that why my mother stayed? I thought they were deeply in love but—perhaps he simply scared her. I catalog random moments, and the look in her eyes, and the truth comes to me in bitter acceptance: She was afraid. My mother was terrified of my father. For the first time in my life, I do not want to be like my mother.

CHAPTER TWENTY-FOUR

My father's hatred of my art ran deeper than his need to turn me into his version of the perfect First Daughter. It was my connection to my mother. She was the one who put my first brush in my hand. She was the one who, to my father's peril, insisted that my talent was a gift that couldn't be ignored while he called it a frivolous hobby. I would be a doctor or an attorney. The end. If I'm honest, denying myself my connection to my mother, forcing myself into law school, most certainly giving up my art, was punishment. I killed her. I didn't deserve a connection to her. Punishment I know my father wholeheartedly approved of. Punishment my father found every way possible to deliver, over and over again.

Knowing all of this, why then would my cover story in Denver be rooted in the world of art, when my father hated that world? Why then would my cover story use my mother's name as my name? There's only one answer: more punishment. He blamed me for whatever happened in Austin. He knew what I couldn't remember.

Of course, I took what would have been a small taunt, and turned into a full-blown body slam, when I'd offered to teach that class when I started to hunger for my art in a deep, passionate way. I'm sure when his confidants, whoever was watching me, reported back to him on my new teaching job, this amused my father, pleased him, in fact, as he knew it would pain me to let it go. Unfortunately for my father, he wasn't the only one working a plan and he was a long way from burying what really happened that night in the bar.

But then, so was I.

THE PAST—MY FIRST NIGHT AS HAILEY ANNE PITT, ART INSTRUCTOR...

Despite my worries about secrets and lies at play around me, especially where Logan is concerned, my steps are fast and light as I head back to the coffee shop to teach my class. For the first time in years, adrenaline that isn't anger, but rather excitement, pulses through me. I arrive thirty minutes early to setup, but upon entry, I'm jolted to find that one of the televisions over the bar is playing the news, with my father and that damn book, the topic. "We have this book on the shelves," Michelle calls out to the general population of about twenty.

Eager to get out of this room before my image is randomly flashed on the screen, and I'm recognized, I dart toward the bathroom sign. I'm instantly down a hallway, wooden walls encasing me, and I quickly search for cover, shoving open the door labeled "Ms. Coffee" of all things. I might have responded to such a name with a snort back in Washington, but here, it's cute. It's real. It's *fun*. Not ready to let go of this newfound place, and identity, I shut the door behind me and lean against it, two sinks to my left, two closed stalls just beyond them.

I step to the sink and stare at myself in the mirror, and there is no doubt that I am Hailey Anne Monroe, complete with dirty blonde hair and blue eyes. If I was in Washington, I'd have been identified already. That I'm in Denver is unexpected, and thus far unrecognized, offers hope that might remain that way. I want it to last and a visual change would help. I could change my hair color, but I nix that idea the minute I have it. Dying my hair is about as appealing as the years in law school I'll soon endure to be my father's version of me. I gave up my art for him. My hair color is the one part of me that I still know as me. I reach behind me and braid the long strands, and upon inspection, I decide that helps. I don't look as much like me as before. Maybe I'll do temporary pink highlights and leave them in long enough to give my father a heart attack, but again, that might draw attention.

Satisfied I've done what I can to hide my real identity, I head for the door when it bursts open and someone runs smack into me. A yelp follows, and I instinctively grip the woman's shoulders to find it's Megan. "You," she says, almost like it's an accusation.

"Hailey," I supply, in replacement of "you," and noting her bloodshot eyes, I ask, "Are you okay?"

"Of course I'm okay," she says defensively, pulling away from me, clearly not worried about upsetting a customer that she still believes me to be, but I have this sense that she feels caged. Trapped. Discovered in some way.

Okay then, I think, stepping aside, to give her the space she clearly demands. She brushes past me toward a stall and I turn just in time to watch her shove a hand through her dark bob, a deep scar running down her arm. Unbidden, my hand settles on my hip, over my own scar. A scar that resembles hers in a way that tells me, like mine, hers is created by steel penetrating flesh, which is not a gentle injury.

She shuts the door and I stand there a moment, wondering about her, about what created that injury and what pain haunts her in the aftermath. I do not remember the last time I wondered what hurt someone instead of who someone was preparing to hurt. Oddly this is far more uncomfortable than the latter, which should be the opposite and I do not like this about me. I look over my shoulder at that stall and wonder if this young girl in a coffee shop might have far more in common with me than either of us might first think. I wonder if she would wish for my life the way I might just wish for hers.

I exit to the hallway and hurry back toward the coffee area. My dash past the television area is quick, my retreat to the art room, a success. Already there are people milling about, waiting for me to get them started. Michelle comes rushing into the room. "You ready?" she asks. "Usually we get everyone seated, take drink orders, and then the instructor gets everyone going."

"Sounds good to me."

"Do you want a glass of wine?" she offers.

"Oh no," I say quickly. "We don't want me to start painting your walls instead of the canvas."

She laughs. "We've had a few incidents."

I laugh with her, but considering my past drinking experiences, I imagine she'd welcome a painted wall over blood and missing a person. Of course, I doubt anyone here is planning to drug me, but that experience is just a little too raw right now to indulge. Shaking off that thought, I quickly focus on the here and now where I want to be, and setup at station for myself at the front of the room. It's not long until I have a full room, and I'm teaching everyone to draw dandelions with lots of laughter in the room as wine begins to dictate the skill on the pages. It's a fun night and at one point, while helping someone turn a weed into a flower, my skin prickles. I'm just leaving Bruno, who indeed looks like a Bruno, to his work, when the air crackles and I look up, seeking the source, to find Logan leaning inside the archway.

I dislike that I notice how good looking he is which I could dismiss as a simple observation of fact. I could, if my heart wasn't racing with his attention, and the fact that I know he came here for me because it's for the wrong reason. I should now be sharpening my wit and caution, suspicious over his motivations and I am and yet, there is more. There is that part of me trying to face the fact that the last two men I was with most likely were on my father's payroll. And the fact that what I had with Tobey wasn't even close to real. Maybe my father even paid him to oversee me. These thoughts have me turning away from Logan. I can't forget that he too could be here to oversee me, and that idea successfully shifts my female instinct to get to know him, into my desire to punch him right in the kisser I will never kiss. My only love affair in Denver will be with art.

I refocus on a pretty blonde named Ivy and help her paint a rose and when she beams with her success, she is even more beautiful. *Like Danielle*, I think. Danielle was a beautiful mess. No. She *is* a beautiful mess which is why she will re-appear any day and revel in her ability to cause chaos. I shake off the crazy thought and glance toward the archway to find Logan has disappeared, but he's not gone far. Of this, I am certain.

For now, I throw myself into my love of art, and I do love art. I love being a part of this place. I love what I'm doing here. In fact, while my class runs right up until midnight, I would happily have continued with my lessons far beyond. Once the last student departs I gather my things and look up to see Logan leaning on the archway. Of course, he's here for me, the *real* me. I'm his job, the woman he's spying on, but there's this small, weak part of me that wants him to be just a man who knows me as just a woman. For once in my life, I'd like to be wanted for me, to know it's really all about me. The way a paintbrush allows me to be just an artist and the class tonight allowed me to be just a teacher.

I walk toward him as he straightens, and I notice how tall and broad he is again, but that's not what really matters. It's the way he owns the space he occupies while Tobey needed me by his side to own anything even himself. He needed *me* to get to the White House. "How was class?" Logan asks, driving away Tobey, and pulling me back to him, his eyes warm with what feels like genuine interest.

"I enjoyed it," I say. "I'm looking forward to the next one."

"Which is when?" he queries.

"Monday night."

"What are you doing now?" he asks.

"Going home."

"How about I take you for a late dinner?" he suggests.

"Why?"

He laughs. "Why? Because we're both hungry."

"I didn't say I was hungry."

"But you are. I know you are. That's what makes me a damn good attorney. I see the unspoken."

It's a lighthearted, innocent remark, unless it isn't. "That wins you no points with me," I say, my half guard now fully erected. "I don't want a stranger to see what isn't spoken."

He arches a brow. "Are we still strangers?"

"Yes," I say.

"And if I want to remedy that?"

"You'll fail," I assure him, and I mean the words, but then, I meant it when I said that woman fell off the cliff, when she was pushed, too. I changed my mind later, and I don't give myself a chance for that to happen now. I walk around Logan and head for the door, stopping by the bar to talk to Michelle.

"Please tell me you're coming back," she says, setting down the wet towel she's holding.

"I will," I say, "and about payment."

"Yes, of course. Let's talk pay."

"How about a brownie for the road?"

"No," she says. "That's not enough, *but*," she concedes, "for now, because it's late, I'll give you the two I have left and some cookies." She hurries away, fills a bag, and returns. "Thank you so much for tonight, Hailey."

"It was my absolute pleasure," I assure her.

She touches my arm. "I am so thankful to you for doing this." She swallows hard. "Gosh," she whispers. "I might choke up." She holds up a hand and seems to gather her wits. "I put my entire life savings into this place. It's very special to me."

Her entire life savings, while I have millions in a trust. If only we could trade places. I shove aside the thought. "What made you pick this place to invest?"

"I used to go to a place like this in Chicago when I was in school. It was a sanctuary for me during a rough time in my life. I could think of nothing better to do with my time but offer that kind of sanctuary to others. My parents are school teachers, they didn't have money to help so believe it or not,

I won the lottery, not the big one, but a small one, fifty thousand before taxes, and here I am."

The lottery. I've never played the lottery. I've never even considered the idea that a random gamble had a place in life. It has always just been this pre-set agenda that myself, and every political youth around me, followed: Go to law school. Support the bigger political cause. Make money. Gain power.

"This is a special place to me," she adds. "And I can't believe I actually made it happen."

"You have an amazing story. How long have you been open?"

"Three years ago, and it's not making me much more than school teacher pay, but it's my dream, you know? I'm living my dream." Someone shouts her name.

"Go," I say. "Take care of business and your dream. I'll stop by tomorrow."

"Thanks again," she says, hurrying away.

Dream, I think, unmoving. She's living her dream and struggling as she does, but she owns her future and her success. A hollow place inside me seems to open up, threatening to swallow me. A hollow place where my hopes and dreams, once blossomed and died. Unbidden, my breath is lodged in my throat and I turn, expecting to find Logan somewhere nearby, but apparently, he's taken the hint and gone away. I hate that I am disappointed, and I hate the story his absence tells. He gave up and that was easy. Maybe it was some surveillance test and I passed. I wasn't easily seduced. I didn't spill the story of my life. It hits me that had I gone for Logan's come-ons, had I slept with him, the only three men in my bed in my adult life would have been hired by my father. My hand settles on my belly where a rolling sensation sickens me.

Needing air and just to breathe past the head games my father plays with me, I rush toward the stairs and walk toward the door. Who is the next person that will be used against me? Because there has to be someone on guard and ready to "deal" with me when needed.

I exit to the street and hear, "Hailey." I freeze at the sound of Logan's voice that tells me he didn't give up. He must get paid by the day.

Slowly I turn to find him leaning on the wall, all long, leanly muscled man. I wonder if my father skimmed a catalog to choose him, and chose based on what? Good looks? His job? His willingness to sleep with me to get ahead?

"What are you doing?" I ask, a bite to my voice that has come from the expectations I've created in my head.

"Waiting on you," he says, his tone unaffected by mine. "It's too late to walk home alone." He straightens. "I'll walk you."

"This neighborhood is safe."

"Are you sure about that?"

It's him that I'm not sure about and I decide to just nip this in the bud. "I'm not in a place to do to this, whatever this is. I'm not. That won't change."

His eyes darken and narrow, but his expression is indiscernible. "I'm just walking you home. That's all."

That's all.

But it's not.

It never is in my world.

Megan bursts from the door, stops dead in her tracks, looks at us—no, *me*—long and hard, and then just leaves. "And there was that," Logan comments dryly.

I look at him. "What *was that?*"

"She's an odd bird," he says. "She watches people and seems to judge them before moving on. Not someone I'd ever want on a jury."

She was watching me, judging me, and I am suddenly concerned that she knows who I am. I turn to try to catch her, talk to her even, but she is gone.

"Problem?" Logan asks.

I rotate to face him again, staring up into his handsome face with a realization. The press is looking for me, not us. Having a hot man by my side, that everyone looks at instead of me, is an asset. I need to put my politician daughter's hat back on and be smart. I need to use him the way he was going to use me. "I need to go home."

"I'm walking you home," he says, and it's not a question. It's what I expect. It's what I setup with that announcement because he might work for my father, but I'm my father's daughter. I know how to manipulate, no matter how dirty it feels. I start to walk down the quiet, quaint sidewalk observing the now silent and dark stores, galleries and restaurants that trail into the surrounding tree-lined residential areas. Logan, as expected and like most arrogant, powerful men, assumes an invitation and he falls into step with me. "Where do you live?"

"Clayton Street," I say, "just six blocks away."

"I'm on Josephine, a few streets over," he replies, offering what I wasn't going to ask for, before he catches me off guard by adding, "I watched you in there tonight."

I glance over at him. "I saw you, remember?"

"You saw me all of sixty seconds," he replies. "I watched you a lot longer than that."

Was he watching me? Had I been so oblivious that I didn't know? I don't like this idea and it hits me that once again, my father's words apply. Keep your friends close and your enemies closer. I need to keep Logan close, but my way.

"I tend to get lost in my work," I comment.

"I saw that," he says. "Can I buy your work? Do you sell in a particular gallery?"

Sell my work. I remember a time when I wanted to sell my work. Now, it's in a storage facility my father doesn't even know I own. "No," I say. "It is not. And I don't sell it."

"Why the hell not?"

I'm suddenly not sure he works for my father, who would not push me to make a career of my art. Never. No way. I stop and look at him. "Because I don't."

"Maybe you should."

He's testing me, making sure that I'm in line with my father's campaign goals and it's frustrating. No. After hearing Michelle's story of dreams and goals, it's infuriating. "Life is full of maybes."

He catches my arm and turns me to him, his hand hot on the bare skin of my arm. "I hit a nerve."

"I have no nerves to hit."

"Liar," he says softly.

Liar.

Now he's not just hit a nerve, he's hit *the* nerve. And I didn't lie anyway. Not this time. He did hit a nerve. I'm a member of an inescapable political cult and he can't begin to understand what that means. He can't know. I look at my arm and back at him, "Let me go, Logan," I order, my voice just as soft as his had been when he'd called me *a liar.*

"What if I don't want to let go?"

I want to tell him to just *go away,* but then there will be someone else, some other spy that will follow. He's insulation to protect me from someone worse. He's necessary. He's the devil I already know. But I can't know this devil right now, this night, when I crave something real that he cannot be for me. He *has* hit a nerve, and I am dangerously vulnerable, when I have not been vulnerable since I recovered from my mother's death.

"Try another time," I suggest, leaving an open door for him in hopes that this makes him back off for now. "This time isn't working for you," I add.

His expression darkens, all hard lines and rough edges, and I sense that he wants to say something else, but smartly thinks otherwise, allowing his hand to slide away from my arm. I don't waste my freedom, of which I have so little. I turn and start walking, but he is quickly by my side, keeping pace, clearly not dissuaded from walking me home. Wordlessly, we turn onto my street, leaving the retail area behind, with only a half a block left to travel. Once we are at my rental, Logan stays with me all the way to my door. I unlock it and turn to face him. "Thank you for walking me home. Goodnight."

He presses his hand on the doorframe above my head. "I will, you know."

"You will what?"

"Try again."

With that, he pushes off the wall and walks away. I stare after him with one thought: I want him to try again, and the fact that I can't stop myself from feeling such things, disturbs me. I don't want things I can't have. This place is changing me, creating a shift inside me. I feel it happening. I *do* want what I cannot have. I want to sell my art. I want to live and breathe my art. I want a man who wants me, not what I represent. I'm emotional, and emotions are dangerous.

What am I doing?

My jaw sets hard. This is Logan's fault. He doesn't get to do this to me.

I open the door and enter the rental that is probably bugged with listening devices. That's the world I live in. I'm watched. I'm monitored. I'm controlled. And everything, is of course, per my father, for the greater good. Logan *will* try again, because power craves power. I'm power in a way I never wanted to be power.

Locking up, like that protects me from anything, I head to the kitchen island and quickly power up my MacBook, waiting impatiently for it to ready until finally, I do what I should have already done. I google Logan who is thirty-three, ten years my senior, a Harvard graduate, as expected, and now in a private practice, and the managing partner of that firm. His track record includes an impressive list of wins delivered to an even more impressive powerful list of clients. He is *absolutely* the perfect candidate for my father's corruption. I look for links to my father and instead find a link to his father. My eyes go wide. His father is a judge, and judges are always political fodder. My heart starts to thunder in my chest and I quickly click the bio to receive another shock. He's not only in the opposite party from my father, he's opposite in views on almost every hot topic.

If Logan is loyal to his father, he would never work for my father. For a moment I feel hope but then I make myself go further. He could be estranged from his father thus working for my father. Or be spying on my father for his father. That makes no sense though. He appeared the same night that I arrived. He's shown interest in my art which my father hates.

I stand up, walk to my art room and spread the sketch I did of Logan out on the floor, studying him, looking for what my mind is telling me about him. There is nothing corrupt in his eyes. Nothing familiar that is, and corruption is what I know. But it doesn't matter, now does it? Thanks to my father, anyone who will ever come into my life could have an agenda. Anyone could form an agenda.

This is my life, no matter what name I call myself.

CHAPTER TWENTY-FIVE

There's a fine line between love and hate. A statement proven by the very real fact that more than half of all murders are committed by a lover or family member. Torment and passion turn people you don't believe can kill, into killers; therefore, emotions become the weapon that transforms love to hate. And in hate all things are possible. I have an intimate understanding of just how powerful and dangerous emotions can become.

My mother and I fought vehemently before she got behind the wheel. Pain and blame ate me alive for the months that followed. Survival mode meant that I shut down emotionally. I became a machine. It was safe. It was a sanctuary inside my own mind. I couldn't hurt anyone. No one could hurt me.

Until Denver.

I woke up from a slumber. The problem is, I didn't know it had happened until it was too late. No. Until it was a bloody emotional mess.

THE PAST...

The morning after my teaching debut, I decide the best way for me to get some space from my father's prying eyes is to work harder at his game and focus on my plan. I have to ensure that he looks away. I have to be a contained problem. I do this by ensuring that whoever is watching me, documents my uneventful behavior. Therefore, I go to yoga class. I then return home, shower, eat a protein bar, and dress in jeans and a T-shirt, along with comfy Keds with the intent of being seen doing nothing interesting. A stark contrast to a Sunday in Washington that would include some formal breakfast, a fundraiser most likely to which I'd wear a suit dress, and make small talk with people my father wanted me to impress.

It's just after noon when I step out of my rental again to a beautiful sixty-something day and head to the coffee shop where I feel certain I will find Logan. He'll know that I know this as well. On the way, I discreetly scout for anyone following me, which I use as an excuse to stop in several galleries, and I allow myself to enjoy the art, to study the craft, to critique and admire painting after painting.

Near two o'clock when I enter the coffee shop, to find the air laced with a smoky coffee scent, while the room bustles with people, laughter, and the hum of voices. I head down the stairs, this time when my gaze scans various televisions, I find sports on every single one. Sports, not news and politics. I love this. It's another liberating moment. I am not in Washington. Everything is not about that world. In fact, it's only now, despite being a rather accomplished world traveler, that I realize there is an entirely *different* world I've never seen. One where caffeine, rather than greed, makes the rules. Well, caffeine, and Michelle, who waves at me from behind the bar, offering me a glowing smile, that is so far from the brittle forced smiles of D.C. that it charms me when I didn't know I could be charmed. I wave back, and yes, I even smile back.

Ashley, a waitress I've met briefly on my first visit here, a pretty blonde in her twenties, also waves. Megan, who is standing next to her does not, but I don't see the recognition of my real self in her face I'd feared either. She simply doesn't like me or maybe she dislikes everyone. My skin prickles and I look left to find Logan—dressed in a navy T-shirt and jeans, sitting at a table, his dark eyes fixed on me, his dark hair rumpled as if he's been running his fingers through it. He still doesn't have his facts, but then, neither do I.

I cross to join him, and I'd like to say that all my years in the press on a public stage could prevent his heavy, watchful eyes from unnerving me, but they do not. He's a man, an impressive one at that, and he's looking at me in a way that I don't remember being looked at in a very long time. Unbidden yet again, and with a jolt, I'm transported back to the night Danielle disappeared, to a moment in a hallway with me against the wall, and Drew standing in front of me, his hand on the wall by my head. Or maybe it wasn't Drew. Was it Tobey?

I stop walking, my hand going to my throat. Did I—was I—with Drew? No. No, I know I left with Tobey, but—there was that moment that I was sitting at the table in the bar, and Drew's leg was against mine, while Tobey was sitting elsewhere.

"Hailey." I blink Logan into view to find him standing in front of me, towering over me, and his hand settles on my waist, steadying me. Do I need to be steadied? "You okay?" he asks, which seems to indicate that yes. I need to be steadied.

"Why wouldn't I be okay?"

"You stopped walking and you're standing in the middle of the coffee shop."

"I did?" I ask, "I mean, I did. Yes. I—had a nightmare that came back to me."

"Must have been one hell of a bad one. Come sit." His hand goes to the small of my back and I let him guide me forward.

We close the small space between us and the table, and Logan holds a chair out for me. I slip into it and blow out a breath. Another half second and Logan is sitting in front of me, his blue eyes warm with concern. "Talk to me."

In that moment, intimacy weaves between us, something fresh and new and undiscovered sparking the air, something *real*. It's compelling. *He's* compelling, different from everyone else in my life, despite all the ways he first appeared the same. I *want* to talk to him. No. I want to be the girl he met, the one who chases her dreams and has nothing to fear but a first kiss and the wrong brush on her canvas. But I'm not that girl and that means he might not be *that guy.*

"Just a nightmare," I say, repeating my prior explanation. "It's sticking with me today."

He eyes narrow. "Okay. Do you have nightmares often?"

"Yes," I say honestly, admitting to him what I have not to anyone else, even Danielle. I have nightmares. They come in spells and then disappear. Some about the car crash. Some from that woman falling off the cliff to her death.

"Have you considered hypnosis?" he asks.

My brows furrow. "Hypnosis? That sound like a magic show."

He laughs. "It's not. It's the real deal. I have a friend who did it to get over a fear of flying. They help you identify the root of the problem and therefore control it."

Identifying the root of the problem isn't the issue for me, but I don't say that. I cut my gaze, and it lands hard on the newspaper next to his arm, with my father on the front page. Real just got really real, and I feel like a fool. "Who reads the paper anymore?" I say, giving him an opening to come at me, if that's where this is leading.

"It's a bookstore," he says, matter-of-factly. "They all like paper and it was here when I sat down." He grabs it and studies it. "Hmm. Look at that."

I hold my breath, waiting for this obvious setup to blow. "Look at what, Logan?" I ask tightly, taking the bait, wanting this over with.

"The damn Broncos cut their quarterback again," he says, tossing the paper in the chair next to him. "I guess I'm going to have to root for the Patriots again this year."

I narrow my eyes on him, wanting to believe that he saw football, not politics in that paper. "I googled you last night."

"Not until last night? Holy hell, woman. What does it take to get some interest? Did you like what you found?"

"Well," I laugh in spite of myself, "there was no proof that you're a serial killer or stalker."

"The stalking charges were dropped years ago which means the neighborhood really is safe. I just wanted to walk you home."

I laugh, and it's been a long time since anyone made me laugh a genuine laugh. I'm still smiling when Megan appears at our table, sets a white mocha in front of me and then without a word, walks away. I blanch and watch her depart. "What was that?"

"I told you," Logan says. "She's an odd one. Back to me."

"There's the attorney in you," I say refocusing on him, despite this Megan situation lingering in my mind. "Back to you," I add. "Of course."

"You *did* google me," he teases.

"Your mother is an attorney."

"A damn good one."

"Your father's a judge," I state.

"He is," he says, his tone as hard as the set of his jaw.

I notice. I let him know I notice. "Was that shift in mood about your father or my question?"

He narrows his eyes on me. "I thought we were talking about me, not my father."

"We are," I say. "Is a bench in your future?"

"No. That's not my thing."

"Why?" I challenge.

"I like to go to war and win, not watch everyone else do it," I say.

"Sounds like a politician in the making."

"Not a chance in hell, sweetheart," he says, reaching for his coffee and sipping. "I want to get paid for my skills, not paid off and told what to think." He sets his cup down and leans forward. "My turn. How long have you been painting?"

"Since I was a teen."

"And you haven't sold any work?" he asks.

"Asked and answered, counselor," I say.

"Spoken like an attorney in the making. What's that story?"

I study him, and it hits me that if he's working for my father, he most likely knows my history. If he's not, he won't know who I am by a school choice that isn't even close to public. "Okay. Yes. There is a law school in my future."

"Stanford."

In that moment, being here and being tortured by all the things I can't have stirs rebellion in me. In this moment, I hope he does work for my father to repeat my reply. I'm going to law school for my father. I'm not going to Georgetown. Period. "Stanford," I confirm.

He arches a brow. "And yet you hate attorneys?"

"Yes. They're arrogant assholes. What better reason to beat them at their own game?"

"Let me guess. You'll be disinherited if you don't do what you daddy wants you to do?"

If only it were that simple. I have a trust from my mother I'll inherit at thirty, and my father wouldn't disinherit me. It would be bad press. "No. No, that's not it."

"Then what is it?"

I can't answer. It's the presidency, but in this moment, I'm not sure why my career is that important. Why am I going to law school? *Because it's expected*, I silently answer. Because everyone around me is going. Because—

"Hailey?"

I blink Logan into view. "It's complicated, Logan."

"Understood. Probably more than you can imagine, but risking overstepping, let me leave you with one thought: Attorneys do what they do because it's their craft. You have another craft. You shouldn't leave it behind. And again, overstepping I'm sure, we succeed when we do what we love. Who made you think that wasn't true?"

"We'd need something stronger than coffee for me to tell you that story."

"That can be arranged," he offers, oh so graciously.

"Why don't I actually help you prep for your filing, instead?" I ask, but I don't wait for an answer. "Did you find those facts to back up your filing?"

"On the case I was working on, yes. This is a new one. A big one actually."

"Let me help," I press again, hating that some part of me needs to validate my decision to go to law school to this man but still I add, "I really am better at this than you think an artist might be."

"Which parent is an attorney?" he says, obviously not ready to let me off the hook.

"My father."

"And your mother?"

"She was a doctor and yes, *was*, she's dead. Don't go there." I move on, to ensure he doesn't. "So, you see. I come from an academic family."

"And art isn't academic, unless you're studying it," he says.

"That would be a statement I've heard before," I confirm. "Yes."

"From your father," he assumes.

"What are we researching?" I ask, pulling my briefcase over my head, and removing my MacBook.

"Based on that reaction, I know what topic is off limits: Your father. And I know what I'm up against. You have daddy issues."

"What are we researching?" I repeat, not about to go down this path with him.

His lips twitch but he finally stops pushing. "Looking for case law to strike down a patent claim."

"Can I read the claim?" I ask. "It's public record at this point, if you're responding to it."

He considers me a moment. "You know more than I expected already."

"I can assure you that I know much more than an average law student."

His expression is impassive, but probing, I would even venture to say intensely probing. This should bother me. I don't need or want this kind of attention but still I sit my butt in this chair and when he asks, "What's your email?" I immediately give it to him,

Obviously feeling empowered, he pushes for more. "What's your phone number?"

"I'm not giving that to you," I say, still dealing with the whole Washington area code problem, I really need to address and quickly.

He studies me a moment and then glances at his computer, punches in what I assume is my email address and presses send. "Now you have the file and my phone number," he says, his blue eyes darkening as he adds, "Just in case you need a friendly neighbor."

Friendly neighbor.

If only this was that simple as well. I start reading the case, glancing up at him as I read the high-profile companies involved. "You're right. It is a big case, and this is going to be a tough one to win on both sides."

"I'll win," he says. "I just need to go into it armed and ready. There's a number of online law libraries for research I can email you."

"I know them," I say, since my father has actually made me take prep classes that amount to law school. "What do you have so far?"

"I just started working this case." He turns a notepad my direction. "That's from my head, before I even start researching."

I read through his impressive list and then write down another case that immediately comes to mind that I believe to be quite relevant to this one. He turns the pad his direction before his eyes lift to mine, his expression impenetrable. "You're smart and knowledgeable, but you know that." He says nothing more, just staring at me, leaving empty space filled with unspoken words we both know that he is thinking, but not saying, a judgment, that I do not like. I am always judged and who is this man, who doesn't know me to judge me anyway? Of course, I know the irony of this thought almost immediately, considering I've been judging him since meeting him.

Worse, I have a distinct impression that his ruling is my failure. I've disappointed him, and this bothers me. Like, really, *deeply* bothers me. This is not a judgment of the persona my father created, and that I have slaved to perfect, but rather a judgment of me, the *real* me, the person that I never allow to be seen, let alone, judged.

And when this man cuts his stare and looks at his computer, it actually feels like a slap that stings and burns, and then stings and burns some more. I don't look away. I open my mouth to demand he say what he's thinking when another prickling sensation draws my gaze left just in time to latch gazes with Michelle, who is clearly watching me. Her gaze jerks guiltily away, her attention stirring unease in me that reminds me of her pimping my father's book. It's now quite possible that my real life, the one that has claimed me as a future First Daughter, has officially destroyed this one.

I shut my computer, shove it in my briefcase, and I get up and leave.

CHAPTER TWENTY-SIX

Nobody sees a flower really; it is so small. We haven't time, and to see takes time—like to have a friend takes time. *In those words, a quote by world-renowned artist Georgia O'Keeffe, I find a piece of me both past and present. Most certainly during that time I first arrived in Denver. It was then that I began to see myself as a flower, yet to bloom, visible but not seen, even by myself. I lived in the shadow of grief, guilt, and my father, and therefore he controlled me, but it wasn't as simple as just me and him, father and daughter. There was so much more than me hiding in my father's shadow. There were revelations about him, my mother, and yes, Danielle yet to be revealed. Revelations that could, would, and did, shatter lives. My father knew, too, and he didn't care. To him, everything was a weapon he used with wicked accuracy and various degrees of force. He would just as easily let us, any of us, wilt and die, as surely as he would rip away one petal at a time until there was nothing left but weeds he'd discard and destroy.*

The question for me though, became, what would I do to survive? Who would I become? Or was I already her?

THE PAST…

My father owns me.

Ten minutes after leaving Logan sitting at that table in the coffee shop, those words radiate through me with every step I travel in my return to my rental house. I do not like these words. I hate these words. I hate that they are true.

Did he own my mother? Was she like me? Am I like her in ways I didn't realize? The wrong ways? I've allowed this to happen because—well—it was expected. I'm his daughter. He's running for President. I have a greater good responsibility and on some level, I accept this and even embrace it. I do. I always have. It's what my mother wanted. It's what she expected. It's who she was. There it is. She wasn't strong and independent.

She was owned.

I'm owned.

The most screwed up part of this, is I know that I'm owned and yet, I still try to please him. So much so that I actually enjoyed sitting across from a man like Logan, knowing that despite being years his junior and without my law degree, I held my own. I'm that good. I made my father proud even if he hates me and I hate him. Therefore, I *will* go to law school and I will be top of my class, but even as I make this vow, it cuts and I bleed. In this moment, I have this sense of being everything and nothing and this is not the first time. I am my father's destiny. My mother was not.

She's *dead*. Danielle is dead.

Maybe my punishment for failing them, is that I lived.

"Stop, Hailey," I whisper, but my mind continues to race. I'm spiraling and I don't know where I'll land if I don't stop. I have to stop. I walk faster and I barely remember entering the rental and locking the door. I barely remember sitting down in front of a blank sheet of paper on my canvas to bare all. Emotions, I hate emotions, but they are here, they are now, and they bleed, like I bleed onto my page. Like my mother bled. Like Danielle bled. Like that woman on the cliff bled. One sheet after another is filled, and then torn away. I don't study anything that I create. I don't let myself. I just create. I don't stop until the sun is lowering beyond the juts of the Cherry Creek rooftops and my hand is cramped, my stomach a dull, hollow ache. There is a stack of papers filled with my craft on the floor, none richly developed or for anyone's eyes but mine—but they exist. They tell a story. A story I am not yet ready to hear.

I walk to the kitchen, pull a bowl of pre-cut fruit from the refrigerator, and open the well-stocked kitchen drawer to remove a fork. I stand there at the counter and eat, and in these next few minutes, with no sound but a ticking clock somewhere, I come back to me. *This* feels like me. The empty me with no emotion, no thoughts, nothing dangerous that can control me. All of those things are on the paper, just like my mother taught me. Only when I have eaten the entire very large bowl of fruit, do I feel as if I can really, truly fully breathe. I have just disposed of my fork and tossed the plastic container when my cellphone rings.

Crossing to the island, I pick it up, and my gut twists in knots at the sight of my father's number. Okay, so maybe I'm not back to that empty place just yet. I know what this is about. So much for Logan being real and wanting me for me. He not only took my bait about Stanford, he clearly works fast. My father already knows. I decline the call and glance at my text messages that would normally be filled with Danielle's musings, but there is nothing. *Nothing.* I wait for the emotion to follow, but I pass the test. My moment of relapse is gone. I feel nothing except good about feeling nothing.

I walk around the island, claim a stool and key my MacBook to life when my cellphone rings yet again, any hope that my father would be easily distracted from his daughter, gone. But then, this call is about Stanford and Stanford is about him, not me, thus it's important. "Hello, father," I say, answering the call.

"I trust you're behaving?"

"I am," I say, and as that deep hollow of nothing fills and overflows with resentment I add, "but based on what I saw on the news, you aren't."

"Discussing your drunken stupor in every interview has certainly been disheartening."

The master at work, turning his bad behavior into mine; deflect, deflect, deflect is his motto, and I've learned well. "That's better than asking about your infidelity," I reply, enjoying the dig.

"You know—"

"The press lies," I supply. "Yes, father. I know."

"I loved—"

"My mother," I say, because we're having the conversation that was in my head early. "I was thinking about law school."

"What about it?" he snaps, sounding irritated enough at the topic that I decide I'm wrong. Logan hasn't talked to him, but I'm here. I'm wading in the water and I go deep.

"Stanford gets me out of Washington which keeps me away from your present wife," I say. "It seems that might be a good thing for all of us."

"You'll be just fine with your step-mother," he says. "Because your affection and involvement with her tells the press this cheating scandal is the crock it is. Say it. Show it."

"And yet I'm here, where I can't do any of that."

"Acceptable behavior considering the expected grief over the Danielle situation. Understandable, in fact. This gives you time to cool off, digest, and think about the bigger picture. The greater purpose we have in life. I expect when you return, you'll be ready to shine."

I suck in a sharp breath and breathe out pure, white-hot anger. "You used that drunken scandal to pull attention from the book, and then sent me away to contain my anger over its contents."

"I'm containing much more than a book and your drunken stupor, now aren't I, daughter? In other words, *behave*, Hailey."

He disconnects.

My teeth grind together. Much more? What does that mean? I tunnel my fingers through my hair and let out a growl. Why don't I know what that means? I push off the barstool and dash for the garden room, picking up the images I've created. The pages are oversized and awkward, but I don't care. I carry them forward and drop them on the living room floor, where I begin to lay them side by side. I stop at one image, my breath hitching in my throat. On this page is Danielle standing with my father at a charity event about a month ago, with my father's hand on her waist.

I press my own hands to my face and sink down to my knees, a memory pushes into my mind, half flashback, and half memory, which seems like an improvement. I'm at the table, and Drew's leg is pressed to mine. Danielle is beside me. I wasn't fighting with her, so I wasn't sure that text was from my father. Not yet, but Drew winked at me, like we'd shared something intimate. It starts to come to me.

Danielle and I are eating dessert, but I'm disoriented, confused. Danielle gets up. Her phone falls to the ground. I pick it up and I read another message: North, South, East, West. That's what I want.

I remember that well. Then, and now, I'm immediately back in a million moments with my father where he says we will own the world: North, South, East, West. But it's a political reference, I remind myself. He's talking politics when he uses those words. He calls *me* honey. Danielle is, *was*, like a second daughter to him, for what that is even worth. She was working for his office or was supposed to work for his office. It could have been work but it wasn't. I knew it wasn't.

Suddenly I'm in a full flashback, sitting at that table, the darkness of the room suffocating, the music louder now, vibrating through me. *I stare down at the phone in my hand and I start to scroll through the messages but before I can Danielle returns. I straighten and shove the phone inside my purse. "I'm going to the bathroom." I stand, and my eyes meet Drew's. He smirks, knowledge in his eyes. He's seen what I've done. He stands up. I turn away, aware that he's following me.*

My cellphone rings and I all but jump out of my own skin, my fist balling over my racing heart. "Calm down," I hiss at myself, my lack of control quickly becoming a real problem and I know it. It's that spiral and I was lying to myself. I do know where this lands, and it is never good.

I cross the room and grab my phone, some small, stupid, part of me expecting to find Danielle's number but instead,

I find Jake calling. Proof that a one-night fling with an FBI agent, or any man with the power of a badge, is also stupid. Jake would be a perfect tool in my father's chest; a man I can't easily tell no.

"Hello," I say, not about to give him the power that knowing I recognize his number would surely give him.

"Miss me?"

"Who is this?"

He laughs. "Should I replay a few of the more intimate places I kissed you to remind you?"

"That's not necessary," I reply tartly.

"Then I'm back to: Did you miss me?"

"Every second of every day," I say dryly.

"And while you miss me, other people are missing you."

"News to me," I reply, and afraid I'm in the press in some way I do not yet know, I sit down on the barstool in front of my MacBook and quickly scan for mentions of my name.

"I hear you haven't been back to Washington," he comments.

"Sounds like you're now working for the press and digging for information."

"You really are a politician's daughter," he says dryly. "Able to talk in circles and say nothing."

"You're really are an FBI agent," I reply just as dryly, abandoning my fruitless internet search. Finding my name in the news is framed with nothing I do not expect. "Able to talk in circles and say nothing."

"Sharp-witted, too," he comments.

"Why are you calling me, Jake?"

"Do I need a reason?"

"No," I say, for no reason other than to lead into my next statement. "But since we both know you're working for my father, we both know you have one."

"I'm not working for your father, Hailey. I hate politicians."

So says Logan as well. It's a theme. I hate themes. "I'm the daughter of a politician," I point out.

"I'm crystal clear on that fact but you aren't your father."

I'm not my father. It's the first time anyone has said that to me in years. "Why are you calling me, Jake?" I repeat again.

"I'm in Washington. Where are you?"

"Is that a question in an official capacity or a personal one?"

"Easy, sweetheart. Let down that guard. I get it. Your friend is dead. Everyone is coming at you, but I'm not one of those people. I'm the guy that helped clear your name."

"What? What does that mean?"

"I saw you leave the bar. I gave a statement to that effect."

"If you were this certain I was innocent," I say cautiously, "why did you show up at my hotel in Austin?"

"I didn't know if you had gone back to the bar. I didn't know when Danielle left."

"But you helped clear my name?"

"Yes, Hailey," he says. "I helped clear your name."

"And you want what in return?"

"To be friends. That's all."

There is that word again: friends. Translation: This for that. Quid pro quo. It is the world I live in. I think now that my father called him, he is supposed to remind me of just what it is that my father is managing outside of my drunken stupor. "Understood," I say tightly.

"I don't think you do," he says.

"Yes," I assure him. "I do."

He's silent a beat. "When do you come back to Washington?"

"I never confirmed I wasn't in Washington," I counter.

"I accessed your flights. I know you're in Denver."

"Of course you did and do. And of course, you pretended you didn't."

"I just wanted to get it honestly from you."

"Then ask."

"I did," he says. "You didn't answer. I have to go but, Hailey? I am a friend. The best one you have right now."

He hangs up and ice slides down my spine. Did he just tell me he knows what really happened the night Danielle disappeared? I believe he did. Of course, my father will use him, and the details of Danielle's disappearance, to control me. The problem for him is that I know, as well as he knows, that he won't allow anything that could hurt him, or his campaign, to go public. It's cold comfort considering I don't, in fact, know what happened that night, but still, it's comfort.

He threatened me and there is no empty place. There is no fear. I won't be my mother. I'm angry and I don't want to draw or paint to control it. I'll just stay angry. It works for me and against everyone else. That's a proven fact.

CHAPTER TWENTY-SEVEN

ONE CAN HAVE NO GREATER OR SMALLER MASTERY THAN THE
MASTERY OF ONESELF,

—LEONARDO DA VINCI

THE PAST…

I paint all night and sleep until noon, expelling my
anger, controlling my emotions. I do not remember
anything else about the night Danielle disappeared, but I
now possess a collage of sketches that tell stories I will use
to trigger memories; images that come from my mind, my
subconscious, that I will try to understand and craft into the
story of that night in Austin.

The minute I wake up, I scramble out of bed, gather my
work, and pin each sketch on a wall in an upstairs office. It's
then that I realize that seventy percent of my sketches are of
two people: my father and Danielle. I've actually plastered
an entire wall with nothing but the two of them together. I
scan them and home in on one partial drawing. This
particular creation is a depiction of what could have been
one of a dozen moments between them, that I ignored at the
time, but could have seen as too intimate; my father is
leaning toward Danielle, his hand on her waist, his mouth
near her ear. Acid burns my throat and I force away denial.
Those intimate moments I captured were just that, intimate.
They were in a relationship. She was sleeping with him,
maybe even spying on me, even without knowing that's what
she was doing. He'd use her like that. I get that now. No. I
admit that now.

"What happened to you, Danielle?" I whisper, but nothing follows. Nothing comes to me but one certainty: That night is drowning in lies, and for once, the lies are not mine.

In the hours that follow, I shower, dress, and study my work; I study Danielle and obviously that is messing with my mind, as I randomly check my phone for text messages, expecting her number, her smart remarks. I *can't stop* expecting to hear from Danielle. I can't accept her death and I will never believe that homeless man killed her. When it's finally time to leave for my class, I do so with my hair braided, my make up heavy, and a need for an escape burning in my belly. Of course, escaping my father is a task that requires herculean powers that I fail at miserably considering he inserts himself into my walk to work.

I'm a few blocks from the coffee shop, passing a small café with an open patio when my gaze catches on a television, my breath hitching when I find my father speaking to a reporter in a sit-down interview. There is a flash across the lower screen that reads: *Claim of infidelity are lies that have hurt my family deeply.*

Tension slides down my spine and I put space between me and a newscast that might flash my image while wondering how step-mother dearest would feel about Danielle and my father right about now. At least that's one area where I owe Danielle appreciation; she played me, but she also dished out a little payback on behalf of my mother. A memory picks at my brain, halting my steps, but when I step to the wall, my mind going elsewhere. I'm in a sea of sharks, and I am a little fish about to be eaten. I can't be the little fish about to be eaten which is why I have to be my father's daughter, which means a master manipulator. I pull my phone from my pocket and punch the call back for Jake, a man who might just know how to fill in all my blank spaces, or at least a few. He answers on the first ring. "Trying to prove you miss me?

"You want something from me," I say, getting right to the point.

"Maybe I just want *you*." His voice is both velvet and promise but I am so damn tired of being used that I cut right past it.

"I'm way too seasoned of a politician's daughter for that approach to work on me," I say. "We used each other that night. Let's do it again. I'm a double-edged sword for you. The one that can cut you and the one that can cut him if he becomes your boss."

I don't have to tell him that "him" is my father. We both know. "Since there's obviously much we need to clarify," he says. "I'd say we should talk. In person. I'll come to you."

"When?" I ask, my tone flat, unreadable by choice.

"When I do," he says, just as flatly.

He disconnects with that little power play, but that's just fine by me. I have what I want. Jake, who has proclaimed he will protect my secret, will come to me. Of course, he's working for my father, and of course, that means he'll paint the visit as one to contain and control me. But I have far more experience in this world, far too much understanding of the people in it than I wish I did. *I am* that double-edged sword and he knows it, while my father never gives me the credit where credit is due. If Jake won't help me then I'll use Jake to scare Tobey into believing that night will soon haunt us all. He'll tell me what really happened.

It's a plan of necessity. It's me taking control.

No fear. I think that my earlier thought was wrong. My mother *would* approve.

CHAPTER TWENTY-EIGHT

If you paint a lie in a million glorious colors, is it still a lie? Or is it, or rather, am I Pandora's Box filled with so many lies that the lid will burst open and destruction and pain will follow?

That's where this is leading so I'll just tell you the answer. It's yes. I am indeed Pandora's Box, and the lid did indeed burst open. I was so busy worrying about what I didn't know, that I didn't feel it happening. I was focused in all the wrong places, outsmarted really, which I blame on one thing: I didn't embrace me. I was still her. I was obsessed with who she was and could be. Angry about what she couldn't be. That girl still thought she could change things, change herself even. Everyone was trying. Why couldn't she?

The me of now is different. I'd have done everything differently, but it wasn't supposed to be that way. That box had to open and someone, more than one someone, had to die. I know that now. That I can even say that from this calm, cool place, is real growth. It's me, helping you. Because remember: That's why I'm telling this story. It's not about me. It's about you. Don't kill yourself over what you can't change. And the truth is, I couldn't tell this if they'd all lived.

THE PAST...

I step inside the coffee shop, and the acid that has settled in my throat evaporates with the flare of my nostrils, and I inhale the rich aroma of coffee beans and chocolate, the tables filled here and there, several repeat students calling my name. This place feels like the cloth of my soul, a place where I can breathe, without asking permission, at least, until my connection to my father steals that away. The minute that happens, and if I stay long enough, it inevitably will, this place will be punished with the press, and then suddenly I'm on the outside looking down on this place from a pedestal of my father's creation. I won't be one of them, as I am now. I'll be *her*. Which is exactly why I am going to guard myself and this place for as long as possible.

I hurry down the steps and scan the bar, looking for trouble, and yes, looking for Logan, and I tell myself that this is necessary, not hopeful. After all, if he's working for my father, he most certainly *is* trouble. He's also not here, at least not in plain sight, but that means nothing. Watching me doesn't require standing in front of me. Manipulating me, attempting to use me, that's another story and one perhaps, he's given up on.

"Hailey!"

I turn toward the bar to find Michelle holding up a hand and offering a smile, before waving me forward. I cross the room, weaving through tables, and greeting several familiar faces, before settling onto a barstool in front of her.

"Coffee?" she asks, resting her hands on the wooden counter, her long brown hair squeezed into a clip at the back of her head.

"Yes, please," I say, and she calls out the order to a tall, dark-haired man behind the bar that I have never seen before. "Eddie! Skinny white mocha."

"Is he new?" I ask when she returns her attention to me. "Or am I just too new to know everyone?"

"He's a college student that's been here a year," she says. "He's only here two nights a week." In other words, he's not a spy inserted to watch over me, just a potential target that could become one, as is everyone, Michelle included. "How are you feeling about things?" she asks, studying me intently.

"Great," I say. "I love it. Why?"

"But you like it here? There are no problems?"

My brows knit together. "What am I missing?"

"It's what I'm missing I'm worried about," she says. "You left abruptly yesterday. Like Logan upset you."

I'm reminded of her watching me yesterday and it hits me that she wasn't watching me at all. She was watching *Logan* with me. Are they a thing? Have they been? Is that why he is here so often? "I had a work situation," I say, managing not to lie. My life, or rather my father's life, is my eternal employment.

"Are you sure? Because he's a regular here, and in case you've heard, we *are* old friends, but if there's a problem, I'll handle it right away. I can't have him running off my art instructor. I've seen his doodling and it amounts to stick people."

"Old friends?" I query, sideswiped by this news for reasons I'll analyze later.

"We grew up in this neighborhood," she says. "But—"

Eddie, who looks to be twenty or so, chooses that moment, to set my cup of coffee down in front of me, moving away without a greeting or look in my direction. No greeting. No recognition. No problem. Which reminds me of her staring at me yesterday.

"Back to Logan," she says.

"I saw you watching us yesterday," I say, getting right to the point. "Are you two—"

"No," she says, holding up her hands. "Not at all. Never. Logan is a good guy, but we've just never had a spark." She narrows her eyes on me. "You're asking because you saw me watching you yesterday."

"Yes," I say flatly. "I am."

"Sorry about that. Honestly, I was trying to figure you out. Not many people would do what you're doing and I just—"

Eddie shouts out a question and she answers.

"You just what?" I press, pulling her attention back to me.

"I just keep thinking I know you from somewhere," she says. "It's been driving me crazy."

Driving her crazy. That is *not* good. "I get that a lot," I say. "All my life." I laugh. "The good part of that is that I'm an inherently private person, and no one remembers me for trying to remember someone else." I grab my cup and stand up. "But you did remember my drink. Thank you." I turn and walk away with the irony of my words. Inherently private. I am and yet my life is always being watched over and prodded by those I don't invite inside. Which is exactly why no one really knows me but me. It's safer that way.

I hurry across the room to the art studio area where random people have started to gather and my mind goes to Logan and I'm thinking again about him not following me. I think—maybe he's really a good guy, and I just—I got up and left. Maybe he's real and I'm so used to fake that I don't even know what real is anymore. I need real. I really, *really* need real in my life right now. I inhale and let it out, grabbing my phone and keying to my email. No email from Logan and it knifes through me. This should please me. He's not here watching me too closely. If I'm lucky it stays that way only it doesn't feel like luck at all. I shove my phone back in my pocket and focus on the only thing that is real: Art.

I glance up and Megan is standing in the doorway. I narrow my eyes on her and take a step in her direction, but she turns and walks away. I fully intend to follow her, but Ashley appears in her spot and rushes my way. "Oh good I caught you," she says. "Tomorrow is Michelle's birthday." She holds up a card. "Do you want to sign and contribute? We're having cake and champagne at closing tomorrow night. It's a surprise since her Special Forces boyfriend is out of the country and her parents are I guess not around or something."

I blink, willing myself to focus on her, not Megan, but something about Megan is bothering me. Actually, everything about her is bothering me. "Of course," I manage, accepting the card. "Let me grab my purse." I hurry to the front of the room, and when I would return with a hundred-dollar bill, to be generous, of course, it hits me that might not be smart. I grab a twenty instead and when I turn around Ashley is waiting. "Is twenty good?"

"It's perfect," she says, accepting it.

I sign the card and offer her that as well. "What's Megan's story?"

She shrugs. "She's odd but she grows on you."

"How fast?" I ask.

"Pretty fast, but between you and me, she really has it bad for Logan. I'm pretty sure we all now know that Logan has it pretty bad for you." When my eyes go wide, she laughs again and holds up the card. "Can you end class a little early tomorrow?"

"Of course."

"Great," she says, rushing away and I let out a breath. It seems I've made an enemy out of Megan, and the last thing I need is another enemy. I think of her eyes as she's watched me from the doorway, the starkness of her expression, the shadows knifing through her gaze. On some deep level she is troubled, and I know now why this bothers me. She reminds me of Danielle. And Danielle is dead.

Class goes well and I find myself smiling and laughing for most of the night. It's exhilarating and yet some deep, dark part of me is clawing and biting, trying to escape. I'm like a baby trapped in her mother's womb, being here is happiness, but it has to end. It's me torturing myself. This can't be my life and yet, I find myself daring to ask—or can it? As I make my final round to chat with my students, I wonder if the crush of my real identity would fade at some point. Well, not if my father becomes President, but maybe if he loses. It's a horrible thing for me to wish for, but one I've secretly nursed for a lifetime it seems.

I want him to lose.

Setting aside that nasty little truth, I focus on keeping the here and now, safe and perfect. I decide I need to talk to

Megan before I leave and pull her into my circle, not outside where she could become a problem. I pack up my bag, exit my art room, and without conscious decision to do so, I look for Logan, but the bar is all but empty, and a knife of disappointment infuriates me. I cannot trust him and right now is the worst time in my life to even try.

I walk to the bar, where that college kid Eddie is wiping down the counter. "Where is Megan?"

"Left for some emergency," he replies, without even looking at me. I do like this quality in this man. Bring coffee. Done. Answer questions. Done. All without nosiness. If only everyone could be just like him.

With my proactive Megan plan smashed, I murmur a "Thanks," and head for the door. Exiting to the street, I cut left toward my neighborhood when I hear, "Hailey."

At the sound of Logan's voice, I suck in a breath and stop dead in my tracks, a rush of mixed emotions inside me. I am glad he is here. I fear that it's because he's truly watching me, working for my father. And yet, I'm back to being glad he's here after I just wished everyone would ignore me. Proof my present state of mind is more than a little messed up.

I turn to find him leaning on the wall, his tie half undone, his jacket gone, sleeves rolled up. "What are you doing out here?"

"I thought you might want someone to walk you home." He shoves off the wall. "Dangerous neighborhood and all."

"Are you trying to get your stalking license back?"

"Only if you're willing to help," he replies, his playful tone charming, but I'm charmed often for political reasons, I remind myself. It means nothing.

"There are a million reasons why I should just say no."

"Is that a yes?"

It's that question that most would have turned into an assumption, that wins me over. "I'm not inviting you inside."

"I can live with that." He pauses. "This time."

"Maybe not ever," I say, and I don't give him time to reply. I turn and start walking. He falls easily into step with me. We don't immediately speak. "Obviously you aren't going to tell me why you left yesterday without me asking," he finally says.

"Let's call it claustrophobia," I say, trying again to be honest. "It hits me at random moments."

"Any particular triggers?" he asks.

"Pretty much it's just about being me." I change the subject. "How'd your filings work out today?"

"Too early to know, but I used that case you gave me. You sure you haven't gone to law school?"

I give a laugh that manages to sound more bitter than I intend. "From the day I could speak," I say. "But I still have to go through the motions and get the piece of paper."

"Because it's expected of us doesn't mean we have to do it," he says thoughtfully. "Not even if we're good at it. And yes," he adds. "I'm speaking from experience."

We turn onto my street and I glance over at him. "Your father pressures you?"

"Like a tidal wave crashing over me *every* single day."

"And your mother?"

"Lost the ability to think for herself a long time ago," he says as we arrive at my door.

I stick the key in my lock and freeze, thinking of my mother. I turn and rest against the wooden surface, my mind going back to the research I did on Logan. "Isn't your mother an attorney?"

"One of the top criminal defense attorneys in the state if not the country."

"And she can't think for herself?" I ask, turning to face him and finding myself eager for his reply.

"Not where my father is concerned. If he wants something, if he believes in something, so does she, thus she believes I should be on a bench."

"Why?" I ask, not sure if I'm asking to figure out my own mother or myself. Or perhaps both. "Why would someone so successful and smart blindly follow him?"

"I'd like to say it's misplaced loyalty to his judicial role but at its core, it's just him. He's the reason and I don't think I have to explain that considering your future job choice, or rather, someone else's choice."

"I'll be a damn good attorney."

"But it's not what you want. It's what your father wants. I said no and if I can just say no, so can you."

My defenses bristle. "You don't know me or my situation."

He presses his hand on the door next to me. "I know more than you think I do."

Adrenaline surges through me. "What does that mean, Logan?"

"It means life is short. Take a deep breath before you move forward before you can't. Consider taking it with me. I'll see you tomorrow night, Hailey." He pushes off the door and walks away.

Now I suck in air, that might as well be glass. I don't know what just happened and that is not a familiar situation for me. He seems to be pushing me to do what I want to do, against my father's will, and yet, those words he'd used: Life is short, and breathe before you cannot, echo a warning. I open the door and walk inside, shutting the door and locking it. I need to get a grip. I can't see anyone clearly and that's not about my life. It's about my panic over that night.

Otherwise, I'd be clear headed. Prior to right now, I have been. I knew Tobey was a user. I was just using him, too. I knew Danielle was—well—Danielle, unpredictable and confused, perfect prey for my father. As for my mother, she loved my father. Love is blind, but I don't believe she was stupid, if she'd have known he was cheating, she would have left him. End of story. I'm done questioning her. That I was, speaks of my state of mind.

I inhale and this time the glass sensation is gone. Calm and resolve settle in my gut. What is my next move? No. What would my next move have been in Austin, after finding out that Danielle was having an affair with my father? I'd call him. I'd call my father and confront him. And, I think as an icy chill runs down my spine, he'd try to silence me and Danielle. I press fingers to my temples. "What are you saying, Hailey?" I whisper. "That he's a killer?"

I drop my hands. I need to know which means it's time to convince him I've remembered everything. It's time to confront him, perhaps for the second time. Then he'll start talking, telling me what I want to know. And I know exactly how to do it. I'll text him my wall of sketches and paintings featuring him and Danielle, my small piece of poetic justice. Any story my art tells about him, any secret, will always be poetic justice.

I race up the stairs, and down the hallway, flipping on the light to the office, and freeze in my steps, air lodging in my throat. Every sketch and painting I've created of Danielle with my father is missing. I stand there for several stunned beats, my pulse pounding in my ears, a dark, heavy sensation in my chest that explodes from me in a growl that turns to a scream, my fingers balling by my sides. "Yes, I know, mother," I bite out. "Ladies control themselves. Ladies are composed, but if you were here right now, even you would be furious."

I start to pace, the idea that I'm not only being watched, but that my private space has been penetrated, *invaded*, infuriates me. The pulse of fury rages inside me and this is not a good me. Anger is good. Fury is not. This is not a me that I want in control. I need to paint. I need to create and I need to do it now. I race down the stairs and cross the living area to my makeshift studio.

I sit down and I skip the pencil, and grab a brush, looking for the true color and vision paint offers me. My hand trembles under the barely controlled rage, yet still it moves, and moves, and moves some more until I drop the brush on the floor and stand up, panting out a breath with what I've painted. It's Danielle, lying in the alleyway, blood pouring from her body.

I swallow hard and I consider snapping a picture and texting it to my father, which would surely freak him out. Yes. I like this idea. "Poetic justice," I call out, delivering his truth, but I'm not foolish enough to do such a thing. Text messages, like my temporary home apparently, are too easily breached by those they are not meant for.

I don't even know why this is what showed up on my paper. Danielle couldn't have been lying in that alleyway. They found her someplace else. I couldn't have seen her like this. I don't remember seeing her like this. She didn't follow me into the alleyway. I didn't do this to her. It's simply me putting my worst fear on paper. That's all this is. It's a lie. I've painted a lie.

CHAPTER TWENTY-NINE

That painting turned out to be Pandora's Box and not in the way you are most likely thinking. That box was me, which I assume you've assumed, but what I'd confined to my mind was not some horrific secret about me. I'd just been conditioned to think I was the root of all evil, but it was a man that was the root of all evil. My father.

THE PAST...

I burn the painting and as the paper frays and shrivels, it is inked in my mind, never to be unseen. I don't know what it means. I just know she's gone. Maybe that's the point. I need closure. I keep going back to the fact that her father wouldn't let me see the body.

Once my creation is ashes, I lay down on the couch, and I have one thought: If there wasn't something to hide about Danielle's death, my art would still be on the wall.

I wake to beaming sunlight in the living room, unaware of the moment I fell asleep, and once again I have one thought: Danielle is dead, and my father didn't cry at her memorial.

By the time I'm in the shower, I'm back to thinking about me. I *wouldn't* kill Danielle. She was always troubled. I was the big sister that kept her sane. I would have been angry over her and my father, I *am* angry, but I would have seen the writing on the wall. He's a manipulator. In fact, I would have been so very furious that I would have called my father that night. My father would have known this cheating scandal was coming. He would have known Danielle to be damning on top of that. Maybe even the end of his campaign.

I fall against the wall, out of the spray of water, barely able to catch my breath. I called him. I know I called him. My mind flashes back to the alleyway. Danielle wasn't with me. No. I was pacing, angry, *hurt*. I grabbed my phone, yanked it out of my purse, my hand shaking as I called my father only to get his voicemail because of course, he was on the plane on his way home. I wasn't. I exploded into his voicemail:

"Danielle? Really? How very presidential of you, father. I wonder what your wife will think? Yes. I know, honey. I read the messages. All of them."

I blink back to the present, and I'm sitting on the floor, knees to my chest. She was a problem for him. She was erratic, unpredictable, a mistake he'd never undo. Someone he needed to get rid of. "No," I hiss, pushing to my feet. He didn't kill her. He was on a plane, headed home. He didn't order anyone to kill her. I laugh bitterly, a choked horrible sound, I barely recognize as my own. She was just conveniently killed the night he found out I knew.

I swallow the acid in my throat. This is crazy. The place in my head is going is crazy. I turn off the water, grabbing a towel. Danielle kept the affair with my father a secret. I wouldn't have told. My father's a bastard, not a killer. All of this careful cover-up is about the affair that could still be damning on the heels of that book.

My mind retraces what I know, confirming this makes sense during which I barely remember leaving the shower or dressing, but somehow, it's become afternoon, and I'm dressed. I'm in all black; black jeans, black tee, black sneakers, the color of grief, because it's time I grieve Danielle. It's time I start accepting what I can't change. Nevertheless, I braid my hair long before I have to leave for class and apply heavier make up. I need to be Hailey Anne Pitt today. I need to be my mother's daughter but I'm not.

With an hour left before I have to leave for work, I once again sit down to paint, setting my alarm to ensure I stop when I need to. This time, when I set my brush down, I'm staring at Danielle again. This time, she's alone, laughing, happy, *beautiful*, and still alive. Yet, in my mind's eye, I can still see the image I created last night; her in that alleyway, bleeding to death, and understanding comes to me. That creation was about me blaming me for telling my father I knew about Danielle. Me wanting to blame him for taking her from me but I'm the one who went nuts on everyone. I did. *I remember.* My lashes lower and I cover my face, transported back to the alleyway.

I end the call with my father as Danielle rushes through the door with Tobey on her heels. "Why would you even read my text messages?" she demands.

There is a jumbled mess in my mind of us shouting at each other. Tobey and Drew are there. Someone else too, but I don't know who. It's all fuzzy. What isn't fuzzy is the moment Tobey steps between us. *"We all need to go back to the hotel," Tobey says. "This is not a fight to be had in public."*

"I'm not going anywhere with you two," Danielle hisses. "Ever again, Hailey."

"Right," I say. "Why do you need me? You have my father."

I blink back to the present. *I left her.* I was drugged, I remind myself. I was *drugged. She* drugged me but that really doesn't matter. *I left her behind. I left her to die.*

I turn away from the painting, shoving my hands in my hair. Guilt can destroy a person. I know this from personal experience and I cannot go down that dark tunnel of hellish torment again. I need to snap out of this. I need to step away from my own thoughts and clear my head but to do that, I need to feel safe. I hurry forward, do a little research and in half an hour, I have the security system activated. Of course, my father's people can breach it, but at least it gives me a layer from reporters or strangers, if I should be discovered.

It's actually rather odd that Rudolf didn't think security to be necessary.

CHAPTER THIRTY

Safe is defined in the dictionary as protected from or not exposed to danger or risk; not likely to be harmed or lost. What happens when the ones who will harm you are the ones protecting you? Were they ever protecting you at all? Maybe they were just trying to shut you up.

THE PAST...

With the house secure, I don't hunker down. That's for tonight, when I return here alone and know I'm safe. For now, I leave and head into the heart of Cherry Creek where I can buy a birthday gift, and explore the artsy neighborhood that reminds me of my mother's love of just that, art. Maybe then I can remember the grace she'd encourage me to have in all situations and figure out what she'd want me to do with this one.

By six, she's frequented my mind often, and I've managed to purchase a birthday gift for Michelle—a smoked glass sand timer with a note that reads: *Because the time is yours and you're living your dream with the coffee shop.* I think it will hit a nerve with her, perhaps because it hits one with me. She's living her dream. I'm not but some part of me knows as I pay the cashier, that Logan was right. Life is short. I'm beginning to think Michelle's little place has opened the door to more for me. I'm not going to stop painting, even if it has to be a hobby. That's what my mother would want. That's what I want.

Pleased with this decision, my steps are lighter as I head toward the coffee shop, but a jewelry store catches my eyes or rather a necklace in the window that reads "Fearless." I walk inside, buy the inexpensive but pretty piece, and slip it around my neck. My mind flicks to Megan, and I buy a second one and stick the little black velvet bag it came inside into my pocket where I can access it easily when I'm ready to give it to her. I'm about to leave when I spy a pen that reads "asshole" and for obvious Logan-related reasons, I buy it as well. If he works for my father, he's an asshole. If he doesn't, I'm the asshole. Which one of us deserves this pen will be decided at a later date.

Done shopping, I decide a dinner of coffee and cookies will be delicious, and I head on toward the coffee shop. Once I'm inside, the smile I now realize is on my lips fades as a couple at a table just inside the bar area is debating my father's infidelity. "What do his bedroom habits have to do with how he runs the country?" a man demands.

"A President has too much power to possess no moral compass," the woman replies, and I walk on by but not before I hear the man, add, "Should I list out all the affairs 'great' Presidents are known to have? Hello, John F. Kennedy and Marilyn Monroe. He also had a teenaged girl brought to his room to have sex and play with rubber duckies in the tub with him. It was in that book "Once Upon a Secret."

"That doesn't make it real," the other person says. "That's nuts."

As is everything in this world of mine, I think, but thankfully their voices fade, and I cut my attention to the bar. Michelle immediately catches my eyes, giving me a wave while Eddie continues to impress me, by ignoring me. I manage a smile and a returned wave, but all I can think about is my father; with the way he's managed to remind me that this isn't my world without even being in this state. Disliking this idea, I hurry forward, entering the art room, where I store my gift for Michelle and my purse. My stomach growls, I can't chat and do nice right now. I decide to skip the coffee and cookies. My hand goes to my new necklace. Like my mother, I'm not fearless. I'm afraid of being me; the girl who left her best friend to die because the truth is, that is exactly what the press has been saying about me. It's what my father said as well.

I rip the necklace off and throw it in the trash and reach in my pocket and do the same with the one I got for Megan. I don't know her. I don't know what she fears, but I saw the scars on her arms. She earned the right to own them or discard them herself, and it seems I have that to envy.

My class is an escape. Students file in and greet me with excitement, and it's as if a pin has pricked my nerves, and the tension slowly slides away. I enjoy every single moment of the students and the art. I engross myself in the people and the roses I have everyone painting. Truly, painting is a sweet, calming balm for my soul. Too soon it seems though it's over when Ashley rushes to the doorway and motions for me to hurry. I nod and end class, offering my farewells. I've just grabbed my gift for Michelle when Ashley is back. "Hurry. She's in the back room. She'll be out any second."

I hurry forward, following her out of the door, to find a crowd of people I don't expect, obviously many of them Michelle's friends. The next thing I know I'm swept into the crush of about twenty bodies and I'm singing Happy Birthday, confetti flying in the air. At some point, I manage to get my gift on one of the half dozen tables pushed together. Michelle is beside herself and as she opens gifts, my skin prickles and my eyes lift to find Logan watching me from the opposite side of the room. His lips quirk and he gives me a barely-there smile, but what makes this smile right and good, is the way it reaches his eyes. It's genuine. You can't fake genuine, not with someone like me, who knows fake like I know my own reflection in the mirror.

"Cake and champagne!" Ashley shouts, obviously closer to Michelle than I realized. "I'll pass it out! Grab a seat everyone."

The huddle breaks up and it's only a moment before Logan joins me, his tie at half undone again but tonight he still wears his jacket. "How about we share a table? Unless you're still angry with me?"

"I wasn't aware I was angry."

"You're always angry with me," he points out.

"And yet here you stand," I say, teasing him, though right now, I hate that he's right. I think I've been unfair to this man.

"Yes," he says softly, those blue eyes twinkling. "Here I am and here we are." He motions to a table and we sit down to have cake and champagne appear almost immediately.

"I actually bought you something today."

"Did you now?"

I smile. I can't help myself. I can't remember the last time I couldn't help but smile. No. That's wrong. I do remember. I was here, teaching my class, absorbed in the world of art. "I did," I confirm of the gift, reaching in my purse, where I've stashed it. I remove the pen and offer it to him. "It made me think of you. I had to buy it."

He accepts it and softly speaks the word, "Asshole," out loud before letting out a roar of deep laughter. I like this reaction. It's genuine like that smile he'd given me a bit ago, but more so, it's him being ten shades of easy going. He doesn't bristle. He doesn't act insulted. He glances over at me, his eyes alight with amusement. "Should I start considering this an endearment?"

After this reaction, *maybe,* I think. And in a rare reach in his direction, or anyone's direction for that matter, I say just that, "Maybe."

His eyes warm, the interest in his stare, warming me, where life has left me frozen, inside and out. He lifts his champagne glass. "A toast to maybe."

I hesitate when I don't want to hesitate, not here, not tonight. I just want to relax and enjoy myself. I know that drinking isn't my issue. I've been drugged. I really do know this as fact but it's hard to let go of what keeps happening to me. Logan arches a brow in question, rooting me back in this world, in his world, at a birthday party, for people who don't care about my father. Danielle isn't here. *She's dead.* My gut clenches and I shove aside the demons, trying to claw in between me and Logan. I reach for my glass and touch his to mine. "To maybe," I say, and then, I dare to sip just a tiny bit of the bubbly.

It's sweet, like this night, and I like it. Like is such a simple word and it feels like an indulgence. I *like* this place. I *like* being normal, or at last pretending for just a little while to belong here, or anywhere, really. I set my glass down and study the cake. "I didn't eat dinner."

"There's a great all-night joint up the road," Logan informs me. "I can take you."

"Maybe," I say, smiling. "I might eat too much cake for that to be an option."

He picks up his fork. "Nothing wrong with too much cake."

We both dig in and eat while sipping our drinks, the sweet and tangy, along with Logan's company, a delicious mix. I ask him questions about his patent case, genuinely interested. I manage to drill him about his practice, more on his family, all of which he answers freely, though I've backed myself into a corner. He's an attorney. It's quid pro quo. He tells. I tell. That can't happen. He sees this realization in my eyes, as he leans in closer.

"Hailey," he says, but it's just then, despite his intense attention that I feel the prickling sensation I know too well. It's all about being watched which I am far too often. I glance up and my attention pulls right to find Megan sitting at a table with Eddie, staring at us. I glance at Logan. "Apparently, she has a thing for you. It's becoming an issue."

He arches a brow. "Does she now?"

"You are not blind," I chide. "But I need to go deal with this." I down my champagne and stand up. The minute I do, Megan does the same and makes a beeline for the bathroom.

I push away from the table and start walking or rather swaying, as suddenly, the room spins. I stop in my footsteps, shaking my head slightly and I tell myself this is about needing to eat. I'm right on this, I decide when the sensation fades away. I pursue Megan and catch up to her right as she enters the bathroom, clearly baiting me to join her.

I reach for the door and blink away spots. I need food. Did I eat at all today? No. Just cake. That wasn't smart. I push the door open and enter to find Megan waiting on me. "I saw you staring at my scars." She yanks up her sleeve. "You want a close up of the freak?"

I blanch at this unexpected attack but recover quickly. "I never even noticed your scars until we were here in the bathroom. And yes, I looked." I unzip my pants and yank down one side. "This is why. Because I know what caused them. Because it hit home."

She sucks in air. "Oh, God. How?"

"Car accident," I say. "My mother died. What about you?"

"Same. Car accident." Tears gather in her eyes, I now know to be brown. "I was training for the Olympics and I can't—it was—no one died. It doesn't matter. I didn't lose what you did. I'm sorry."

"It was a different kind of loss, but a loss that was life-changing," I say, understanding, thinking about losing my mother and my art in one fatal sweep.

Droplets pour down her cheek and I pull her close, hugging her, understanding her but then my vision is blurry and I'm—I don't know what just happened. I lost time. Oh God. I *lost time*. Now Megan is gone, and Logan is pulling me into my art room, pressing me against a wall, out of the view of the bar. "I know who you are," he says. "I know who your father is. I know who you are. I know you're hiding from that book and the loss of your friend."

Adrenaline surges through me and I grab his lapels. "What do you want, Logan? What's your price? Because there is always a price, right?"

"Trust," he says. "Trust me enough to help you carry the secret."

"How do you know?" I demand. "How did you—"

The room spins. I lean into Logan and I have this moment, when I'm certain he's holding me close, worried even. I sense him there. I smell his now familiar cologne. I can't seem to see him though when I know that he's *right here*, in front of me. I can't make the room stop fading in and out until it does. Everything goes dark. Time fades away.

Suddenly I'm back, but now, I'm blinking into daylight. Where am I? What is happening? I glance down and my hand is on the bed—I'm in my new bed—and there is a heavy weight at my back, on my hip. A *hand* is on my hip and my gaze rockets to the nightstand where I find a gun and a badge. An FBI badge. I eye that hand where it rests on my body, and the watch is familiar. This is Jake. I'm in bed with Jake and I'm fairly certain I have on no clothes. I suck in a slow breath, trying to remember how this happened. I was with Logan. I *wanted* to be with Logan. There was cake and champagne. I drank champagne, and—no—no, no, *no*. This can't be real. Jake was watching me, waiting for the right moment. I was drugged again. *Jake* drugged me and then dared to take me to bed like this. Anger explodes inside me and I reach for his gun.

CHAPTER THIRTY-ONE

Now would be a good time for a confession and not one of a killer, but rather a victim. I know how to handle a gun. Actually, I know how to handle a variety of firearms and quite well. When I was twenty, I was grabbed in a shopping mall by a man who wanted to blackmail my father. Therefore, I am technically a kidnap victim though it lasted all of ten minutes. An armed, off-duty police officer saved me. Needless to say, I was shaken, even more so than I let on to those around me.

At that time, I'd given up my emotional outlet of painting over my mother's death. Considering I was crawling out of my own head and skin while trying to complete a yoga class, that replacement recreation wasn't working. I needed something, anything, and I found that in a newly minted friend: Tobey. Well, not actually in Tobey himself, but his surprising obsession with target practice at the gun range, which speaks of his passive aggressive nature few understand the way I do. He convinced me that the firing range, or rather mastery of a weapon, would deliver focus and control that would overflow into the rest of my life. And so, I went along for a visit, and the rest is history.

I became as obsessed with hitting my mark as he was. I still am. Shooting accurately requires the kind of focus that allows nothing else to exist but the trigger and the target. Of course, as far as protection goes on a college campus, and in attendance at a political event, you can't carry a weapon, therefore, my skills were not useful.

Until that morning with Jake.

THE PAST...

With the gun in my hand, I slide out from under the blankets and climb out of the bed. By the time I've turned around, Jake has rolled to his back. Ignoring my state of undress, I climb on top of him and the blankets, straddling his hips to point the gun at him. "Wow, sweetheart," he says, holding his hands up, his green eyes fiercely alert. "What the hell are you doing? And just to be clear, this is not one of my erotic fantasies."

"You drugged me," I bite out. "I know you drugged me. I don't know how you pulled it off but you're the one with a connection to Danielle. *You* did this."

"Drugged? I have no idea what you're talking about and I never met Danielle. *Put down the gun.* This is not going to end well for you, Hailey."

"In case you didn't study me well enough, agent and slave to my father that you are," I cock the gun. "I'm an excellent shot with a get-out-of-jail-free card. I could kill you right now, and we both know that my father will just clean up the mess. Hell, your best buddies at the FBI will bury you, quite literally."

"I'm well aware of your skills or I'd already have taken my gun back. I'm also aware that you didn't feel you needed it the last time you were naked and on top of me which was only a couple of hours ago."

"Taunting me right now," I promise him, "is like begging me to kill you."

He grabs the barrel of the gun and my heart leaps to my throat. "Shoot me or give me the gun," he says. "Decide now."

"I *want* to shoot you."

"That's a no to shooting me," he says, and in a blink, he's rolled me to my back, and somehow, he's out from under the covers, on top of me. "Don't fuck with me, woman." He doesn't give me time to reply. "I am *not* your enemy. We established that last night. We're *friends*. And I earned that title, remember?"

"Because you gave me an orgasm, if that, since I can't remember last night? That doesn't earn you friend status, especially not in DC."

He narrows his eyes on me. "You really don't remember, do you?"

"No," I hiss. "I *really* don't remember because *you drugged me*."

"I didn't drug you, Hailey." He stares at me, his green eyes hard, penetrating and intense, before he abruptly curses, and then rolls off of me, reaching in the nightstand and tossing me an envelope. "My offer of trust, which you already accepted last night. Open it, look at it, and put some damn clothes on so we can talk." He sets the gun down, grabs his pants, and starts getting dressed.

Unease rolls through me with some vague memory I can't quite form, and a sense of him telling the truth, but it's not him I'm remembering right now. It's Logan, "I know who you are," he'd declared, right after I'd decided I might actually like him. Right before I'd blacked out and he had access to my drink. Did I go to Jake, to do damage control and end up naked?

"Hailey," Jake snaps.

I glance over at him to find him already dressed in jeans and a T-shirt, his gun now holstered at his side. Feeling naked inside and out, I sit up, give him my back, needing my feet on the ground. I'm pretty sure the fact that I feel comfortable giving him my back says something, too, but right now: the envelope. I open it, pull out a photo, and suck in air at the sight of Danielle having sex with my father, confirmation of an affair, and what feels like betrayal, that some part of me didn't accept as real. I drop the envelope and photo as if burned, a wave of nausea coming over me. I push to my feet, grabbing a robe from the chair, and pulling it on, even as I rush to the bathroom. Oh God. I'm so very sick and I don't even try to shut the door. It's all I can do to land on my knees in the right spot before I heave over the toilet. I'm recovering, gripping the seat when Jake appears kneeling beside me. "Water?" he asks, handing me a bottle. "I'm not drinking anything you give me," I murmur, shifting to rest against the tub, my back against the cold surface. "Why would you show me that?"

"You wanted to know what was covered up that night," he says. "You wanted to know I was with you, not your father." He squats in front of me. "Are you sick from booze or that photo?"

"Does it matter?" I ask, defensively.

"I am many things, most of which this job has made me, Hailey, but I don't get naked with a drunk or drugged woman. You were neither of those things last night. You were as coherent as you are right now."

I hug my knees to chest, pulling the robe to my ankles. "Considering I just threw up, that isn't a statement that supports your case."

"Is this how you felt the night Danielle died?"

"According to the newspapers, I was stumbling all over the place. That also doesn't fit your description of me last night."

"But you don't remember?"

"Does it matter now?" I ask, not about to admit what I've been told not to admit.

"Were you drunk the night Danielle died?"

"Do I need a lawyer, Jake? Is this an interrogation?"

"Danielle's dead, and her killer is in jail," he says. "I'm trying to understand your blackout last night. How much did you drink then and now?"

I shove fingers through my hair. "I've drank three times in my life. Two times with Danielle. Once with you."

"You didn't drink with me," he says. "Not a drop. Tell me what you remember about last night."

I look up at him. "I remember the first few swallows of champagne. I don't remember drinking more than a glass. I'm not a drinker. I was fine and then I wasn't."

"You're telling me you've drank three times, and each time you blackout?"

"Yes, but you know this. That's why you—"

"What I know," he says, "is that this is medical. Most likely—you're allergic to alcohol."

I blanch. "What?"

"This isn't a professional observation, Hailey. I have a buddy, or did in college, that had the same issue. He saw a doctor. Google it. It's a real thing."

"No," I reject. "That's impossible. You can't be allergic to alcohol."

"You can. It's a known phenomenon. Rare but known."

"No," I say, rejecting this idea yet again, clinging to the one thing I've been certain about in all of this. "Danielle drugged me," I push back. "Someone who knew what she'd done to me in the past drugged me last night. That means *you*. Someone told you. Maybe *she* told you."

"That didn't happen. Any of it. Not where I'm concerned."

"Then *what did*? How did I even end up in bed with you?"

He offers me his hand. "I'll fill in the blanks. Including the naked parts if you like, or we can just repeat those."

"Don't joke right now," I say, and my tone is earnest. "Honestly. This is freaking me out and," I eye his holstered gun again, before meeting his stare, "I might just pull your gun again if you continue to joke about this."

"We both know you aren't that foolish. And we both know you were scared when you woke up." He softens his voice. "I get it now. Let's go talk." He stands up and helps me do the same. "Talks are best with coffee."

"And donuts?" I joke.

"Cop joke. Good. You're feeling better. You *do* keep coffee in this place, right?"

"Of course," I manage, the topic of coffee and conversation, somehow feeling far more uncomfortable than me naked, straddling him and holding a gun on him and I have no idea why. "What normal person doesn't have coffee in the house?" I add.

He laughs and that sound rings with normalcy that I've never attributed to Jake and for the first time since meeting him, I actually consider him human, not a badge. He laughs. He smiles. He drinks coffee. He's *human*. Not that I trust him. I trust no one, but he's now the man with the key to huge chunks of my life. His eyes are my eyes and I want everything I can get from him. That means I need to think before we talk. I need to try to process anything I'm missing. "Let me brush my teeth and put on real clothes."

He studies me a moment, the probe of his eyes deep, which makes him a little less human and a little more agent. He's trying to read me, trying to see things I might not want him to see, which I now know is why coffee and conversation make me nervous, but finally, he gives a nod. "I'll be waiting on you downstairs." Without further preamble, he turns and leaves.

I press my hands to the sink and will myself to remember how I got here to this moment but there is nothing. I have not one single memory of Jake before this morning. And *allergic to alcohol*? I can't be allergic, can I? If I am, then that changes everything. It shifts the way I've viewed myself and others, and I'm not quite sure what to do with that. It doesn't matter, I decide quickly. Or it does but not this very moment. What I do know, is my plan prior to that champagne remains. Jake knows things beyond last night that I don't know, and I need to change that.

I shove off the counter and run into the closet, pulling on sweats and a T-shirt, as well as Keds. I wash my face, brush my teeth and hair, and ignore how crappy I look right now. I just need answers and my phone. After a quick search, I decide it, my purse, and my computer are all downstairs with Jake, who could look at any of them which wouldn't be a problem, except that I don't remember anything. Except for Logan: *I know who you are.* Which means I might be leaving Denver today.

I start for the door when my gaze catches on the envelope. I snatch it and the photo up, scanning more of the same types of photos. "Oh, Danielle," I whisper. "Why him?

You knew what he is." But she was also needy and insecure, vulnerable in ways that allowed someone like my father to take advantage of her. I drop the envelope on the bed and head downstairs.

I find Jake in the kitchen, resting on the counter by the refrigerator, a cup of coffee in his hand. "How are you?" he asks, back to studying me, but there is what seems to be genuine concern etched in his tone, his eyes even, but I don't believe it. I don't believe anything anymore.

"I'm fine," I say, walking to the pot, and starting a cup to brew for myself, while hyper-focusing on the stream of coffee. Jake doesn't say anything, but I feel the heavy weight of his stare, concrete on my shoulders, crushing and intense. He wants me to look at him. I don't.

My brew is complete, and I pour creamer in my cup, add Splenda, and then stir. When finally, I've turned to lean on the counter to his left, he breaks the silence. "You still don't trust me," he comments.

"I don't trust anyone. That's called politics."

"We at the FBI call that the CIA but that aside, I gave you the photos."

"And that proves what? Danielle was having an affair with my father. I know that. If you want something from me, you're going to have to give me more in trade."

"You said the same thing last night."

"And you said what?" I challenge.

"You don't remember, *at all*?"

"No," I breathe out, admitting to him what I have to no one else, but then I made my memory loss rather obvious this morning. "No. I don't."

He sets his cup down and walks to me, taking mine from me as well, before his hands come down on the counter next to me. "I said, and I'll say now, that I want *you*, thus the way we ended up naked again."

"That's it? That's all that happened?"

He grunts and pushes off the counter, running his hand through his sandy brown hair and in that moment, he is once again human. "You're killing me here," he growls, frustration etched on his handsome face, but handsome doesn't mean honest. "That's *all* that happened?" he continues. "Not exactly a reaction a man wants a woman to have the morning after."

"It's obvious that we got naked," I say. "I'm missing everything else. I need to know what else happened. Can't you understand that?"

He gives me one of those probing stares of his again, his expression masterfully unreadable. "You were upset when you walked in the door and found me here," he says. "You were not pleased that I entered without permission. You accused me of doing so on another occasion, and stealing your paintings of Danielle and your father, despite me handing you photos of the real deal."

"Did you take them?"

He folds his arms in front of his broad chest. "As I told you last night, no. I did not take them, but your father wants this thing with Danielle to go away real bad, sweetheart. I'm not surprised he's monitoring you."

"By way of you?" I accuse.

"No," he says. "Not me. Rudolf."

"Who now knows you're here," I say.

"Only because I let him know. I made friends with my badge, and then told him to back off, I got you a little space, but it won't last."

"Why? What do you really want from me, Jake?"

He presses his hands on the counter on either side of me again. "Nothing that you don't want to give."

"That's not an answer."

"I'm not asking you for anything," he assures me.

"But one day you will," I assume, because that's how this works.

He studies me a few beats. "One day I might." He pushes off the counter. "For now, I gave *you* something. I gave you the gift of control. You and I have what your father doesn't want anyone to have. Use it wisely, if at all. Wait for me if you can, but if you can't, make sure he knows that you have a resource to send those shots to the press, if it becomes necessary."

My breath lodges in my throat and I plant my hand, that I think might actually be shaking, on the counter behind me. "What aren't you saying?"

"Your father will do anything to win this election, and I do mean anything. I think you know that."

"Be direct," I say. "Spell it out, Jake."

"I don't think that's necessary, now is it?"

My pulse thunders in my ears. "Are you saying he killed Danielle?" I demand, adrenaline surging through me to the point that I now know I'm shaking. "Did he kill her or rather have her killed?"

His hands settle on my shoulders, and the touch is not sexual at all. It's grounding. It brings me down a notch, which is clearly his intent, but he doesn't hold back. "I can't prove that he ordered her murder, but the minute I headed that direction with my investigation, I was shut out."

"And yet you covered for me, or so you say."

"I made an effort to prevent you from becoming a fall guy," he confirms. "If your father did this, he needs to own this, not you."

Not me.

"You know I don't remember that night," I point out, needing to know everything. Needing to know where this is headed.

"I know you called your father and confronted him about Danielle."

"How? How do you know that?"

His lips set hard. "I know."

"And yet the photos are supposed to mean something to me."

"We both know those photos are trouble for your father," he counters.

I'm back to the confirmation that I called my father. I stroked the fires. I made Danielle a problem for him. "Just to be clear," I say, "You don't believe the homeless man did it." It's not a question.

"No," he says. "I do not."

No, he does not.

"Which brings me back to you," he says, and with those words, my throat starts to close off. This is where everything lands. He's stripped me naked to play with my head. He's baited me, reeled me in and I invited him here to do it. I'm a fool and this is where it all ends.

CHAPTER THIRTY-TWO

"YOU DON'T TAKE A PHOTOGRAPH. YOU MAKE IT."

—ANSEL ADAMS

THE PAST...

I become aware of Jake standing between me and the exit of the kitchen. I'm also acutely aware of the fact that I am far more naked with Jake than simply taking my clothes off. I have no idea what I did with him. What I said to him. What I confessed. "I thought we were talking about Danielle," I say. "Not me."

"You're connected," he says. "Right along with your father and I know for a fact that your father had a conversation with his Chief of Staff about the value of the sympathy vote. If he's down in the polls, what will he do to get back on top? Think about it."

Any relief I have at the realization that he's not accusing me of something, fades with the blade of memory that transports me back to that balcony in Austin. To that moment when I'd rejected a dive to the ground out of worry I'd hand my father the sympathy vote. I wasn't willing to give him that then or now.

"Have you thought about it, Hailey?" he asks, pulling me back to the moment. "I have and the minute I figured out where that leads, which is you, was the minute I was with you, not him."

"What does that mean?"

"It means," he says precisely, "until you give me a reason otherwise, I'm your friend but I'm not his." He eyes his watch. "I didn't know we'd have to repeat last night today. I have to go. I have a situation to handle but I'll be back as soon as I can." He starts to turn away.

"What's your end game, Jake?" I demand, not ready to let him off that easily.

"Right now. Keeping you alive."

"And later?"

"To be decided *later*. What's *your* end game, Hailey?"

"Not my father's."

He narrows his eyes on me. "And what of the White House? Are you eager to get there?"

Aware that he could still be working for my father or working both sides, I tread cautiously, "I'm not of any value to you if I don't, now am I?"

"A cautious reply, by someone who thinks I want that tit for tat you offered me. I don't. It must suck to know that you'll never have a relationship you trust until he's done and over." And with that, he heads for the door, but he's only halfway there when he turns back to me. "I'm sending you something. Watch for it." And with that, he walks to the door and exits.

I let out a heavy breath trying to digest what just happened when my phone buzzes with a message from my purse. I mentally tick through a list of who might text me: Not Danielle. She won't ever text me again, and that twists me in knots. Tobey? Maybe. My father? No. Rudolf? Maybe. Probably something to do with Jake and that sets me into action, closing the steps between me and the island where my purse sets, to dig out my phone. I grab it, glancing at the message screen, surprised to find an unfamiliar local number. The message reads: Why'd you leave?

I inhale sharply, certain this is Logan, who I apparently gave my Washington number, which was foolish. It's like saying: Yes, you're right. I'm that girl you think I am. For all I know, I admitted my real identity. I'm still trying to deal with Jake and now this, a real problem considering I have no idea where his "I know who you are" declaration landed us last night. With Jake, the photos align him with me, at least for the moment. With Logan too much is unknown, and I can't take unknowns right now. That's a problem that has to end today but even as I consider Logan my biggest problem, I replay Jake's words: *Until you give me a reason otherwise, I'm your friend.*

In other words, until he digs around and finds out something that turns me into the hunted instead of my father. If he really wants my father. I need to help Jake get my father which serves me well. It saves me four to eight years of my life in the White House. As for law school, I might attend just to know I have my own money and power, but my art will be in the background. My art will be the future I'm trying to make my real tomorrow.

I stare down at the message again, and reject any mode of communication   that can be printed off, copied, or recorded as a reply. If Logan wants to talk, we'll do it in person, and on my terms. I glance at the time to find that it's already ten in the morning, which means I've left Logan free with my real identity for far too long. I head toward the front door that I lock, setting the alarm before I rush up the stairs. I need to shower and think. I walk into the bedroom and stop at the sight of the unmade bed, where I slept with Jake; shaken by the complete blank I still am on how that happened. I can't even fully gauge how much I trust, or don't trust him. I am missing hours with him while I have maybe only forty-five minutes where I was coherent this morning. I shake off this thought. Right now, he's gone, and Logan is here, as well as a potential problem. Well, one remnant of Jake still remains.

I walk around the bed, snatch up the envelope, ensure the photos are safely inside and debate where to hide them. Experts like Rudolf will look in every odd place in existence. I can't leave the photos here. I need someplace else. I need to just keep them with me at all times but even that could be tricky. My purse isn't locked up at the coffee shop. I walk into the bathroom and set the envelope and my phone on the counter. I'll find a place for the photos and that place won't be here. I check my messages again and I still have that one message: Why'd you leave? Obviously, Logan decided he'd move forward based on my reply or lack thereof. How he moves forward is a big issue though, and time sensitive.

I quickly strip, shower, and do all my normal girl stuff to my hair and makeup before I redress in black jeans and a black T-shirt and tennis shoes. If I end up at Logan's office as planned, I'm not going to look like the future First Daughter, or anyone worth knowing. Of course, I may stand out this way too, but at least I don't look important. All but ready to go, I pack up my purse, grab the envelope and head downstairs. Once in the kitchen, I pause at the island and power up my computer to look up Logan's office number. I dial the receptionist. "Is Logan in?"

"Yes, ma'am. May I tell him who's calling?"

"Actually, I have another call. I'll call right back." I disconnect and text the address to myself, while Logan has remained silent in the aftermath of his text and my non-text.

I'm about to shut my computer when my conversation with Jake comes back to me with his claim that I'm allergic to alcohol. I resist my next move, but I have to know. I type in "alcohol allergy" and pant out a breath when plenty of results pop up. I start reading and most of the links talk about allergies as in a physical illness; hives and so on. That is until I type in: *I black out almost every time I drink.* And there it is. A forum of people talking about this rare occurrence, and I begin reading posts that fit my exact reaction to drinking. Of course, there are those calling them foolish, and accusing them of drinking too much, but there are too many like me for me to dismiss this as nonsense.

I glance at the time in the corner of my screen. It's nearly noon, and Logan could leave his office for lunch, if he hasn't already. I shut my computer, but for a moment, I am paralyzed. Danielle didn't drug me. Jake didn't drug me. Guilt knifes through me. If Danielle drugged me, I had a reason for leaving her behind. She caused me to be out of my mind. I also had a reason for being angry with her, outside of the affair, which this realization doesn't change. I still thought she drugged me. And Jake didn't prove my father was behind the murder. He only validated my certainty that the homeless man did not.

"I didn't kill her," I hiss, packing up my briefcase with my computer and the envelope. *Just like I wasn't drugged*, I think, but quickly reject the negativity of that thought. I'm done twisting guilt into anger in illogical ways; blaming Danielle and myself, when the guilt lies one place: My father.

Going forward, I'm going to protect myself and where that leads me. Do I make my father pay for his sins against my mother and my best friend? How can I not make him pay? I *will* make him pay, but before I can even decide what that means, I have to deal with Logan.

I head to the door, already thinking of ways I can use Logan against my father as I exit, lock up, and listen to the security system arm, with what I now know is a false sense of relief. It was on last night when Jake managed to enter the house before I got home. In other words, any time I arrive home someone could be waiting on me. Now I wish I'd kept Jake's gun. I *need* a gun and I need a gun that won't lead back to me.

CHAPTER THIRTY-THREE

Trust.

Google that word and you'll find the dictionary has a long list of possible definitions. Any word with that many definitions can't be trusted. Just like the word, a person cannot be trusted. Think about it. Is there anyone in this life that knows everything about you? Everything. Someone that you can say knows your deepest, darkest thoughts we all have but want to deny?

If you say yes, you're lying and you can't be trusted.

I think this truth is why the show Dexter *was such a big hit. We all have something hidden, and we know this means other people do as well. We know there could be a serial killer amongst us, in the mostly proverbial sense. Now I'm not saying trust doesn't exist. I'm simply saying it requires insurance and Jake understood this, which is exactly why he gave me those photos. He gave me a gift, a tool that I could use to protect myself, and that is exactly what I did.*

THE PAST...

Ten minutes after I lock up my rental, and a short walk later, I discover the building Logan bought to live and work in is right on the edge of the residential area, as are many businesses in the Cherry Creek area. It's also a black glass high rise, that wouldn't come cheap. Translation: Logan has money and while some might find this appealing, I don't. Money, power, and an "I know who you really are" declaration equal a threat, not a turn on. I enter the building

261

and walk to the directory on the wall to discover floors one through fifteen are all businesses, while sixteen to twenty are residential. Logan's offices include levels nine through fifteen.

With a plan to hide my envelope, I head to the stairwell and enter, starting my walk up while looking for a sliver of insulation or anyplace that might become a hiding spot, but nothing works. I reach floor three, and exit, in search of a ladies' room, and find it. Once I'm inside the two-stall room, I find the ceilings to be flat and sealed. There's not even a cabinet under the sink. This just isn't going to work.

My phone buzzes with a text and I dig it from my purse, to find a message from Logan's number that reads: WHY did you LEAVE? WHY WHY WHY WHY WHY WHY WHY WHY.

My eyes go wide. What the hell? That is a crazy message. Almost child-like. This isn't Logan. I don't believe that anymore. Suddenly I'm jolted with the memory of following Megan into the restroom last night. I remember her confronting me over her scars and her confession about her car accident. Even more so, I remember the way she'd felt lost and needy, in that same way Danielle so often did. Then there was the hug that felt like I was hugging Danielle. Then nothing. I have no idea what comes next.

I glance back down at the text message. I was so consumed with Logan's confession about my identity, that I just assumed he was the one texting me, but this has to be from Megan. I must have given her my number. That has to be what is going on. I punch "dial" on the number texting me and immediately get a voicemail with no greeting. "Megan. It's Hailey. Can you call me back? Actually, I'm going into a meeting. I'll try you back right after it ends."

Just in case she calls right back, I stay my ground, waiting a full minute. "Damn it," I whisper, certain now that Megan is really quite troubled. I'm now officially torn between hurrying to the coffee shop to check on her and staying here to deal with Logan. Of course, I can't help

Megan if I'm not there, and I won't be if Logan stirs the pot. I stick my phone back in my purse, and head for the elevator.

In a short ride up, the doors open to a gray wall inked with the words "Casey Law Firm" in thick, silver letters that confirm I'm in the right place. I cut right and enter a typical lawyer-style office with a fancy leather furniture framing a glass reception desk. "Is Logan available?" I ask, stopping in front of the forty-something redhead manning the post.

She presses her black-rimmed glasses up her snooty nose. "Can I tell Mr. Casey who is here?"

"Hailey."

I look up to find Logan standing to the left of reception, his three-piece blue suit, as sharp as his blue eyes focused on me. "Do you have a few minutes?" I ask.

There's a pregnant silence, a coldness about him that contracts every one of the many war moments I've shared with this man. "This way," he says, which I assume means yes to having a minute, and that were headed back down the hallway behind him.

Afraid he might just change his mind, I hurry forward, and the minute I join him, he indicates a hallway to the left, which we travel side by side, a sharp energy jutting from him to me. He's pissed and I'm not sure why. Because I came here? Because of last night? I want to know and I am quick to cross the second lobby we enter, and allow him to motion me into his office. I gladly enter first, which gives me about sixty seconds to take in the wide black desk, leather seating area, and floor-to-ceiling windows with a mountain view.

By sixty-one seconds, the door is shut and I'm stunned to be pressed against the wall, his big body crowding mine. "No more games," he bites out. "What the hell is this?"

"If I wanted to play games I wouldn't be here," I snap back, not as easily intimidated as he might think.

"After last night," he replies. "I don't believe you."

"Right," I say, and then I just dive in, offering him an olive branch with the truth. "I don't remember last night."

His eyes narrow sharply. "What does that even mean?"

"I remember pieces but not all of it."

"Well let me refresh your memory. You called me a user, who was after your father's power, and volleying for a position, right after you kissed me like you wanted to—"

"Enough," I say, pressing my hand to his chest. "I don't know if you deserved that so I can't apologize. I think I was drugged or—it's more complicated than that."

"You drank the same champagne I drank and after last night, I'm going to need a lot more than that to continue this conversation."

"I want to hire you."

His withdrawal is instant. His jaw flexes and he pushes off the wall, his hands settling under his jacket on his hips. "I don't need your money and I have plenty of clients."

I have this crazy urge to grab him and step into him that I have never felt with Jake, or Tobey for that matter. And yet I ended up in bed with both of them. "I remember the champagne and cake," I say. "I remember talking to Megan and then I was suddenly just in the art room with you. You were declaring you knew who I really was in a public place which you had to know was going to freak me out."

He draws a subtle but distinct breath. "I'll admit that was poorly timed, but the idea was for you to know you don't have to hide from me. Instead, I got attacked."

"I might not remember everything, but I know I felt sideswiped and trapped." I step to him and grab his lapels. "There are things happening. Things that make it impossible for me to trust anyone and I repeat, you chose *a public place* to tell me that you knew who I was."

"What things are happening?"

"You want answers? Let me hire you. Be my legal confidant and representative should I need you. That protects you and me."

"You don't need to hire me to trust me."

"I can't give you that." My hands fall away from him and I step back. "That's not the world I live in and I don't know you well enough. And even then, I can't just trust anyone. We sign a contract with legal confidentiality or I leave. And you draw up the contract. It has to have my real name on it to be valid and I don't want anyone else seeing that."

He studies me for several beats. "Have a seat," he says, and then without another word, he turns, walks to his desk, giving his attention to his computer.

Inhaling, I let out a calming breath and then make sure he knows that if he's in, I'm in. I walk to the sitting area, and claim a cushion on the black leather couch, sitting my briefcase and purse next to me. My phone buzzes with a text message and I pull it out to read: Why would I even consider calling you?

I type: Let's meet in person.

No, she replies. I shouldn't have even texted you. I know why you left. We both know it was HIM.

She's scaring me. She's obsessive. Scary obsessive. I don't know what to say. I have nothing. Logan stands up and I stick my phone in my purse again. He sits down next to me and sets the contract and a pen on the coffee table in front of me. "The retainer is one dollar. I don't want your money. I have plenty of my own."

I glance over at him, the look on his face unreadable, but I believe him. He doesn't want my money. I wish that meant he didn't want anything else. I think it does, but that's not enough. Not with so much on the line. I pick it up and read the simple one-page document. I grab the pen and sign, *Hailey Anne Monroe*. I slide the paper toward him and reach into my purse, pulling out a twenty.

"You can buy me coffee with rest."

He doesn't take the bait and invite our familiar banter. He takes the twenty and stuffs it in his pocket, and we shift to face each other. "Talk," he orders. "I'm listening."

I hesitate, but I decide I'm all in. This man's father is not my father's friend or political ally and your enemy's enemy is your friend. If he burns my father, I really don't care. In fact, I might just celebrate, as long as he doesn't get killed. I really don't want Logan to die.

"I'm still here," he says, snapping me into action.

"Right. First, how do you know who I am?"

"I was watching the news and I recognized your photo," he says. "But I wouldn't worry about others figuring it out. I've been up close and personal with you. We've talked. I've looked at you closely."

"Too closely if this goes wrong," I say, reaching in my briefcase and pulling out the envelope. "What I'm going to ask of you could be dangerous. So that one-dollar fee isn't enough but I also don't want you to be motivated to get rid of me so I'm going to let that fee stick."

He leans closer. "Talk faster."

I offer him the envelope. "I'm being watched. I need you to protect this and if anything happens to me, be it now or later, I need you to use this in the most vicious of ways. I need you to make it count and don't get killed doing it. If that scares you—"

"It doesn't. What is it?"

"You can look, but please not in front of me." I cut my gaze and swallow the knot in my throat. "My best friend that was murdered, was having an affair with my father. You have graphic proof that on the heels of that book that just released would hurt him."

"Are we talking about a murder cover-up?"

"I don't know. I don't believe a homeless person killed her but—"

"You were drunk that night."

"No," I snap. "No, I was not. This was a bad idea." I try to get up, but he catches my arm.

"I shouldn't have assumed anything I saw in the media. Tell me your truth."

My truth.

I press my hands to my face and then flatten them on my knees. My truth. Here it goes. I told Jake. I can tell Logan, who is now my attorney. "I've drank three times. At a high school party. At the bar the night Danielle died. Last night. I've blacked out every time. I thought Danielle drugged me. She was—a unique person, troubled. It wasn't farfetched. Then when I woke up this morning and I didn't know how I got home, I thought someone who knew Danielle was screwing with my head."

"What's the 'but' because there is one, right?"

"I googled the topic and it's possible that I'm just allergic to alcohol, but that's not the point. The point is that I can't remember the night Danielle died in its entirety, but I found out about the affair that night. I remember that much, and I remember calling my father. And then she was dead."

"You think your father might turn on you?"

I tell him everything. The push to send me here, the missing art I'd created, and my interactions with Jake, minus the part where I got naked with him not once but twice. "So you see," I conclude. "I need insurance. I need to tell my father I have proof and I'll use it."

He rejects that idea. "If you do that, you could trigger a reaction that isn't what you want. That's not the answer."

"Part of me just wants to release the photos anonymously and pray it ends his run," I say. "I'm sure your father would be happy. But my father is Teflon and if he doesn't win this time, he's young. He'll have a recovery plan for the future."

"Agreed on the negatives of that action, but to be clear. Politics isn't a part of this for me, though I get it. If you want your father out, my father, being your father's adversary, actually makes you feel safer with me." He doesn't wait for confirmation that isn't required. "As for what comes next, the photos are more moving parts in a weapon that needs to be broader. Luckily, I'm good at developing broader weapons and thanks to my father, if, and I mean if, we needed political backing to help wield our swords, we could get it." He sets the envelope aside. "Let's be completely frank and not talk in circles that seem to say one thing but could be another. What's your goal here? Survival and getting to the White House or ruining him?"

"He cheated on my mother. He slept with Danielle and most likely had her killed. He would use me as political cash. So, no. I don't want to go to the White House and yes, to be clear, I know that ruining him is what that takes."

He considers me for an eternal moment and he must not like what he finds because he doesn't close the deal. He takes a proverbial step to the side and then wide. "I need you to give considerable thought to that answer. I'll ask it again before I take actions." He glances at his watch. "And right now, I'm on limited time. I need to be in court in an hour and we need to talk about how to keep you safe."

"I have to convince my father that I'm all in with him and I haven't. It's the only way. I know that. Now, let's talk about your safety. Stay away from me. If they come after you, this ends, and it could end badly for both of us. They can't know you're helping me." I pause and add, "Stay away for now, Logan."

"Agreed. *For now.* I'll still come to the coffee shop or it will seem unusual but this visit to my office will have been monitored. What are you going to say if you're asked about me?"

"Megan's sending me some crazy text messages. I'll say I was looking for her."

He frowns. "What crazy text messages?"

"About you, I think. She's jealous. It's not healthy. Did I tell you anything that happened with her last night?"

"You did not," he says. "We jumped right into the conversation about who you are when you got back from talking to her. You left angry. The end, and right now Megan is not what's on my mind. You and my court hearing are. I need a way to contact you. I'll buy you a phone and leave it in your art cabinet at the coffee shop tonight."

"You don't have to do this, any of this."

"No," he says. "I don't, but I am. And you owe me a painting for my living room wall when I give you the freedom to be an artist. Now leave, before I kiss you, because that will just make things more complicated."

"Thank you, Logan." I stand up, slipping my briefcase on my shoulder and for just a moment we look at each other.

"I said go," he orders softly, and I listen this time. I hurry to the door, but I don't exit. I turn around to find him facing my direction now, watching my retreat. "I'm glad you didn't kiss me, because when, and if you do, I want to know that neither of us has anything to gain. I can't give you the White House and you can't give me freedom." With that, I turn and leave, and it's not until I step into the elevator that the levity of what I've just done hits me. I've decided to stand between my father and the White House, but I don't feel guilty. Not one ounce of guilt. It's me or him and he made it that way, not me.

CHAPTER THIRTY-FOUR

Guilt.

This is an emotion you feel when you believe you should have done something differently. This is an emotion driven by an eternal belief that we can change the future. We can't, at least not the eventual outcome. If you're meant to become famous, you will become famous, even if it takes a random person on the street discovering you. If you're meant to die, you will die.

I still didn't get that back then. I was still of the belief that my actions made a difference. If you look back at every action I've taken, you'll see guilt driving me. If I hadn't gone to the party in high school, my mother wouldn't have died. If I hadn't gone to Europe with Danielle, that woman on the cliff wouldn't have died. If I hadn't called my father, Danielle wouldn't have died. There were a lot of "what ifs" with Danielle, actually.

Megan reminded me of Danielle. That would become a problem for me.

THE PAST...

As soon as I leave Logan's office, I walk to the coffee shop, where I find Ashley and Eddie working a small crowd. I hurry to the bar, where Ashley is waiting on an order. "Is Megan in?"

"She quit, and Michelle is sick today. She sounded like walking death. We don't want to call her and freak her out.

She never takes off and I got a fill-in. A girl that used to work here is coming in any minute."

I'm still digesting the most important part of what she just announced. "Megan quit? Why? When?"

"She didn't say. She told Eddie. I tried to call her back, but her line is disconnected. I think that's a pretty clear message. She's done with us."

And yet she is texting me. "Did you try her alternate numbers?"

"I grabbed the one in Michelle's rolodex. Her files are locked up."

"When is Michelle back?"

"Hopefully tomorrow morning," she says. "Like I said. She's really sick."

"Do you know where Megan lives? I can run by there."

"I actually do," she says. "She rooms with a couple of girls in the apartment right behind the Cherry Cricket Inn. Number 476."

"I'll go by there. I'll let you know if I reach her."

"Why bother?" she asks. "She's gone. We'll move on. She's trouble anyway."

"More like troubled," I say. "And you don't look away from those people." *Like I did Danielle*, I think, heading for the door. What did I say to Megan last night? Did I make her quit? I shove my hand through my hair. Logan said I kissed him. I kissed that man and don't remember, which is truly an injustice but aside from that, Megan must have seen it and reacted in an irrational way.

Like Danielle would have, I think, back to the comparison.

I'm on the street in sixty seconds, and since I know exactly where the hotel is, I don't lose a step. I try to call Megan and end up leaving yet another message. "It's Hailey. Please call me. Please." I disconnect and will back every moment with Megan in the bathroom, but I don't remember anything after the hug. I don't know how we ended that encounter.

In a few blocks, I'm at the apartment. I knock and a thin brunette girl in jeans and T-shirt opens the door. "Is Megan here?"

"She left. Gone. Forever."

Gone.

Forever.

I really hate those words spoken together. "Where did she go?"

"She said it was time for an adventure. And poof. She took one."

"Do you know how to reach her?"

"If I did I wouldn't tell you."

I reach into my purse and pull out a hundred-dollar bill. "Now do you know?"

She takes the money. "No." She shuts the door.

I huff out a breath and give up, heading back toward the main sidewalk. This was a place she shared with friends and I hope she's gone home to a good family, wherever that might be. I'm almost back to the hotel when my cellphone rings. I stop walking, yanking it from my purse, in hopes that it's Megan. One glance at the caller ID tells me it's Rudolf, and the timing, right after my Logan meeting, says this is trouble. I answer the line to hear, "The enemies of your friends are not your friends."

That twist on my father's words can mean only one thing. I'm right. This is about Logan. "And that says what about you?"

"Logan Casey has connections to your father's enemies which makes him an enemy."

He's just validated Logan as the right person to ask for help. "I know nothing about that man," I say, and when I would snap back with more, I remind myself that I'm supposed to be supportive of my father. "He upset an employee at the coffee shop. I headed to her apartment to try to get her back to work."

"You were in that building a long time."

So much for that space Jake claimed to give me from my father's pack of wolves. "I had to wait on him," I say, without missing a beat, "and my days are not exactly filled with activities right now. If you're calling mc on this, how bad of a problem is he?"

"He's only a problem if you make him a problem."

"I'm not making anyone a problem," I say. "I'm careful. He has no idea who I really am. He thinks I'm an artsy chick, just like you wanted."

"You're being very agreeable," he says, obviously suspicious, but he says it anyway. "This makes me suspicious."

"Because I like my artsy job at the coffee shop. I don't want to leave right now and we both know my father doesn't want me back either. We're set up here. I don't want to do this all over again."

"That's right," he says dryly. "You do like art."

"Which we both know is why my father chose to make my cover in the art industry," I say. "I'm being taunted with what I want, what he doesn't intend to let me have."

I imagine him giving me a three-second deadpan stare, and then he just says, "Stay away from Logan."

"He comes into the coffee shop. If I act like a total jerk that will get more attention than any of us need."

"We're watching."

"I'm quite aware of that, Rudolf."

"*Don't* forget." He disconnects.

Certain eyes are on me right now, I stick my phone back in my purse, despite a deep need to warn Logan of trouble. I start walking, knowing Rudolf will monitor anything I do right now. I don't even want to go to my email and open Logan's message to get his phone number. A warning is going to have to wait until tonight.

I turn onto the sidewalk and this time when I start walking, I try to sense being followed but I don't. I don't and it's frustrating because I am. My pace is steady and my walk to my rental, short. Once I arrive, there's a box wrapped in brown paper sitting at the door, which I assume is Jake's promise of a delivery. I kneel in front of it to find my fake name and address with no return label.

I open the door, and enter the house, taking the small box with me. I lock up and head to the island, depositing my briefcase and purse on a stool before sitting the box on the counter. Opening it is like breaking into Fort Knox, but finally, I pull out a shiny box that I know is a gun safe. The lock code is taped to the top and I enter it to open the lid and stare down at my favored weapon: *A Sig Sauer P238 Lady Barbara*. You don't just guess and produce my favored gun. It takes intimate knowledge of my personal shooting habits and I'm not sure how I feel about that.

There's a card taped to the inner lid with my name on it. I yank it free and remove a plain white card that reads: *This is me trusting you in a big way considering you pulled my own gun on me. Don't shoot me, but I'm certain you'll know who to shoot when the time is right.*

That's when I realize the security system wasn't armed when I entered.

CHAPTER THIRTY-FIVE

"I NEVER PAINT DREAMS OR NIGHTMARES. I PAINT MY OWN REALITY."

—FRIDA KAHLO

THE PAST...

I grab the gun with the ease of someone who knows it and knows it well, as I do, while moving inside the kitchen to ensure no one is at my back. I load the Sig Sauer and consider my next move. I could search the house, but what I know of the people that work for the government, and my father, is that they're skilled in ways I am not. I also know that I've been warned I could be in danger, and those people might not be my friends. I grab my phone from my purse and dial Jake.

He answers immediately. "You got the gift."

"Did you come in my house again?"

"Why?" he asks.

"The security system was off."

"And yet you entered the house," he says tightly.

"How do you know that?"

"This is my second gift to you," he replies. "A lesson. Know your surroundings a hell of a lot better than you do."

"Where are you?" I demand.

"Nowhere close, and before you ask, I use a remote device to disarm your system. It's worthless. That gun is not."

"And yet you know I entered the house." It's not a question.

"I assumed you did based on our conversation."

My jaw clenches. "I don't like this game, Jake."

"Better to learn your lessons from me than from someone else."

"About that," I say, thinking of Rudolf. "What happened to the breather you were—"

"Think before you speak," he says. "*Think.*"

In other words, my line is being monitored. Of course. I know it is.

"Hang up now," he says.

I suck in air, angry at him, angry at everything and everyone right now, but I hang up on him. My phone rings again and I answer the line without even looking at the number. "Daughter."

God, not now. "Father," I say, my grip on the cold steel in my hand tightening.

"I hear you've been mingling with the enemy."

"I heard that, too," I say. "And while I had no idea, now that I do, I'll be careful. And as you've said, keep your friends close and your enemies closer."

"Is he your friend or enemy?" he asks.

"Is he *your* friend or enemy?"

"I don't know. His father is the polar opposite of me politically, but he doesn't align well with his father. He could be turned, though he could be thinking the same of you."

"I've invested my entire life in supporting you politically, father. I'm not throwing that away for some man. I'm with Tobey anyway."

"He doesn't seem to think so."

"He needs to suffer a little for sins that are between him and me, not you and me. But we both know he wants the White House, and he aligns properly with that goal."

He's silent two beats in which I know he's calculating my risk. "Let's talk about Logan."

"I'm listening," I say, holding my breath.

"Are you sure he doesn't know who you are?"

"If he does, he's given me no indication that he does."

He's quiet, thoughtful. "Get close to him. See if you can get him talking politics and party positioning. Do this and do this well, daughter."

Relief washes through me. Logan is, at least for now, safe. "If I do—"

"Don't negotiate. Not when I'm still cleaning up your mess." He disconnects.

I slip the phone into the pocket of my jeans, but I don't put the gun down. I walk toward my art room, check for any intruders, and then because I really have no option but to move forward with, or without my weapon, I work my way through the rest of the house. I check every room and end in my bedroom, where an envelope rests on the center of the bed. I set my gun on the nightstand and pick it up. Inside I find nothing but a card that reads, *The gun is registered in Danielle's name. Poetic justice is in the works.*

Poetic Justice.

My own words.

My eyes go wide. Did I say them out loud? I must have, which means, he's telling me that my efforts to search for listening, and perhaps video devices failed. I flip the card over and read: *I handled it. That's your breather. I'll know if it's a problem again.*

In other words, he put in his own listening and video devices and that's how he knew I'd entered the house. For all I know everyone has been watching my every move, even when I undress. This is not what I want my life to be, and yet my father allows it. He creates it. *Poetic justice*, I repeat in my mind. Was he suggesting I kill my father? No. Of course, he wasn't. But what was he suggesting then?

I'm tired of all of these men. Lord help me, if I was back in Washington dealing with my step-mother, too. It's really time I get a grip on all of them. I grab my gun, march downstairs, and enter my studio. The gun goes on a table next to me and I start painting with a purpose. When I'm done, I've created a gift for Rudolf. I've painted him sitting on my couch, on a barstool, on my bed. I then snap the photos and text them to him. He calls me of course. "What was that?"

"You said I'm into my art. I am. What do you think?"

He's silent a moment. "That wasn't about your art."

"No," I say. "That was me telling you to stay out of this house when I'm not here, and as you know, the cameras are gone. Make sure they stay gone and if you recorded when I was naked—"

"I didn't. I wouldn't do that."

"This is the world of politics—"

"I'm not that guy," he says sharply.

"You're just the guy that does whatever my father wants."

"And you think that includes filming his daughter while she dresses?"

"Look. I'm not the enemy. I have done nothing but support my father. I'm grieving over my friend, but I'm strong. I know this is go time, but what you're doing—stalking me—is making me claustrophobic."

"We're protecting everyone involved."

"I know you're paid to look out for my father, but please, I beg of you, Rudolf. At least let the house be my sanctuary. I won't paint those specific paintings you don't want me to paint. I promise. They were just—my way of coping privately, with what I can't ever allow to be seen publicly. That's all. They were actually good. They were a calm private way for me to vent and be done with it."

He's silent several beats. "The house," he finally says. "Agreed but let's talk about Jake."

"What about him?" I ask.

"Are you fucking him?"

"Yes," I say, hoping this is confirmation there were no cameras in the bedroom. "Is that a problem?"

"No. He's with us. What about Logan?"

"I thought you didn't know Jake?" I challenge, remembering a prior conversation.

"I do now. Back to Logan."

"I already told you, I barely know Logan."

"But your father told you to get close to him. Logan doesn't strike me as a man to share. Keep that in mind." He disconnects.

Oh my God. Did the man just tell me that my father wouldn't want him to film me naked, however, he's just fine with me sleeping with Logan for information? I grab the gun, if only I could claim that poetic justice, but my mother would not approve, and I'm not going to jail for my father.

I walk back into the kitchen, and place my gun in my purse, closing the safe and placing it under the kitchen sink. That's when I realize with much guilt, that I haven't heard from Megan nor have I thought about her. I dial her number and it goes directly to voicemail again. I text her: I'm worried about you. Can you please tell me you're okay?

Her reply is instant: Why did you have to leave?

I'm really sorry, I type. I didn't realize how much you needed to talk.

You knew, is her answer.

I didn't, I reply quickly. "Let's talk now. Can you call me? No. Never again.

I don't give up and our exchange turns lightning fast.

Me: Where are you?

Her: Why does that even matter anymore? I'm not there. I can't be there.

Me: Did you go home?

Her: Yes.

Me: To your mother?

Her: How did you know that?

Me: I assumed you'd go to family.

Her: I was in love with him

Me: I was afraid you'd say that.

Her: You can't even begin to understand. There is more to the relationship than you know. I can't talk about this. I'm going to get upset. I need to go.

Me: Please just keep talking to me.

I wait and there is no reply. Nothing. I type: Hello. Megan? Hello?

I wait.

Still nothing.

I sigh. Maybe I'm making this worse by talking to her. I glance at the clock realizing I need to get to the coffee shop. It's later than I thought and I have a class to teach. I hurry upstairs, braid my hair, darken my makeup and as I feel a little extra obvious today, I pull on a baseball cap. A few minutes later, I've locked up, secured the house the best I can, of course, and head out with my briefcase, my purse, and the gun nestled inside.

My walk is short, and I do indeed try to be more aware of my surroundings, but I still sense nothing and no one watching me. Good thing I'm well versed with a gun. I won't know I'm in trouble until someone is on top of me. For now though, I think I'm safe. Everyone is working everyone, with me in the center and right this minute, that makes me necessary.

I enter the coffee shop to find Michelle behind the bar, and she looks like walking death. I hurry across the room, waving at several people before I stop in front of her. "What are you doing here? You clearly don't feel well."

"Megan quitting put us in a bind. I have to be here."

"Do you have any emergency number for her? Can I try to contact her?"

"She never gave me any and the one number I had is disconnected. I have two new people starting tomorrow. I just need to get past today."

"What can I do?"

"Teach class," she says. "You do enough." She reaches under the counter and hands me a bag. "Cookies and something that was left for you from a delivery driver."

"Thanks."

I grab the bag and head toward the art room, where I place my briefcase under the cabinet, but I keep my purse. Tonight, it, with my trusty Sig Sauer inside, goes across my chest to rest at my hip. My phone goes inside my pocket, just in case Megan calls. I sit down in a chair in the corner, out of the view of the main coffee shop, open the package to find something wrapped in brown paper, which makes me think of Jake, but it's not from Jake. Inside is a fully charged phone. The note attached reads:

Call me. My number is in the favorites.

—L

I tap Logan's name. He answers on the first ring. "Any trouble?"

"Nothing I didn't handle but they know I visited your office."

"And?"

"They want me to get close to you and figure out your agenda."

"That's interesting," he laughs. "That makes life easier. In light of that information, are you going to be at the coffee shop tonight?"

"Yes."

"I'll walk you home from class."

He disconnects and with my gun in my purse, I decide to stick the extra phone in my briefcase under the cabinet. I've just hidden it away when my phone buzzes with a text message. I yank it from my pocket and read a message from Megan: You aren't as stupid as you're pretending to be. I suck in air, a chill racing down my spine. These words are familiar. They're my father's words. It's a coincidence, of course, but it shakes me that Megan used that exact phrase. I don't even know why she would say such a thing. She doesn't know me. I'm trying to decide how to reply when a group of about fifteen people swarms the room. It's a good fifteen minutes before I settle the group, that turns out to be a birthday party, into their places, and I pull my phone back out again and stare at the message, reading it again: You aren't as stupid as you're pretending to be.

I have a sudden flashback to six months ago at a fundraising event. Danielle and I were working the crowd when a billionaire political mastermind had cornered me about my father's positions on offshore drilling. I knew the answer he wanted. The man hated environmental dangers. I knew the answer to give him. No to offshore drilling, but I didn't want him to support my father. I didn't want to go to the White House. And so, I'd said yes to offshore drilling.

"No," my father says, joining us, his hand settling on my back, his fingers digging into my flesh. "She loves to freak people out by stating the opposite of what's expected with a completely straight face. No to offshore drilling. Isn't that right, honey?"

Danielle laughs and downs her drink. "She's funny, right?"

Once we are free of the pair Danielle laughs again, this time for real. "You're evil. I love you."

"It was an accident."

"Liar," she teases.

A few hours later, Danielle and I are standing near the door when my father corners us, or rather me, and snaps. "What the fuck was that?"

"I got confused. I'm sorry."

"You are not as stupid as you pretend to be. Don't cross me. There's a lot more than you on the line." And then he walks away.

Danielle looks at me, and as if nothing had happened, says, "Want to get some dessert?"

I blink fully back to the present and stare at the message. I don't want to talk to Megan anymore. I stick my phone in my pocket.

CHAPTER THIRTY-SIX

The famous poet and philosopher Ralph Waldo Emerson once said, "There is an optical illusion about every person we meet." In other words, I'm not the only one who is a sum of a dozen lies. Perhaps the biggest lie of all is when we pretend we don't know lies exist as a necessary vein of life to the point that we do not believe they are real anymore. Denial becomes the ultimate illusion or no—it's truth that is the illusion. Our own denial might even make everyone else's lies seem worse than our own, bigger, grander, more nefarious when the truth is far simpler. The most nefarious lies are the ones that everyone finds out about.

THE PAST…

My class that I normally love drags on forever, and when I finally leave my art room to find Logan nowhere in sight, I know he will be outside waiting for me. I am eager to leave, and my goodbyes are quick. I hurry to the door, exiting and sure enough, Logan—still in the same suit I'd seen him in earlier, is leaning on the wall by the door, waiting on me.

"Hi," I say, turning to face him.

"Hi," he says, pushing off the wall to face me and this time I don't feel the need to back away and I know why. Just having him here calms me down. It's his energy, I think. He's strong but not cutting. He's steady. He's reliable. He does what he says he will do when no one else in my life does. "You okay?" he asks.

"Now I am," I say, meaning it. And he's the only person I've ever said that to. "Any news?"

"Let's walk."

"Okay."

We turn and fall into step, walking several feet without words. I sense hesitation in him, something he doesn't want to say. "Just say what you want to say."

He motions to a bench and we sit down. Close. We sit close, which tells me he's not withdrawing. He's still in this with me. "I don't have a problem with your people coming after me, if that's what you think."

"Are you sure about that?"

"Yes, but while I'm not close to my father, I don't want him attacked."

"Protecting your own," I say. "God. There's a concept."

"I'm not saying I won't help."

"I know and honestly, it's refreshing that you're worried about your father, and that you're vocal about it. I get it, too. Protect him. Just do this, please. Promise me that if I die, you'll go after him with the photos. I have a trust fund coming to me at thirty. I'll will the money to you and—"

"This isn't about money. I have money invested diversely enough that no one can attack me and wipe me out. I learned that lesson from my father. I'm going to help you, but we need to do this through a third-party and well-shielded for both our sakes. That is going to take some time."

"There isn't a lot of time."

"Here's what I know: If he's damaged and the opposing party feels it's damning, they will let him earn his party nomination. They want him locked in so the pain comes when he can't be replaced. But Hailey, we're talking about destroying your father. Is that what you really want?"

"Yes," I say. "Yes. How many times do you need me to say it?"

He studies me several long moments and then nods. "Okay. I'll make the proper calls."

My phone buzzes in my pocket and I don't even think about looking at it.

He lifts a brow. "You need to check that?"

"It's Megan. She's being very—frustrating. I've hit a limit." And for no reason other than I don't want him to feel distrust, something I live with, I grab it. "She walked out on Michelle," I say, glancing at the message that reads: No reply? The truth never did work for you.

Unease rolls through me. This is *not* Megan. I look up at Logan and force myself to read him some of the earlier messages, the ones I thought were about him: I was in love with him. I glance at him, expectantly, but I know what his reply will be.

He shakes his head. "That is *not* about me. I barely know Megan and if it is about me, she's scaring me, and you need to stop talking to her. Get someone involved who can handle her."

"I tried. We have no contact information at all."

His phone buzzes and he grabs it, glancing at a message before putting it away. "My client just had the police show up at his door with a search warrant. I'm going to have to go."

"That sounds like a criminal case."

"It does now," he says, "but he pays me well enough that I'm going to step up and get him help." He stands and offers me his hand. "Come on. I'll walk you home."

I stare at his hand, hesitating, this sense that the minute I take it, I've formed one truce, and left everything else in my life behind. But I still take it. I let him pull me to my feet and when my eyes meet his, I know I'm right. This was the moment he decided I was with him and he was with me. His phone buzzes again and he releases me. "Go," I say. "I'm close to home. Take care of your client. You can call me later if you want."

His eyes warm. "I will."

He turns and starts walking and my phone buzzes in my hand. I look at the message: You know who this is. We both know you know who this is. Washington Park. It's walkable for you right now. The boathouse at Smith Lake.

My heart leaps and blood rushes in my ears. I dial Danielle's father. "Hello," he answers as I hang up. He said he saw the body. I'm crazy. This isn't Danielle. Megan must have figured out who I am and she's lashing out at me. I don't want to hurt him.

I inhale and consider my options. If it's Megan, and it has to be, she's crazy, and I need help. I dial Jake. He doesn't answer. I dial him again. I leave a message. "I need you. Desperately. I have a problem. Meet me at Washington Park at the boathouse at Smith Lake. I know this sounds crazy, but I think it's Danielle. I think she needs help. *I* need help. Meet me there."

My phone buzzes again and I glance down to read: Come now or I will tell the world what happened in Europe, the real truth. Why wouldn't I? I have nothing left to lose.

My heart freezes and shatters into a million pieces. It *is* Danielle. I don't know how, but it is because no one else knows that secret. I dial Jake back. This time he answers. "Talk to me," he says. "What's going on?"

"Meet me at the house instead of the park. Can you?"

"Yes. What is this?"

"Not on the phone," I say.

"Okay. I'll be there." He hangs up.

I start walking. I need to get to Danielle and zip her mouth before Jake decides to look for me at the park, after all. I pull up google maps and directions to the boathouse, and damn it my hand is shaking, but I find it. I start walking, nearly running. It's eleven o'clock, and a weeknight, the streets nearly vacant which makes me easy to follow. I can't be followed. I turn into a Mexican joint, and I walk to the back door exiting to the alleyway and waste no time darting behind cars, zipping in and out, until I'm down another alleyway, and into a neighborhood. It's a starless, moonless night, and the street is dark, trees offering shadows, yards pitch black. That's where I stick. People's yards, out of view.

Finally, I make it to the park, and I stand on the opposite side of the highway staring at the boathouse. I unzip my purse, readying my gun but I don't reach for it. This is

Danielle. I am not going to kill my best friend. I'm going to hug her and help her. I dash across the highway and head toward the lake, walking the long path around it, under trees and into the shadows but I never make it all the way. Danielle steps into my path, looking frail and thin, her hair a mess, her face gaunt.

"My God," I breath out. "You're really—I can't believe your alive." I step toward her and she holds up a gun, pointing it at me.

"Don't even think about it," she warns, her voice quaking. "You called him. You ruined my life. It's always been about you. Europe. You made me lie."

I hold up my hands. "Easy, Danielle," I say. "I didn't make you lie. I didn't make you do anything. You're not thinking straight. Let me help you."

"No. No, I'm done with your help."

"Tell me what's going on," I say. "Make me understand. Your father said he saw your body."

"Because Terrance, being Chief of Staff and all for your father, convinced me that your father loved me and if I loved him I had to disappear for a while. Because *you* knew about us and *you* had to be controlled. Because you were upset. But when I got to New Zealand and my mother tried to commit me. Five million dollars they paid her to commit me. They were made to believe that I'd done terrible things that I didn't do. They believed I did those things. My own parents."

"But your mother didn't commit you," I say.

"Oh, she tried."

"What does that mean?"

"It means she's no longer with us. I found a cliff. We're good at that right?"

"No," I say. "We are not. Let's go somewhere. Let's talk. Let's figure this out. I'll help you. You know I always help you."

Her face messes up, tears starting to stream down her cheeks. "But you didn't help. All I did was fall in love with him."

289

"I didn't know what they did to you. I swear to you."

"You promise?"

"You *know* me. That's why you're here. You know deep down, I'll help."

"Yes," she breathes out, the gun lowering.

I take a step toward her just as footsteps sound and Danielle jerks the gun up and toward the sound but it's too late. A gun fires and Danielle falls to the ground. "No!" I scream, as the man who fired steps into view and to my shock, it turns out to be Tobey. "Tobey! What have you done? What *the hell* have you done?"

I start toward Danielle but he's suddenly in front of me, pointing the gun. "What my father, Chief of Staff, should have done. Killed her. That's what your father wanted. Now it's done. Now you die, and the rest of us go to the White House."

"You're crazy," I say, my hand going to my purse, but he closes the space between us quickly, already a mere foot away. I can't pull it out fast enough. "We're supposed to go to the White House together."

"You broke up with me."

"I was just punishing you. I'm still with you. Put the gun down. What are you going to say anyway? I just happened to die with Danielle who is supposed to already be dead?"

"We're creative. Danielle won't show back up. You'll disappear and be found in the lake which delivers the sympathy vote."

More footsteps sound and Tobey must not expect them because he jerks right. I reach for my gun, but I never get the chance to pull it. Tobey falls to the ground and Jake charges forward. I don't wait on him. I run for Danielle and check her pulse, but it's too late. She's gone this time. She's gone, and I can't bring her back.

I fall over the top of her and start to cry, deep hard tears that rock my entire body. I have a vague realization of Jake pulling me close and it's then that I remember something that Rudolf said to me: *He's with us.*

CHAPTER THIRTY-SEVEN

THE BEGINNING OF THE END

After the FBI swooped down on the park, chaos feeding more chaos, I am now sitting in the back of an SUV waiting on Jake. Exhaustion has taken hold and my emotions are just beneath the surface, the pain festering into anger. I reach into my briefcase and I pull out the phone Logan gave me, noting his attempts to call me a half-dozen times. I punch in his number. "Hailey," he says. "Are you okay? I saw the news."

"Yes, but this is going to get ugly, dirty, bad. Really, really bad. You need to stay away."

"I can handle all of those things."

"But I don't want you to. Remember when I said that if you kissed me again, that I don't want it to be because we want anything from each other?"

"Of course I remember."

"I still want that. I want you to be that escape from this place. I don't know how long that is for me. I'm not asking you to wait, but if I get free, I'll call. And you can decide if you want to answer."

"What makes you free?"

I laugh bitterly. "If he's arrested, which I doubt, or if he loses. Then I'm free."

"And if he wins."

"I'm in hell forever."

"Hailey—"

"I'll call. You decide if you answer." The door opens, and I hang up and turn the phone off, sticking it back in my briefcase.

Jake slides inside and shuts us in the backseat alone. "What's happening?"

He scrubs his jaw and rests his elbows on his knees, turning his head my direction. "Danielle will get a proper burial. Her father will be arrested, but I talked to the New Zealand officials. Danielle's mother is dead, but it appears to be a suicide, not a murder."

She didn't push her off a cliff like she'd said. Even a mess, she was baiting me. "What about Drew Ellis? Where does he fit in this?"

"He's missing. I'd assume he saw too much. We'll keep looking but my gut says he's dead. We'll never see him again."

Dead. I do not like dead. "What about Megan?"

"Danielle was at her house. She's missing. We're concerned."

My hand goes to my belly. "Oh God. No. Please. She has to be okay."

"We're looking. I'll let you know when we know." He sits up and shifts my direction. "This is going to get dirty, messy, and just overall shitty."

I laugh without humor at his play on what I said to Logan. "I know."

"Whatever you might think, I'm one of the good guys."

"They said you were with them."

"Who?"

"Rudolf."

"Good. I want them to believe that. They're all going down. Terrance is going down now. I don't think I can arrest your father, but I want him. I will get him. If I can't get him legally, I'll get him politically."

"I thought you were one of the good guys?"

"The good guys get the bad guys," he says. "End of story. Are you in or out?"

"In," I say, knowing this is my time to be fearless and for real this time.

"That means staying by his side. That means accepting the bullshit he feeds you about tonight. That means—"

"I'm in."

"I'll give you immunity."

"I'm in already."

"It might not happen by the primaries," he warns.

"Please make it happen before then."

"I can't promise, but I will promise that he'll never be President."

"I'll hold you to that."

He studies me several beats and then nods. "Then let's go to Washington."

TWELVE HOURS LATER…

I've managed to pull myself together in a simple black dress and heels, with my hair sleek and professional. *I'm professional*, and grief-worthy, as should be a good future First Daughter. I'm also managing to hold myself together as I sit in my father's living area with him and Terrance while they explain to me that Tobey was rogue and behind everything. The two of them sit side by side on the couch, while I sit to the side on a chair, as if it's them against me, which of course it is.

"I'm sorry," Terrance says, his voice croaking out, his face all hard lines and grief, while his suit is perfectly pressed, as is my father's, of course. "I can't even believe my son would do these things," Terrance adds.

My father cups his shoulder. "We'll get through this."

I almost feel sorry for Terrance for what's about to happen to him. Almost. Not really. He's just as guilty of Danielle's murder as his son. Almost as guilty as my father. The door opens and shuts, and Rudolf appears in the entryway. "Sir, the FBI is here." That's all the warning there is.

Jake and four additional agents sweep into the room and they go right for Terrance. "Terrance Johnson you're under arrest for conspiracy to commit murder, fraud, and—" the list goes on. I tune it out.

I'm staring at my father's pale face, trying not to smile. He stands and starts his indignant routine. "A lawyer is on the way, Terrance. Help is on the way."

Terrance sobs, actually sobs, but then the man has lost his son and freedom in a matter of hours. I almost feel bad again. It's a full twenty minutes of activity before Jake steps to my side, and lowers his voice. "We found Megan. She's fine."

Relief washes over me, but that joy is doused as my father joins us. "Sir," Jake says, facing him but staying by my side. "I want you to know that I'm available if you need me. I've taken to your daughter and I'll be looking out for you and her."

My father narrows his eyes on me and then Jake, and it's clear in those conniving, intelligent eyes, that he thinks what Jake wants him to think: Jake saved him for me. It's the beginning of his end.

SIX MONTH LATER, PRIMARY ELECTION NIGHT...

I walk onto the stage with my hand in my father's, my step-mother is at his opposite side, as is my step-brother, and the crowd roars at the sight of us. My father kisses my hand and then that of my step-mother dearests before he claims the podium and his acceptance speech begins. He's now the candidate of his party. I'm numb. I feel nothing. I barely hear anything. I go through the motions as I have for months, sticking with Jake while he works his plan. Terrance is working with him. Others are too, though Drew never showed up and while it's doubtful he will, it could still happen. The time to end my father is not yet. As Logan suggested, it's after the primaries.

It's hours later when I'm finally back in my apartment building. Security escorts me to my door because that's how this works. We have Secret Service. I walk in the door and shut it, the sound of silence welcome but inside I'm screaming. He's too close to winning. I push off the door and walk to my bedroom, reaching under the mattress to the phone I keep there, the one that has Logan's number inside. I want to turn it on. I want to call him and tell him I haven't forgotten him. Because he's not a part of this place, this world, and I want out so badly. But that's just it. That would seem like the reason I'm calling is because I want an escape, not him. I said I didn't want us to be about wanting something from each other and I don't. I can't have him right now, anyway, even if he still cares. There's a knock on the door—actually three fast knocks—which means Jake. I stick the phone back under the mattress.

I hurry to the door and open it, and he grabs me, pulls me to him and kisses me. I sink into the kiss, because the thing is, he's a part of this world, and this is my world. And we both want something from each other and we know it. It works.

For now.

NOVEMBER, TWO WEEKS BEFORE THE ELECTION...

Jake and I are sitting on my couch eating pizza, waiting for the bombshell to hit the news. When it finally happens, he turns up the volume on the television, as the announcer says: *The bombshell dossier on Monroe is filled with troubling information that is most scandalous and criminal, if it proves true. Allegations of an affair with his daughter's best friend, who was murdered last year, insider trading, offshore accounts, payoffs and more.*

Jake turns off the sound and we just look at each other, the sense of an end coming, for us and my father, in the air. It's surreal. It's sad. It's pure joy. I will miss Jake, but I always knew he was temporary, and he knew the same of me. I will not miss my father, but I'm not yet convinced we've won.

Election night says it all.

TWO WEEKS LATER, ELECTION NIGHT, CAMPAIGN HEADQUARTERS…

After hours of watching the polls, of close calls, of narrow wins and losses, I'm standing backstage when my father pounds a wall and drops his forehead to the hard surface. Step-mother dearest touches his shoulder and he shoves her hand away, turning to face forward. "We'll be back," he says, as if he didn't just melt down. Let's go tell them we'll be back."

He's lost, and I happily follow him onto the stage to revel in this moment. This time when we walk the stage to the cheering crowd, my heart is filled with joy. It's over. He's lost. It's not true justice, but to my father, it's the ultimate torture. I stand on that stage and listen to him deliver his speech, congratulating the new President who is not him, and when it's over, he leaves without even saying goodbye to me.

I exit the stage and Jake is waiting at the bottom of the steps. He kisses my hand. "We did it."

"We did."

"I have to go," he says. "I need to know what he does next." But he's not talking about tonight.

"I know," I say. "We were good together."

He gives me a nod. "Maybe one day we will be again."

"Maybe."

But we won't. We both walk away and I hurry through a curtain to a private area, digging out that phone Logan gave me from my purse and now I turn it on. I dial and hold my breath. He answers on the first ring. "I wasn't sure you'd answer. I'm free now."

"And I'm here."

"What? Where?"

"The back door. Come to me."

I hang up and hurry that direction, cutting through people and rounding a corner for what feels like an eternal walk. I reach the back exit and push through the door to find Logan standing next to a black sedan, looking his perfectly handsome self in a black suit. I rush toward him and him toward me, and there is no question what comes next. We kiss, of course, because now I'm free to be in his world, or rather, make his world my world.

My father's reign has ended.

And that was almost the end but of course, you know that my father doesn't live. He's not dead, and my world isn't really all rainbows and roses, so the story isn't over.

PART THREE: THE END

CHAPTER THIRTY-EIGHT

We're back to almost present day, six years after my father's big loss. I didn't go to law school, I now own an art gallery in Cherry Creek, and my work has become quite in demand. I, of course, married Logan but my father was not invited to the wedding. It was small, cozy, and in the art room of the coffee shop.

Logan is good for me. I was right about his calming effect. He soothes that dark part of me that is far too much like my father. Between him and my art, I am able to forget, that the old me even exists. The girl that found her way to trouble at a party and lost her mother. The girl on the mountainside with Danielle. The girl that lied for her father and herself. I really have become the girl who is an artist and a wife. Someone who loves, in the only way I can love, which I'm not sure is the way Logan loves, but maybe one day.

It was perfect until the day my father showed up at our apartment door...

THE PAST...

I'm sitting at a canvas in my studio that Logan has built for me in our apartment, right off the kitchen, when he appears in the doorway. "I need to run downstairs to the office to finish up some work. How about dinner at the new Italian place?"

"I'd love that," I say, and he crosses to inspect my work, which is a depiction of the Cherry Creek neighborhood I'm unveiling in a show next weekend.

301

"Stunning Hailey," he says, and I beam. I love when he loves my work.

He kisses me and heads to the office, and I must be painting for another hour when the doorbell rings. Assuming it's my supply delivery, I hurry to the door, and when I open it I suck in air at the sight of my father. The years have been kind to him, his hair a little grayer, his eyes a bit more lined, but he's fit and handsome; his suit, of course, is expensive. "What are you doing here?"

"I want to see my daughter. Can I come in?"

A dark sensation claws at me, but I back up and allow him to enter. I don't wait on him. I turn and walk toward the kitchen and head straight to my gallery. I sit down at my work area, and he appears in the doorway where Logan was earlier. He glances around at my room, the mural I've painted on the walls, a fancy paint-splattered floor beneath our feet. "Nice setup," he says. "I'm going to make some coffee. You want some coffee?" He doesn't wait for an answer. He enters my kitchen, and this infuriates me. This isn't his home. I don't get up. I tell myself I won't, but I last about two minutes.

I follow him, which is what he wants, but I am still his daughter apparently. He offers me the cup in his hand. I ignore it. "Why are you here?"

He sets the cup down. "Right to the point. Okay. I'm running for office again. I'd like your support."

I laugh, my head tilting backward with the force before I look at him. "That is never happening, though I'd almost like to help just to watch you suffer another loss."

"You liked seeing me lose?!" he demands.

"I loved it. You are a horrible person."

"You," he says, walking toward me. "Are a spoiled brat that—" He grabs his chest and grunts. "You," he tries again, but his eyes start to roll back. "I'm—I need—help."

"So you said," I say, turning away and walking into my studio where I sit down and stare at my work.

"Hai—ley," he groans and I'm pretty sure the thud that follows is him hitting the ground, but there is this tiny imperfection on the painting. It's driving me nuts. I pick up my brush and dab at the spot.

"Hai-ley."

This time my name is a whisper. I puff out a breath and set down my brush before I stand up and walk to the kitchen. He's on the floor, on his back, and there seems to be foam coming out of his mouth, which I think I read means heart attack. I walk back into the art room, grab my phone and dial 911. "My father is having an event. He needs help." I give them the address and I don't wait for instructions. I hang up. I seem to blackout, but I haven't had a drink. It's just like when those old blackouts happened though. I completely lose time. I don't remember what happened between the time I make the call and when finally, they are covering his face, pronouncing him dead.

And so, the story ends. Do I feel bad about waiting so long to call that ambulance? No. It was finally poetic justice. I painted and he died. It was his time. He was going to die. That's the point. The story is already written, so just live it while you can because one day, you'll be dead too, and it might be sooner than you think.

THE END

WANT MORE LISA RENEE JONES MYSTERY?

CHECK OUT MY LILAH LOVE SERIES!

As an FBI profiler, it's Lilah Love's job to think like a killer. And she is very good at her job. When a series of murders surface—the victims all stripped naked and shot in the head—Lilah's instincts tell her it's the work of an assassin, not a serial killer. But when the case takes her back to her hometown in the Hamptons and a mysterious but unmistakable connection to her own life, all her assumptions are shaken to the core.

Thrust into a troubled past she's tried to shut the door on, Lilah's back in the town where her father is mayor, her brother is police chief, and she has an intimate history with the local crime lord's son, Kane Mendez. The two share a devastating secret, and only Kane understands Lilah's own darkest impulses. As more corpses surface, so does a series of anonymous notes to Lilah, threatening to expose her. Is the killer someone in her own circle? And is she the next target?

TURN THE PAGE TO READ CHAPTER ONE OF BOOK ONE: MURDER NOTES!

CHAPTER ONE OF MURDER NOTES

There is blood in the ocean.

I don't notice it at first, but then, most people don't. It's called denial. We refuse to see what we eventually have to cope with, or perhaps even confess. For the innocent, they don't expect the brutality of the actions required to take a life, so they simply cannot process the inconceivable. For the guilty, it's all about denying your own ability to do such a thing, and denial can be a slow, brutal sword that carves you inside out. Though there is another class of people that are more animal than human. Those so sick, so demented that they feel a fleeting joy from death, and then seek more joy by doing it again. And again. You won't find guilt in their eyes. You won't find remorse. There are times when I've felt like one of those animals, but then the guilt starts again.

But you see? There is no remorse. I'm not sure what that says about me.

And so I walk on the beach, not seeing what is there, and it's like so many other walks along East Hampton's Beach. Cool sand between my toes. The taste of salt on my lips. A gust of wind lifting my long brown hair from my neck. I see it happening, like I'm above the scene, looking down. Like I'm dead and that other person on the beach is alive. Sometimes I can almost hear that wind whisper my name, too: Lilah. Lilah. *As if it's calling me to a place it knows I must travel, but I continue to refuse. It is a gentle, soothing caress of a whisper, a seductive promise that acceptance will bring relief, even forgiveness.*

The wind lies. It always lies.

But then, that's why it wants me. Because of my lies. Because it knows how they haunt me. It knows my secrets when no one else knows. Only that's a lie, too, and I blink to find the only other person who does know in the distance and closing in quickly.

He walks toward me, graceful and good looking, his suit ridiculously expensive; the wet sand beneath his black lace up shoes impossibly smooth everywhere he steps. But then, he's a man who easily convinces people he walks on water, so why not sand? A man whose accomplishments are second only to his arrogance, while his charisma is just one of his many weapons. He can kiss a woman and make her crave more—he certainly did that to me—but I remind myself that this does not make me naïve, as he also has the power to utter only a word and have grown men follow him. He is the picture of perfection that very few see is framed with broken glass. But I see. I know things about him no one else knows.

Like he does me. And therein lies the problem.

Rejecting him, I turn away from his approach, facing the ocean, a new dawn illuminating the sky, a strange red spot tainting the deep blue of the water. It begins to grow, and grow some more, until the lifeblood of someone gone, and possibly forgotten, spills through it like oil, set on destruction. Blood is now everywhere. There is nothing else but it and the guilt that I've tried to deny.

And suddenly he is behind me, his hand on my shoulder, and I shiver with that touch. He did this. He spilled this blood.

Only...no. That doesn't feel right. I think...I did this.

I wake from one of my freak-show nightmares, which I thought were finally over, to a dark room, my cellphone ringing on the nightstand and my body aching from the need for sleep.

"Rich," I murmur, shoving against the big, hard body that has managed to drape over mine. "Get off. My phone's ringing." He doesn't move, which is a problem that reaches beyond this moment, and more directly to us working in the same field office and hopping into bed together. "Rich, damn it."

He gives a groan and rolls in one direction while I go the other and grab my cell, glancing at the caller ID. It's the local PD. "Special Agent Love," I answer.

"We've got a body off the Santa Monica Pier and need your assistance," the man on the line says. "Early morning jogger made the discovery and called it in."

I glance at the clock, five AM, and wonder what idiot jogs at four in the morning, in the dark, on the beach, but this isn't my job anyway. "That's the local authority's territory. You've got the wrong girl."

"You are Special Agent Lilah Love, correct?"

"You knew that already," I say irritably, and since this clearly isn't going away easily, I sit up, preparing to fight for my need to sleep.

"Then you're requested by name. Director Murphy sent the directive."

My boss is meeting me there? This is more than me lending my profiling skills to the locals if he's joining me, and my exhaustion fades into concern. "I'll be right there." I end the call and throw off the blankets, grimacing when I realize I'm wearing Rich's shirt, which is not sending him the non-committal message I need to send after dodging last night's "talk." But it smells good, the way he always does, I think as I push myself onto my feet and stumble toward the bathroom.

Stepping into the tiny bathroom, a cracked tile scrapes my foot, and I grimace, taking up residence at the equally tiny, ancient sink and grab my toothbrush.

"When are we going to finish that talk we started last night?"

At the sound of Rich's voice, I start brushing my teeth, making sure I'm as incapable of talking about moving in with him now as I was when we were having sex last night. "Lilah," he says impatiently, my reprieve lasting all of ten seconds.

I glance over at him through the long drape of my messy dark brown hair to find him leaning on the doorway. Naked. The man is all kinds of blond, hard-bodied goodness, but still. Good grief. "Why don't you have clothes on?" I ask, though I'm not sure he can understand me with my mouth full of foam.

"I'm serious, Lilah. We've been hot and heavy for six months. We need to have this talk."

"You're naked," I say, yanking the toothbrush from my mouth, since clearly he didn't hear me the last time. "I'm not talking to you naked." I go back to brushing my teeth.

"You aren't naked. I am."

"Aren't you funny," I say, turning on the water and rinsing my mouth, and since he's still standing there when I'm done, I face him. "I'm serious, Rich. You're naked. I have a dead body waiting on me. The two do not compute. Now is not the time."

"You're one of the top FBI profilers in the country," he states. "You always have a dead body waiting on you. Which is why we never talk."

I turn and press my hands to the sink, showing the white ceramic more interest than it deserves, while his naked body might deserve more than I can afford to give it right now. "Everyone has their fetishes, I guess."

"You don't like dead bodies. Why do you say shit like that?"

Because I want to scare you off, I think, and I might actually really freak him out if I insist I do have a fetish for dead bodies. Of course, as logical as Rich is, he'd know it's because they help me catch killers. Instead, I just say, "I'm getting dressed," and hope he takes a hint and does the same, I turn to walk into the closet. Thankfully, his sound of frustration is followed by a shift in the air that tells me he's finally gone to dress. Wishing for the shower I don't have time to take, I yank a pair of faded jeans and a black V-neck

310

t-shirt from their hangers, get dressed, and then lean on the wall to pull on black combat boots.

All of three minutes later, I re-enter the bathroom to find Rich back in the door frame, and while he's not naked, his low slung black jeans aren't doing much to cover his assets, which I really want covered right now. I toss him his shirt, which he catches and pulls over his head. Seizing the momentary distraction I've created, I head back to the sink to wash my face, brush my hair, and contemplate how washed out my pale skin is without the make-up I'd prefer to be wearing right now. I'm a girl. I like being a girl despite this job and I pretty much fucking love how that, mixed with my "potty mouth," as my mother would call it if she were alive, confuses the hell out of people.

Ready to get out of here for more reasons than one, I step to Rich and he doesn't budge, his big body blocking my petite one. "So about that apartment," Rich says. "You've been in Cali for two years. This place is the size of a Cracker Jack box and it's a dump, Lilah. It's time to make a change."

"You're right. This place is tiny, a point driven home by the fact that you're presently suffocating me. I need something bigger and if it came with a toilet that doesn't require me jiggling the handle every time I use it, that would be a plus."

"I'm glad you agree."

He's glad I agree? Okay. That didn't go as planned. He's not registering what I'm telling him. I see it in his face and I need to shut up before I dig myself in deeper. "Move, Rich. I need to go."

Still, he blocks my path. "I have a long-term lease and a toilet that doesn't need to be jiggled," he says. "It's not your fancy Hamptons place of old, I'm sure, but it's a step up from this shit hole. Move in with me. I want to wake up and look into those gorgeous brown eyes of yours every morning for now on."

Yep. Officially screwed this up big time. "Did I mention I have a dead body waiting on me? And Murphy?"

His brow instantly furrows. "Murphy's meeting you?" He backs away. "What the hell is going on?"

"I'm clueless," I say, walking to the chair in the corner of the bedroom and slipping the satchel I carry to all my crime scenes over my head and chest.

"If Murphy's at the crime scene," he says, "we're taking over."

"Most likely," I say, and not about to invite more conversation, I leave it at that and make my way to the door for my escape, but frustratingly, Rich steps in front of me.

"Move in with me," he repeats, his hands coming down on my shoulders. "I'm crazy about you."

"I'm not a relationship kind of girl."

"What do you call what we're doing?"

"Sex. Friendship." I'm confusing him and I think me, too. I should have left out the friendship part, except I do like him. Quite a lot actually. Frustrated at myself, I add, "I don't know."

"You just described a perfect relationship, Lilah. That's what we all want. Sex and friendship in one place."

Note to self: Friendship is a really bad word with men. "Look. Rich. I mean, you're like the perfect Cali surfer dude: gorgeous and sweet, but-"

"Surfer dude and *sweet*? Holy fuck." He drops his hands from my shoulders and scrubs one of them through his longish, curly blond hair. "That's how you see me?"

I hold up my hands. "No. God no. I'm sorry. See? I suck at this stuff." I toughen my voice to make sure he knows how serious I am. "You're an all-American G.I. Joe bad ass. You would die for just about anyone. You are amazing, Rich. Absolutely fucking amazing. Too good for me. I'm the one that's the problem. I have issues. Big issues. That's why I don't do commitment." I shove a strand of hair from my face. "And I can't do this now. You know I can't do this now."

His jaw sets hard and he gives me a disgruntled, reluctant nod. "Go. Deal with Murphy."

I don't argue. I step around him, and dart for the living room, pausing in the doorway long enough to say, "Lock up

when you leave. Sick fucks love me." I take off for the front
door.

"What the hell does that make me, Lilah?"

"The exception," I call out, and he has no idea how true
that statement rings.

Thanks to that early Wednesday morning jogger getting
us all out of bed at the crack of dawn, I travel from my Los
Feliz neighborhood to Santa Monica in thirty minutes,
which would be unheard of any other time of the day.
Parking my gray Ford Taurus in a lot near the beach is just
as easy. I step out of the car, slip my FBI badge over my neck
and fight a gust of September seventy-something wind and
head down the sidewalk toward the pier. Weaving my way
through the now sleeping perpetual carnival of the
boardwalk, I make a beeline for the Ferris wheel certain to
lead me to the end of the pier. Turns out, the growing crowd
around the yellow tape on the nearby beachfront does the
job just fine.

I approach several uniforms and show them my badge.
"Who's the detective in charge?" I ask.

"Oliver," one of them tells me.

Great, I think, moving on along the sidewalk. That man
hates me. I've made it all of ten feet across the sidewalk,
about to hit the sand, when I hear, "Special Agent Love."

At the sound of Detective Oliver's voice, I grimace and
turn to find the forty-ish "Gray Fox," as the ladies on the
force call him, joining me. And yeah, I guess he's good
looking. If you like the stereotypical, cigarette smoking,
perpetually-wrinkled-suit-wearing good cop with a bad
attitude.

"Detective."

"Are you going to do a better job for me this morning
than you did two days ago?"

And here we go. "It was a professional hit, Detective Oliver," I say tightly. "You don't just get a read on him, or her, with a snap of your fingers."

"You didn't get me a read at all."

"This isn't a thirty-ish perp with two kids and a dog you can track down in the suburbs. There are papers written on this shit. They don't fit profiles."

"I don't give a fuck about papers, college girl. And if you and your people are coming onto my scene, you had better find a way to get me a profile." He starts walking, exiting the sidewalk to hit the sand.

Irritated, I whirl around and pursue him, catching up quickly. "My services are volunteered as a professional courtesy, not to invade your personal space."

"Funny," he says dryly. "I don't remember being given an option this morning when I declined your services." We reach the dock area where various officials have gathered several feet from another taped-off area. One of the badges motions to him, and he in turn motions toward the cluster of people gathered by the dock.

"Go. Get me answers this time," he says before showing me his back.

Grinding my teeth, I face forward and walk, pushing through the layer of personnel to find Joe, the red-headed forensic guy–which is actually what everyone calls him–leaning over the victim, his thick-rimmed glasses inching down his nose. "Hiya, Agent Love."

"Hi Joe," I say, but it's not him that has my attention at present. It's the dead, naked male body in the sand, water washing over his bare feet, a chill racing down my spine, and not because I'm squeamish. Because this is exactly how we found another victim only two nights ago, and we never found the victim's clothes. I don't expect to now either. The absence of clothes on the body, or anywhere to be found, is assumed by most on the scene to be an effort to hide evidence. But not by me. My gut said there was more to it two days ago, and it most definitely does now as well.

I step closer and Joe moves to the dead man's head. "Bullet between the eyes," he says, glancing up at me, and indicating the clean hole center of the brows. "Look familiar?"

"All too familiar," I say, removing plastic gloves from my bag as I squat in the sand and inspect the remains.

"Clean entry," Joe adds, "perfect precision, no mess, no fuss."

"Were the clothes taken off before or after the murder?"

"Before."

I don't ask his reasoning. He'll detail it in his report.

"And the case two days ago?"

"Also before, and pending blood splatter analysis and confirmation, of course, this case is a virtual clone to that one."

"Only that was a woman," I say, looking for any signs of struggle he might have missed, while I struggle myself with my hair I should have tied back in this damn wind.

"But that doesn't rule out a serial killer, right?" he asks, sounding a bit too excited about the prospect.

"Serial killers and assassins are different breeds," I say, "and we're at two victims, which does not equate to a serial killer, at least by definition."

"Assassin? You think this is an assassin?"

"Yes," I reply simply.

"What kind of assassin takes off the victim's clothes?"

"This one," I say absently, my gaze catching on the tattoo on the man's arm, the arm not shoved half under his body and into the sand, a foreboding knot forming in my stomach. "Can I see that ink?"

"Oh yeah," he says. "I wanted to look at that, too. It looks interesting." He moves to the side of the man, shifting the arm, and the ease of movement says I'm right. The guy is practically still warm. "I'm thinking of getting a tattoo myself," he says.

"Time of death?" I ask, focused on the case.

"He's fresh," he says. "I'm estimating three AM, maybe three-thirty." He changes the subject. "I'm thinking Superman. Do chicks dig Superman?"

"What?" I say, looking at him.

"I was thinking I'd get a Superman tattoo."

"If you're trying to embrace your resident geek status, it works."

"Who says I'm the resident geek?"

"Everyone except you, apparently. Embrace it. It works for you."

He glowers. "Seriously, Agent Love. Could you just-"

"The tattoo, Joe," I say, feeling that knot in my stomach growing.

"Right. Tattoo. His. Not mine."

He flips the arm just enough that I get the full view of the tattoo and I hear nothing else he says. I see the Virgin Mary with blood dripping out of her mouth, and suddenly I am back on another beach. My lashes lower and I'm living the exact moment I was grabbed from behind. I had twisted around, and thrown an ineffective defensive move. The ineffective part, and the punishment I'd received for being that weak, is the reason that I now train just as hard in my physical combat skills as I do on constantly honing my profiling abilities. I'd gone down hard on the sandy ground with a heavy male body on top of me, big, muscular arms caging me. One of his beefy forearms had been etched with a tattoo moving and flexing with his flesh while he assaulted me. A tattoo of the Virgin Mary, bleeding from her mouth. Praying to her or anyone else did nothing to save me.

"Special Agent Love."

At the sound of my name, I snap back to the present to find Detective Oliver standing behind Joe, glowering at me, not the dead body. "Are you sleeping or getting me my answers?"

I inhale and stand up, turning to find Special Agent-in-Charge Murphy a good twenty yards away. Yanking my gloves off, I start walking in that direction, only to have Detective Oliver catch up with me. "Hold on there, sweetie."

316

Anger officially ignited, I whirl on him. "Sweetie? Well, look here, *honey*. Unless you want me to shove that sock you have in your pants in your mouth, back off, Detective Oliver. I get it. This is your turf and I'm just some twenty-eight-year-old kid, while you're the seasoned vet. But I've been in and around law enforcement since I was in diapers, and I'm damn good at my job."

He arches a brow. "Are you done?"

"No," I say, "but you are. We're trying to catch the same damn monster, so back the fuck off."

He stares at me long and hard, to the point that I move to leave. He gently shackles my arm and turns me around. "Don't touch me," I snap.

He holds up his hands. "Understood." His eyes narrow. "You want to talk about what set you off back there?"

"Aside from you," I lie, "I don't know what you're talking about."

He slides his hands to his hips under his jacket. "I challenge you every damn time you come onto my crime scene-"

"Challenge? Is that what you call it?"

"Every time you come onto my crime scene," he repeats, "and you never let me rattle you. What got you back there? Because it wasn't me."

"That's an assassination," I say, moving away from the topic of me. "And this is an opinion and working theory, not a fact, but I say he takes their clothes off at the directive of a client."

"None of that answers my question. What set you off?"

The sound of footsteps has us both looking up to find my boss approaching, and there is something about his full-on gray hair, which is as perfectly groomed as his tan suit is fitted, along with his carriage, that radiates authority and control. His control, not that of Detective Oliver.

"Special Agent Love, Detective Oliver," he greets, stopping in profile to us, and glancing between our warring expressions. "Do we have a problem?"

"You and I should talk, Director Murphy," Detective Oliver states.

"After I talk to my agent, who graciously got out of bed yet again to aid one of your cases."

"The case you took over," Detective Oliver reminds him.

"Oh I did, didn't I?" my boss replies, and then more firmly, says, "I did. I need to talk to my agent. Alone."

Detective Oliver scowls and leaves while Director Murphy looks at me. "What was all that about?"

"Typical turf war when we take over. Nothing I can't handle."

"*I'll* handle it," he promises, and then thankfully moves on. "New York has a case that has enough similarities to these two here that we may be looking at a serial killer who's crossed state lines. That makes this our baby."

"This isn't a serial killer," I say, repeating what I told Detective Oliver. "It's an assassination."

"Or a serial killer obsessed with assassination-style murders. Profile the victims, then talk to me."

I hesitate but can't let this go. "You said New York?"

"That's right. Your home state, which aside from your profiling skills, makes you the right match for this case."

That's debatable, but I don't tell him that. "I've seen the tattoo that's on the arm of the victim before," I say instead.

"Where? And in what context?"

"It wasn't in a professional capacity and it was many years ago. Back home in the Hamptons, actually."

"That's Mendez Enterprises territory," he says. "A family and empire based in the Hamptons. Notoriously legit and yet not legit at all. Very soap opera-ish. I read up on them when you joined our team."

A frisson of unease slides through me. "Why would you read up on them when I joined the team?"

"I like to know where my people came from and what influences them, directly or indirectly."

I'm not sure what to make of that comment, but he doesn't give me time to try to figure it out, already moving on. "I understand the son, Kane, took over after his father was murdered a few years back. Do you know him?"

"If you researched as you say, then you know, that you simply can't grow up in the Hamptons and not know the Mendez family," I say remaining as non-committal as possible. "We all knew them. And yes, I knew him."

"Word is he's a smooth operator, but then, so was his father."

"I would say that description fits," I agree, thinking that Kane is that and much more, which I won't elaborate on at this point.

"Always squeaky clean when investigated, too, from what I understand. The kind of people who get others to do the dirty work. Like perhaps the assassin you feel we're dealing with. That along with a tattoo that connects the body to the Hamptons. Sounds like a connection to investigate."

"I certainly think there's a connection to the Hamptons and we should have it checked out."

"So go," he says. "Check this out."

I blanch. "What? No. With all due respect, Director Murphy. I left that place for a reason."

"And you're going back with a bigger one. Your job. Go pack." He looks at his watch and then me. "It's not even seven yet. Call the office on your way home. With luck, our team can have you in a bird by noon." He starts walking and I stare after him, seeing nothing but an ocean of blood. I'm going back to where those nightmares started. And back to *him*.

LEARN MORE AND BUY HERE:

HTTPS://LILAHSERIES.WEEBLY.COM/

ABOUT THE AUTHOR

New York Times and USA Today bestselling author Lisa Renee Jones is the author of the highly acclaimed INSIDE OUT series.

In addition to the success of Lisa's INSIDE OUT series, she has published many successful titles. The TALL, DARK AND DEADLY series and THE SECRET LIFE OF AMY BENSEN series, both spent several months on a combination of the New York Times and USA Today bestselling lists. Lisa is also the author of the bestselling the bestselling LILAH LOVE and WHITE LIES series.

Prior to publishing, Lisa owned multi-state staffing agency that was recognized many times by The Austin Business Journal and also praised by the Dallas Women's Magazine. In 1998 Lisa was listed as the #7 growing women owned business in Entrepreneur Magazine.

Lisa loves to hear from her readers. You can reach her on Twitter and Facebook daily.

Made in the USA
San Bernardino, CA
04 July 2019